THE
ENEMY
YOU
GNOCCHI

AN ITALIAN CHEF MYSTERY

CATHERINE
BRUNS

Poisoned Pen
PRESS

Published by Poisoned Pen Press, an imprint of Sourcebooks
P.O. Box 4410, Naperville, Illinois 60567-4410
(630) 961-3900
sourcebooks.com

Library of Congress Cataloging-in-Publication Data

Names: Bruns, Catherine, author.
Title: The enemy you gnocchi : an italian chef mystery / Catherine Bruns.
Description: Naperville, Illinois : Poisoned Pen Press, [2021] | Series:
    Italian chef mysteries ; book 3
Identifiers: LCCN 2021003840 (print) | LCCN
2021003841 (ebook) | (paperback) | (epub)
Subjects: GSAFD: Mystery fiction.
Classification: LCC PS3602.R857 E54 2021 (print) | LCC PS3602.R857
    (ebook) | DDC 813/.6--dc23
LC record available at https://lccn.loc.gov/2021003840
LC ebook record available at https://lccn.loc.gov/2021003841

Printed and bound in Canada.
MBP 10 9 8 7 6 5 4 3 2 1

For my mother, who taught me to love books.

ONE

WHEN I WAS A YOUNG GIRL, I always associated the smell of Italian food with my grandmother's house. Tomatoes and onions. Garlic and homemade bread fresh out of the oven. Brown sugar and melted butter from her mouthwatering ravioli sauce. By the time I was ten, I'd decided her kitchen must be a little bit like heaven—warm, sweet-smelling, and full of love.

Twenty years later, as I mixed the same sauce on Anything's Pastable stove, I still delighted in the fragrances that brought back fond memories of cooking with my grandmother as a child. Kitchens would always be my happy place. But now there was a new kitchen in my life. The kitchen of my very own restaurant.

Creating delectable dishes in my own establishment was a dream come true. I enjoyed coming up with new recipes when I had the time, and every week I would feature a different dinner special on my menu. This week's was ravioli with a pumpkin puree, ricotta and parmesan cheese filling, covered in a brown sugar sauce like my grandmother's. A cozy, seasonal dish perfect for the holidays. As a trained chef, I enjoyed making several different entrees, and this one had always been a personal favorite to prepare, loving the smell of the brown sugar as I mixed together the filling in a large silver bowl.

Stephanie Beaudry, my assistant, chattered on gaily about the show she was performing in at Harvest Park's Little Theater. My cousin Gabby—who'd stopped over on her lunch break—and I listened attentively. The rehearsal schedule for *A Christmas Story* had left me shorthanded on a number of occasions. It was difficult to manage everything in the kitchen on a normal night, let alone during the busy holiday season, and my anxiety level would often rise like dough in the oven. Sometimes I would stop and wonder why I was putting myself through this. Then I would laugh out loud and remember that cooking and the holiday season were two of my greatest loves.

"Tessa, I've been having so much fun," Stephanie gushed. "I always wanted to try local theater, but of course Ryan would never allow it while we were married."

Gabby raised her eyebrows at me when Stephanie's back was turned. She was never shy about expressing her opinion. Yes, Stephanie had already mentioned the show several times this week, and I'd even gone to see it the week before, but I was happy that she was enjoying herself.

"Steph, you did a fantastic job. You're a natural on the stage. Has Zoe been to see it yet?"

Zoe was Stephanie's adorable six-year-old daughter, a

miniature copy of her mother with green eyes and short, curly auburn hair. She had a sprinkle of freckles on her cheeks that I often teased her was fairy dust, and she loved hearing it.

Seeing Stephanie and Zoe together was always somewhat bittersweet for me. My husband had passed away last year, and sadly we hadn't gotten around to having children. During the last eight months that Stephanie had been in my employment, I'd grown fond of Zoe and envied her mother. I'd even babysat a couple of times when Stephanie had rehearsal. Zoe loved helping me "cook" in the kitchen. I didn't know if children were in the cards for me, but my mother was always quick to remind me that my biological clock was running out of time.

"She's coming to tomorrow's matinee," Stephanie answered. "If we're not too tired afterward, I plan on taking her to the Festival of Lights."

The bells on the front door jingled merrily, and I glanced down at my watch. Two o'clock on the dot. There was usually a lull in clientele at this time of day with only one couple in the dining room and the dinner rush not picking up again until around four.

"I'll seat them," Stephanie offered. She brushed her hands on her apron and went into the dining room.

Gabby sipped from a bottle of water. "You look tired, Tess."

"That's because I am," I smiled. "Thank goodness that Stephanie doesn't have rehearsal tonight. And you have no idea how much I'm looking forward to sleeping in tomorrow. I love the holiday season, but it wears me out."

She puckered her lips together. "Gee, I don't know why. You work like—I don't know—five 12-hour days, plus you're usually here on days off as well. Then there's the Festival of Lights, which you agreed to make Christmas cookies for, and your Breakfast with Santa event on Christmas Eve morning. You really need to stop slacking off." Her mouth dropped open as she feigned shock, and she wiggled her eyebrows, making me laugh.

"Very funny."

"Are you going to the meeting at Town Hall tomorrow afternoon?" Gabby asked.

"Yes, I promised that I'd be there. It's kind of weird to have one on a Sunday, though. Do you have any idea what it's about?"

Gabby shook her head. "All I know is that only Harvest Park business owners are invited. The community wasn't even told about it."

"It must have to do with the festival then." The Festival of Lights was a huge annual affair in Harvest Park, topped only by the Apple Festival in the fall. Every year the proceeds went to a needy charity. It wasn't required that business owners donate something, but the town's merchants were generous with their money and time. "Maybe they need more volunteers. Will you be there?" I stirred the sauce in my stainless steel pot and then turned the burner down to simmer.

Gabby sniffed the air and sighed happily. "I'm planning on it. And that smells so good." She stared at me with pleading eyes. "Any chance of grabbing some of your ravioli before I go back to the store?"

I removed the pot from the burner and went to the freezer, withdrawing a sealed bag full of ravioli that I'd prepared and frozen the other day. When water in another pot reached a boil, I tossed the pasta in. "Hmm. I suppose I can spare a *little*."

She grinned. "You're the best. Don't tell anyone, but you're my favorite cousin."

"I'm your only cousin," I reminded her. "Well, at least in New York."

"Don't worry, I won't tell my brother." Her expression soured, as if she'd eaten a lemon. "Gino's been such a Scrooge lately."

"He's tired. It can't be easy with a newborn at home, especially around the holidays." My cousin Gino and his wife, Lucy, had three boys—six-year-old twins Rocco and Marco and a two-month-old baby named Lucas who refused to sleep most of the time.

Gabby watched as I plated the ravioli and covered it with brown sugar sauce. "It's so great to see you happy again, Tess. I know it's been a tough year for you."

Her words were an understatement. My husband, Dylan, had been murdered fourteen months ago, and it had taken me a long time to come to terms with my loss. Last Christmas had been depressing, but I finally felt like I could start to enjoy the holiday season again. "I couldn't have done it without your help." Of course, there was also my mother, Gino, and Justin, a good friend of mine.

Stephanie came back into the room with an order pad in hand. She ripped off a page and placed it on the metal wheel beside me.

"One order of your, I quote, *delicioso* ravioli and a glass of Chardonnay." She gave an exaggerated cough. "Your fan club awaits, Tess."

A groan escaped from between my lips. "Oh no. Is that who I think it is?"

"Yep." Stephanie tried to conceal her grin. "Mario Russo is looking forward to seeing, and I quote again, 'the prettiest chef in the entire state of New York.'"

I shook my head. "Please tell him I'm busy."

"You know Mario won't buy it," Stephanie remarked. "He always insists on seeing you when he comes in."

The corners of Gabby's mouth quivered. "I guess we'll have to add the new barista in town to Tess's growing list of admirers. Of course, he comes after Justin and that sexy landlord of hers."

"I think you're exaggerating." I transferred more ravioli to another plate and ladled sauce on top of it.

Stephanie sliced into a fresh loaf of Italian bread still warm from the oven. "Vince is so dreamy," she sighed. "Say, what's the Italian phrase for ooh-la-la?"

Gabby laughed. "Unfortunately, Tess and I don't speak the language fluently, not like our parents."

A familiar clinking sound came from the dining room. Stephanie pointed at me and I sighed in resignation. "Never mind. I'll bring his plate out myself."

"I knew he wouldn't give up until he saw you," Stephanie said.

Gabby stared from me to Stephanie, puzzled. "Mario's making that racket?"

Stephanie nodded. "He taps his fork against the water glass if he thinks he's been waiting too long."

"He must be great at weddings," Gabby snorted.

Mario Russo had moved to Harvest Park about three months ago when he opened The Espresso Lane, a coffee bar located right across the street from my good friend Archie Fenton's Java Time. At first, I hadn't been too concerned since Archie's cafe was beloved in the community. After all, it was the longest running business in Harvest Park. However, it didn't take long for most of the residents to be swayed by the cheaper prices at Mario's shop, his bigger selection of drinks, and the Christmas contest he was currently running. Not me, though. My loyalty belonged to Archie. If only Mario would take the hint.

I set the bread basket on a tray next to the ravioli, and Stephanie handed me a wine goblet filled with Chardonnay. "I can't afford to be rude to him. He *is* a steady paying customer. Steph, you might as well slice a piece of the tiramisu I made earlier. He always takes some home with him."

Gabby's eyes lit up at the mention of her favorite dessert. "Can I take a piece back with me? I'll pay you, of course."

"Don't be silly. Steph, please wrap one up for Gabby and Liza as well." Liza was Gabby's lone employee at her bookstore, Once Upon a Book.

"You're a doll." Gabby grinned. "See you at the meeting tomorrow."

"Mario *is* demanding," Stephanie said in a low voice as she sliced the cake. "But he's also kind of cute. If you could save some guys in this town for the rest of us Tessa, I'd appreciate it."

She and Gabby laughed as I rolled my eyes at them. "Oh, you two are a riot." I left the kitchen and went into the dining room with Mario's plate. The other couple was lingering over their coffee and dessert as I placed Mario's food in front of him. "Here we are, Mario. Would you like anything else?"

"Ah, the beautiful Mrs. Esposito. How are you today, my dear?" Mario reached out and grabbed my hand, covering it with a kiss. Irritated, I snatched it away quickly. I didn't want to be rude, but Mario was starting to try my patience with his advances.

In his early forties, Mario was exceedingly attractive and aware of it, with ebony colored hair streaked with silver at the temples and ice blue eyes that were striking against his Mediterranean skin tone. He'd once told me that his maternal grandmother had been born in Ireland, while his father's family came from Sicily, like mine. He seemed to think this meant we were kindred spirits and destined for each other. We definitely were not.

He grinned slyly when I pulled my hand away. "What's the matter, love? Can't you spare some time for your best customer *and* boyfriend?"

"You may be a steady customer, Mario, but you're not my boyfriend," I said politely. Rule number one—never make a scene in front of other customers. The man was a wolf on the prowl with arrogance aplenty. "Shouldn't you be at your shop? Midafternoon is a popular time of day for people to want a pick-me-up coffee."

"Not to worry. I've got it covered, *bella donna*," he crooned in a voice as rich and smooth as chocolate. "Sit down. Talk to me, *Bellissima*."

Mario threw around Italian phrases like they were after dinner mints. Maybe other women found him romantic, but not me. Still, I didn't want to offend anyone. "Sorry, but I'm very busy. I have Christmas cookies to bake for the Festival of Lights."

The Festival of Lights was an annual holiday tradition in Harvest Park. People drove through an amazing array of Christmas figurines from gingerbread houses to an ornate Santa's sleigh lit up in the park. This year, there were over seventy different holiday displays, the most we'd ever had. The town's maintenance crew had been working on it since well before Thanksgiving, and this year's show promised to be the best one yet.

"Oh, right." He shoveled a forkful of ravioli into his mouth and swallowed so fast I doubted he'd had time to taste it. "That starts tomorrow night. I'm looking forward to playing Santa for all the little kiddies."

I blinked. "*You?* I thought that Ernie Reynolds was playing Santa. He does it every year." Ernie even had his own suit.

Mario puffed out his chest. "Well, not for a few days at least. Old Ernie's in bed with the flu. His dry-cleaning store has been closed since Thursday." He gave an obnoxious laugh. "Ernie's so cheap, he must be on his death bed. The guy's got the first dollar he ever made."

What a rotten thing to say. I spoke calmly but couldn't resist getting in a jab of my own. "Are you sure the job is yours? Archie played Santa once before in a pinch, and he did wonderfully."

Mario wiped his mouth with a napkin. "While we're on the subject of that old codger, Tessa, I have to say that I'm very disappointed in you."

My eyebrows drew together. "What are you talking about?"

"You're always at Java Time for coffee," Mario complained as he swallowed more ravioli. "I mean, what are people going to think? My girlfriend can't be going to the competitor." He chuckled, but I didn't find it amusing. "You come in for a coffee, and I'll give you extra scratch-off tickets for the contest. One of them is bound to be a winner."

Was this guy for real? Mario's twelve days of Christmas giveaways ranged from a free turkey to the grand prize—a new computer. Stephanie had won a Keurig from him last week. Where he'd gotten the money for all these items was a mystery to me.

I counted to five in my head before I spoke. "Mario, we are not a couple. I have no clue where you got this idea. You're always welcome here as a customer, but—"

Maria stabbed another piece of ravioli with his fork. "I heard that you're looking for someone to play the big red man at your Breakfast with Santa event. When is it again?"

"Christmas Eve morning. But I already have a Santa." Okay, this was a teensy lie. I was hoping Justin could do it, and he wanted to, but he hadn't been able to find anyone to cover his work shift that day. "I won't be needing—"

Mario cut me off, another thing that irritated me about him. The man never let anyone finish a sentence. "Look, baby. I'll do it. I love playing Santa for the kiddies. It gets me right here, you know?" He patted the lapel of his gray pinstriped suit.

My teeth clashed together in annoyance. "I'm not your baby, so please don't call me that. Thanks for the offer, but—"

Mario acted as if he hadn't heard me. He put down his fork and patted his trim stomach while emitting a loud belch. "Oh, Tessa. That was so good. Better than my own mother used to make." He made the sign of the cross upon his chest. His white shirt had the first three buttons undone, revealing a mass of dark chest hair with a thick, gold chain partially hidden within. "Tell you what I'm gonna do. I'll give you the special Mario rate." He winked. "I only do that for people I really like. No cash needed. All you have to do is give me free lunch for a week, and you know—" He leaned closer to me and winked. "Some other fringe benefits."

I backed away in disgust. This man was revolting. It was bad enough that Mario's cafe was putting a sizable dent in Java Time's profits, but there were rumors he was infringing on other local business owners as well. I'd dress up in a Santa suit myself before asking him to help me out.

With a smile, I picked up his empty plate and started to walk away. "Enjoy your day."

Mario was not about to be ignored. He grabbed my wrist in a tight grip. "I haven't finished talking yet, sweetheart."

Startled, I stared down at his hand. "Please let go of me."

He smirked as if he found me mildly amusing. "Now, Tessa, that's no way to treat a paying customer. Where's your loyalty?"

"Hey, Russo." A deep male voice sounded from behind me. "I believe the lady said for you to take your slimy hands off her."

I whirled around in surprise. My landlord, Vince Falducci, was standing behind me, watching the interaction with a steely glare. His fists were clenched at his sides and his gaze was frozen on Mario. Uh oh. I was afraid that World War III was about to commence.

Mario's face froze in fear as he observed Vince's bulging biceps peeking out from under the short-sleeved black T-shirt he wore. There was an intimidating scorpion tattoo on his left arm. Vince's eyes smoldered with anger as he clenched his jaw, but his voice was level and calm. "You've got exactly ten seconds to leave before I throw you out the door."

When Mario released my wrist, I backed away and the two men sized each other up. Vince tapped his foot on the floor and waited. The room was so still that you could have heard a piece of penne drop.

Mario's chair scraped against the floor as he slowly rose to his feet. After giving Vince the evil eye, he reached into his pocket and threw two twenties down on the table. "Keep the change, doll." He winked at me, turned his nose up at Vince, and headed for the front door, while whistling "Santa Claus Is Coming to Town" under his breath.

Vince followed Mario and my chest constricted with fear, sensing another confrontation. Both men were terribly head-strong, and I'd witnessed Vince's fiery temper firsthand when we'd started working together. I scurried after them.

Vince stopped just inside the door, and I almost plowed right into him. We watched Mario stride across the parking lot to his vehicle, hands stuffed deep in his trouser pockets, nose in the air as if he didn't have a care in the world. A vein bulged in Vince's forehead, and he pushed against the bar of the door.

I placed my hand on his arm. "Please don't. He's not worth the trouble."

Our eyes met and Vince's stoic looking face relaxed along with his grip. His eyes, as dark as two pools of coffee without a hint of cream, softened. He placed his hands on my shoulders, the warmth from them seeping through my sleeves. "Are you okay?"

"Yes, I'm fine."

Tires squealed on the pavement and caught our attention. Through the glass door, we saw a long, black sedan screech to a halt right next to my would-be suitor. The man on the passenger side rolled down his window and said something. Mario's back stiffened, and he fumbled with his car keys. The man leaned out of the window farther and spoke again. Mario's shoulders slumped forward, and he glanced around the lot, searching. He then turned, walked over to the sedan, and got into the back seat. Before he'd even shut the door, the vehicle zoomed off.

My mouth dropped open in shock. "Who were those guys? They didn't look like they were having a friendly conversation."

Vince frowned as he stared after the car. "I don't think it's anything to worry about. Mario can handle himself."

"Well, it looked suspicious to me. I'm going to call Gino." My cousin was a police detective in Harvest Park.

Gino picked up instantly. "What's up, Tess?"

"I'm not sure," I said honestly. "Mario Russo was walking across my parking lot when two men pulled up in a car next to him. I couldn't hear what they said, but he got into the car and it sped off."

"And?" Gino asked.

I stared at the phone in disbelief. "You always told me that if I saw something suspicious, I should report it. This felt off to me."

Gino blew out a sigh. "Okay, fine. Did you get a good look at the men? Or the license plate?"

"Not really," I confessed. "They both had dark hair. The one leaning out of the car looked middle-aged, with a thin build. Well-dressed."

"This doesn't exactly come as a surprise," Gino said wryly. "We've got good reason to believe Mario might be involved with a loan shark. I appreciate that you worry about your fellow towns-people, but there's a lot you don't know about this guy. And the less you know, the better. If it makes you happy, I'll stop over at The Espresso Lane in a little while to see if he's back. All right?"

"Wow. That's so considerate of you to check on him. Let's hope that he *does* come back."

Gino grunted in response. "Lose the sarcasm, cuz. Jeez, you get more like my sister every day." He clicked off.

"Unbelievable," I seethed. "Gino didn't even seem concerned. He acted like it was normal."

Vince suppressed a smile. "I can see Gino's point. Mario's about as phony as they come."

"Do you think that he's involved in something shady?"

He nodded grimly. "I know his type, Tessa. Remember what happened to my restaurant."

Yes, I remembered and knew Vince spoke the truth. He'd seen plenty of shady dealings and characters at his own expense. Before the inception of Anything's Pastable, the building had been a dumpy pizzeria called Slice, attracting folks involved with drugs and other illegal activities. Vince had owned the building then but was innocent of the goings-on. And in another string of bad luck, he had also co-owned a five-star restaurant in New York City with similar problems, through no fault of his own.

Vince leaned against the door. "Remember what I told you when I found out the truth about my partner? I felt like an idiot. Everything happened right under my nose. Since then, I've learned a thing or two, and I'm never going to let anyone take advantage of me again." He pinned me with a dark, unwavering stare. "Mario Russo is a disgrace to the entire town of Harvest Park. Between you and me, I don't believe he's come by that coffee shop of his honestly."

My mouth went dry. "Gino thinks that he's involved with a loan shark."

He gave a solemn nod. "Or worse if you know what I mean. Whatever the case, you should refuse to serve him if he comes in again. Stay away from him. He's bad news."

I exhaled sharply. "I can't refuse to serve him. He comes in every day."

Vince ran a hand over the day-old stubble surrounding his sensual looking mouth. "Tessa, I don't want Mario making trouble for you. I've seen the way that guy looks at you. My mother had an old saying, 'The man who looks like an angel is often the worst kind of devil.' She warned me and my brothers that we'd better never act that way with women, or she'd tan our hides." He flashed me a saucy grin. "This is technically still my building until you buy it outright from me. So, I say that you can't serve him."

I stiffened at his comment but decided not to say anything. After all, Vince had come to my aid, and I was grateful for that. In the past year, I'd gotten to know him fairly well. A trained chef like me, he was used to getting his way, in and out of the kitchen. "Did anyone ever tell you how stubborn you are?"

Storm clouds brewed behind Vince's eyes for a second, and then he barked out a laugh. "Seems to me that it works both ways."

It appeared that Vince knew me pretty well too.

His tone turned serious. "Tessa, please humor me on this. Except for a few women in this town who have fallen victim to his charm, Mario Russo has managed to make a lot of enemies, especially among fellow business owners."

"Yes, I know. Archie's place is suffering most of all."

Vince folded his arms across his chest. "You know those prizes Mario is giving away as part of his twelve days of Christmas contest?" When I nodded, he continued. "It wouldn't surprise me if the stuff is hot."

"You think he's dealing in stolen goods?"

Vince gave a casual shrug. "You of all people should know it takes a lot of hard work and preparation to get a business off the ground. Not to mention a while before you begin to make a substantial profit. That wasn't the case with Mario's shop. Trust me. Things don't add up with him."

As much as I hated to admit it, the scenario did fit. "That does explain a lot. I'd love to know what else he's up to."

"It's only my opinion but take it for what it's worth." Vince's voice softened. "Stay away from Mario Russo because he's nothing but trouble."

TWO

SUNDAY MORNING, I SLEPT IN UNTIL ten o'clock, a luxury I rarely allowed myself. As I yawned and stretched, I lay there, listening to the tap of sleet hitting the windowpanes. The house was still and quiet, something I'd resigned myself to during the past year. Sundays were still somewhat painful, for they were the one day of the week that had belonged completely to Dylan and me. We always looked forward to lying in bed, talking and cuddling until late morning. Afterwards I'd cook a large brunch, and then we'd either go for a long walk, a movie, or a drive in the country. Those memories would always hold a special place in my heart.

Unconsciously, I moved my hand over the top of the pillow next to me and heard a chirping sound. I peeked underneath, and Luigi, my tuxedo kitty, stared up at me with an accusatory expression. I knew that look well. He leaped from behind the pillow onto my chest, and I groaned, then laughed as he nudged my hand to pet him.

"Yes, I know. Your breakfast is late, but I was tired." He meowed again and moved off while I rolled out of bed. He stood expectantly in the doorway and waited as I tied my bathrobe, then led the way downstairs.

While my Keurig heated, I filled Luigi's food dish with star shaped crunchies and gave him fresh water. As he ate, I took my mug of dark roast into the living room and sat in the window seat, watching the sleet as it changed over to snow and started to stick to the ground. The Christmas season was my favorite time of the year and filled me with a serene contentment.

Last year that peace had been lost. Dylan's death in the autumn was followed by a tumultuous stint working at Slice, and then months of renovations on the building before my own restaurant opened in the spring. I'd been too busy to think about the holidays last year, which somehow made it easier to cope. I'd cooked the usual Christmas dinner for my family, made hundreds of cookies for friends and neighbors, but that had been the extent of it.

This year Christmas already had a different, unique flavor to it. Justin had brought and helped me decorate the six-foot fir tree, which stood a few feet away from the window seat, enhancing the room with its glorious pine scent. I plugged in the multicolored lights and watched them twinkle, surrounded by strands of silver garland. My fingers touched various ornaments—treasured pieces that triggered powerful memories and made me smile.

Dylan and I had been married for almost six years and dated for three before that. Every Christmas since we'd started dating, he had given me a special ornament. They were a standing joke between us that began the first time I ever made him breakfast. I'd been distracted by a phone call and burned the toast, which had started a small fire in the kitchen.

My ego had taken a severe beating that day. I'd hand prepared my own pappardelle with a gorgonzola cream sauce the night before. I *never* burned anything, let alone toast, so I'd been mortified. But Dylan thought the incident was hilarious. When Christmas rolled around, he'd presented me with a toaster ornament, two burned slices of bread peeking out of the slots. My name had been engraved along the bottom. I'd laughed until the tears ran down my face.

Every year afterward, Dylan had always bought me some type of cooking related ornament. One year it had been a food processor, another time a pasta machine. I had no idea how he'd managed to find such unique ones. They were usually custom made and always engraved. I knew he put a great deal of time and effort into finding the perfect one. Dylan had always been generous about gift giving, and I received many other things of greater value, but this was the one present I looked forward to every year.

Last year, for the first time, there had been no ornament. Dylan had died two months before Christmas. All the "firsts" without him had been difficult, but thankfully they were over now. My mother had warned me about how hard the "firsts" could be. After six years, she still missed my father terribly.

I stared down at the text that had arrived from Justin at five o'clock this morning. He sent one every day and was better than clockwork. More often than not, they contained some corny joke that always made me smile, like today's: Good morning. Why did the chef add extra oregano to the sauce?

I chuckled as I typed my reply. No idea. Why?

His response came instantly: Because she was making up for lost thyme.

I let out an audible groan and typed, you really need to work on your stand-up routine.

Speaking of chefs, how's my favorite one today? Would you like to go to the Festival of Lights with me tonight? Say about seven?

My mouth quirked in a smile, and my fingers flew over the keyboard as I quickly typed out, I'd love to. The only other thing on my calendar for today was the meeting at Town Hall.

Justin seemed to know whenever I needed a pick-me-up. Despite his busy work schedule, I could always count on him. He was strong, dependable, and caring, the perfect partner to see the dazzling light display with. I was determined to make this Christmas a good one. I started making a mental list of all the things the holidays would bring: the festival, cozy Italian food, Christmas baking, and feeding all my friends in Harvest Park. All I needed was a Santa for my breakfast and everything would be perfect.

My brain skittered back to Mario's offer. I couldn't believe he had swindled his way into playing Santa at the festival. Vince's comment about Mario still concerned me, as did the two men who had confronted him in my parking lot. Who on earth had agreed to let him have the job? I hoped it was a joke. If there was one thing our town didn't need, it was more of Mario Russo.

Four hours later, I stood next to Archie in the meeting room of Town Hall, laughing as he told me how his granddaughter Ella had asked her parents for a reindeer for Christmas. Archie's face lit up like a Christmas tree whenever he talked about any of his grandchildren, but I had a sneaking suspicion that four-year-old Ella, named for his deceased wife, was his favorite.

Archie was in his late sixties, balding and a bit on the stout side with kind brown eyes and large jowls that drooped whenever he smiled, which was often. Archie had recently completed renovations to Java Time in hopes of drumming up more business. He'd bought new machines and had new flooring installed this past summer, which had set him back quite a sum, plus a more efficient display case for the baked goods he carried. He'd felt confident that he could recoup the expense in no time. But that was no longer true, and I was sure the stress was taking its toll.

"Are your grandkids coming for Christmas?" I was tempted to ask how Java Time was doing but decided it wasn't the place or time. Even though Harvest Park was a warm and cozy town, the grapevine was always in search of fresh dirt.

He shook his head. "Brandon has an ice hockey tournament the following morning so I'm going to drive out there on Christmas Eve." He undid the cap from the Java Time coffee box he'd brought and filled my waiting cup with dark roast. "Have one of those doughnuts, honey. Or how about a bagel?"

I glanced down at the goodies Archie had brought with him. He was generous to a fault and always donated food and drink for meetings. Besides the bagels, there were glazed, cinnamon, and Boston cream doughnuts. I spotted a lone apple fritter, my favorite, and reached for it. "You're still carrying items from Carlita's bakery?"

"Only doughnuts and a couple of varieties of pastries. Carlita wants to bring in more, but nothing is selling well for me lately." His lips thinned.

"I'm sure things will pick up soon," I said hopefully.

Archie smiled as he picked up an olive-green handled knife to slice his bagel in half. "I'd like to think so, but—" He broke off. "Never mind. Let's talk about something else."

My curiosity piqued. "What's wrong? Is this about Mario?"

Archie hesitated, his usually jovial face taking on a stern look. "I didn't want to say anything, but it seems that he's been spreading rumors about me and Java Time. Ernie was in the other day and told me that Mario's blabbing to his customers that my place recently failed a Department of Health inspection."

My jaw dropped. "You're kidding, right? Java Time is always immaculate."

He smiled sadly. "That's not all. Mario told customers that I use imitation coffee, which is why I won't sell it to them by the bagful. Truth of the matter is, I've never sold it. Besides, you should never grind a whole bag of coffee at a time. It doesn't stay fresh for long once the beans are ground. But somehow that guy always manages to twist things around and make me look like the bad guy."

"I don't understand why people believe him instead of you. You have a great reputation and always treat customers fairly."

He heaved a sigh. "Well, honey, if you tell a person something enough times, they start to believe it. Mario seems to be good at brainwashing people." He leaned in closer. "Did you know he's been selling baked goods in his shop as well? I don't know who the supplier is, but they're at least fifty cents cheaper than what I charge, and his coffee is almost a buck less a cup than mine. What I want to know is how this guy is making a profit? I don't understand. Sure, I've had competition from other coffee vendors before, but none that went to such slimy means to get ahead. And I'm getting old and too tired to fight anymore."

He sounded defeated and it saddened me. I squeezed his hand. "Don't talk like that. It's the holidays and people are spending money on presents. Maybe they're looking to save a few bucks and will come back after Christmas." I didn't mention that I'd seen an increase in my business at the start of the holiday season.

"I hope so," Archie said.

"Next thing you know, he'll start buying pans of frozen lasagna and ravioli from the grocery store and open his own restaurant." I took a large bite from the fritter, savoring the taste of fresh apples and cinnamon.

Archie didn't laugh. "I wouldn't put it past him. Please don't think this is sour grapes on my part, honey. I know Mario wants to put me out of business, but he's not making any friends with other merchants either. You know how we all try to support each other, but Mario refuses to patronize any place in town except your restaurant."

"I wouldn't mind if he came in less," I admitted.

His voice barely above a whisper. "I'll bet that Mayor Randolph brings him up today. I think that Mario was purposefully not invited."

I mulled this over while Archie greeted another store owner. Matt Smitty walked in and flashed me one of his boyish grins. He nodded to Archie and then went up front for a seat.

"Seen much of him lately?" Archie asked.

"Not really. He came into the restaurant before Thanksgiving with his kids, but I haven't seen him since." Matt and I had dated in high school, long before Dylan had entered the picture. The relationship only lasted for a few months and then ended after senior prom. "I'm glad that we're friends again."

"Rumor has it that Matt's got himself a lady friend," Archie remarked.

This came as a surprise. "Seriously? But what about Lila?"

"The divorce was final a few weeks ago. He told me so himself last time he was in Java Time. I guess they're splitting custody of the kids."

"That must be hard on him." After we'd broken up, Matt had struggled with a drug addiction for years, but finally managed to turn his life around. And I knew how much those kids meant to him.

Archie nodded. "I'm sure it is. Anyhow, Bruce Morton couldn't wait to tell me that, when he dropped his car off at Matt's shop for repairs the other night, a woman was in the front seat with him. It was after hours, and Matt was leaving."

"Maybe it was Lila."

"Don't think so. Bruce said they were kissing. It just about killed him that he couldn't see who the mystery woman was," Archie chortled.

Bruce Morton owned Meat and Greet, a grocery store in Harvest Park. He was about Archie's age but without the kind and sweet demeanor. Bruce was short on patience and long on gossip. Still, if the rumor about Matt and a new woman were true, it explained why I hadn't seen him in a while. He and Lila had separated shortly after Dylan's killer was found. I suspected Matt being a primary suspect had something to do with it, but he'd assured me they'd been having problems for a while. Nonetheless, I still felt guilty.

"Good for him," I said. "I'm glad that he's getting on with his life."

Tyler Randolph appeared, and a momentary hush fell over

the room. He approached our table and good-naturedly slapped Archie on the back. "Mr. Fenton, sir, you're a godsend. I was just telling my wife that I needed a good, strong cup of coffee. Everyone knows yours is the best in town."

Archie beamed as he passed the sugar and cream to Tyler's waiting hands. "Stop by tonight for a cappuccino on the house. I know they're your favorite."

"I wish I could, but Alexandra and I are hosting a small gathering at our home. Or at least Alex says it's a small gathering. Knowing my wife that probably means one hundred of our closest friends," Tyler said dryly.

We laughed as Tyler selected a glazed doughnut. "Too bad you don't have a catering service, Tessa. We'd be your most popular customers. Are you still having Breakfast with Santa at your restaurant?" he asked.

"That's the plan. As long as I can find a Santa. Who are you using for the Festival of Lights?" It was the perfect opportunity to see if the rumor about Mario was true.

Tyler set his coffee down on the table and looked disappointed. "Darn. I was hoping you had a name for me."

"What happened to Ernie Reynolds?" Archie wanted to know. "He loves playing Santa every year."

Tyler ran a hand through his prematurely gray hair. "Ernie's sick with the flu, so I need someone else for at least tonight and tomorrow. My assistant lined up—" He hesitated, and I knew why. Like most people in town, Tyler was aware of the friction between

Mario and Archie. "Anyhow, I was hoping to find someone with more—ah—experience."

Archie tugged on his whiskers thoughtfully. "Gee, I wish I could help you out tonight, but Jake's got the evening off, so I need to stay put at Java Time. Who's filling in for Ernie?"

"Tessa," Tyler smiled, changing the subject. "I've been meaning to tell you that the takeout we got the other night was superb. Alex is in love with your penne and tomato sauce, and the pumpkin ravioli was amazing."

My chest swelled with pride. "Thank you. I'm so glad that you both enjoyed the food."

The crowd had grown louder while we were talking. Tyler glanced around the room and then raised his coffee cup to us. "Please excuse me. We should get started."

Archie went up to the front row to sit and chat with Bruce, while I sat in the second to last row and finished my apple fritter. There was no one behind me and I had a great view of the entire room. I enjoyed people watching, even if it was only the back of their heads.

My phone buzzed with a text from Gabby. Can't make the meeting. Jodie Livingston is coming in with a large order so I'm opening the store for her. Can't pass this up. Fill me in later. Going to the Festival of Lights tonight?

Jodie was an avid bookworm with fifteen grandchildren she loved buying books for, so I could understand Gabby's decision. I typed out a quick response. Yes, I'm going with Justin. We'll probably be over about eight. See you and Lou around then?

She sent me back a thumbs-up.

Tyler gave an exaggerated cough, and the few people who were still talking immediately fell silent.

"Thank you for joining me today," he said. "I wanted to let you all know how much I appreciate your dedication to the Festival of Lights every year. As you know, it's our second largest event, only succeeded by the fall Apple Festival. This year's recipient of the proceeds is our local Humane Society. We hope that after all expenses are paid, there will be at least two or three thousand dollars to donate to the organization, which is desperately in need of the money."

A murmur of approval went up from the crowd. Tyler continued on about activities in place for the festival, vendors who would be selling items in the Lake House, and the new light displays featured this year. He was in midsentence when a click-clacking sound on the linoleum in the hallway caught my attention. I turned in my chair as Wendy Summers, Tyler's assistant, slid into the seat next to mine. She was breathing heavily, her pale, almost transparent skin red with exertion. I glanced with surprise at her fiery hair. I almost hadn't recognized her.

"The color suits you," I said.

She flushed appreciatively. "Thanks. I always wanted to be a redhead. Sorry to sound crass, but it's no fun being a brunette, Tessa. Then again, if I looked like you, I probably would have taken my chances."

"Stop it. You always look pretty," I told her.

Tyler shot Wendy a dirty look and she immediately fell silent.

"Crap, he's going to kill me." Wendy pulled a notepad out of her purse. "He specifically told me to be here on time to take notes."

I sipped my coffee. "Is it really necessary? The *Harvest Park Press* covers the town board meetings." Why would Tyler need to bother his employee with the task as well? If you asked me, she catered to her boss way too much.

"Try telling him that," Wendy whispered as she pushed her long hair back behind her ears. "First off, he calls me a secretary." She gave a proud toss of her head. "I'm not a secretary, I'm an administrative assistant. Second, he believes that any meeting he has to attend means I should be there as well. Unless it's out of town, which he does a lot lately. Third, he wanted this special meeting kept top secret so that the *Harvest Park Press* didn't catch wind of it."

I scanned the room, looking for the college-aged reporter, but he was missing. "Why, what's the deal?"

Tyler cleared his throat loudly and glared at us. *Uh-oh.* My attempts at being discreet had fallen short. Wendy froze in her chair and we fell silent. I sympathized with her. She was in her midtwenties and had worked for Tyler for three years. Rumor had it, despite his outwardly pleasant and charming demeanor, our mayor was difficult to work for.

A hand shot up in the first row, and Bruce stood before Tyler even acknowledged him.

"Hey, Randolph, is that the only reason you've called us here?" He tugged on his light-brown beard, which always reminded me of Grizzly Adams. "To go over the activities and what else you still need? This is a busy time of year and, for most of us, our bread-and-butter season. If you've got something else to say, please get on with it."

"The older that guy gets, the more impatient he becomes," Wendy noted.

Tyler shot him an icy stare. "Well, I was getting to that Bruce but certainly wouldn't want to hold you up, since your time is more valuable than the rest of ours."

"Oh, he's ticked off," Wendy whispered. "Look at the way he's clenching his jaw."

Tyler made a point of glancing around the room for several seconds. "You all may notice that one certain business owner isn't here."

"There's several people who aren't here," Bruce grunted. "Larry from Suit Yourself, Greg from Pie Carumba, and Molly from Spice and Nice. But I've got a feeling you're talking about Mr. Russo."

A murmur ran through the room.

"Here it comes," Wendy said. "Tyler can't stand Mario." She leaned in closer and darted her eyes up at the mayor on his podium. "Alexandra was having an affair with him, you know."

My mouth fell open. "Are you serious?"

Wendy nodded and dropped her voice even lower. "Oh yes.

But he got tired of her and moved on to greener pastures. Now that Ernie's sick, Tyler made me in charge of finding a new Santa Claus. Mario came into Town Hall on Friday and agreed to do it when I asked him."

"Why would you give Mario the job when you know that Tyler dislikes him?" Boy, that must have gone over well.

She gave a careless shrug. "Tyler was a little upset, but he'll get over it. Mario's a good guy, and he wanted to do something nice for the kids. I think it's so sweet."

"Are you kidding?"

Startled, we both turned around. Claire Dunsbach, who worked in her family's florist shop, The Flower Girl, was staring at us wide-eyed. She and her mother must have sat down while we were talking and had obviously overheard part of our conversation.

Claire smiled sheepishly, as if she'd guessed my thoughts. "Sorry, I wasn't trying to eavesdrop, but couldn't help hearing what you said about Mario playing Santa." She narrowed her eyes at Wendy. "Why would you give the job to *him*?" she asked. "Santa is the main attraction, besides the light show. We want someone who embodies the spirit of Christmas and Harvest Park. Not that phony."

Wendy flushed as heads started to turn in our direction. "Claire, we can talk about this later—"

Claire jumped up from her seat. "Hey, Tyler, is it true? Mario Russo is playing Santa at the Festival?"

A few gasps and some snorts came from around the room.

The smile faded from Tyler's face. "Where did you hear this?"

Claire pointed at Wendy, who immediately shrank down in her seat.

Tyler's face grew scarlet as he and Wendy exchanged glances. She folded her arms across her chest and stared down at the floor. They clearly had a great working relationship.

Tyler continued. "I was planning to address that topic next. It's only for a couple of days, while Ernie recovers, but I thought all of you should be told ahead of time."

Archie spoke calmly. "Tyler, with all due respect, we're the ones donating our time and money to this event. Shouldn't we have a say in who plays Santa?"

"Archie's right. It's our decision," Claire added furiously. "Anyone would be better than that pond scum! He's been selling poinsettias in his coffee shop and telling customers that my bouquets are overpriced. The job should go to someone who supports our town, not someone who is trying to profit at everyone else's expense!"

Claire's elderly mother, Ruthie, roused herself from her seat. "It's an outrage. Archie would never do something like that!"

Everyone began talking at once, so Tyler rapped his gavel against the podium. "Please! One at a time. Now, it's only for two nights, people, and then Ernie will be back. *Hopefully*."

"What's Mario going to do," Claire taunted, "hand out coffee club cards to the kids instead of candy canes?"

Tyler's dark eyes thinned to tiny slits. "Look. I realize he wasn't everyone's choice. And he certainly wasn't mine. But we're losing sight of what's our main concern, the animal shelter. Helping those in need. That's what Harvest Park is all about. We're expecting our biggest crowd ever this year."

"Mario's not that bad," Bruce protested.

Everyone in the room turned to look at him. Bruce rarely had a nice thing to say about anyone, so this came as a surprise.

Archie raised an eyebrow. "When he moved into town you were the first one to say you didn't trust him."

"Yeah, Bruce," Ruthie cackled. "You told me he was a phony. Mellowing in your old age?"

Bruce held up his hand in a "stop" motion. "Hey, I'm not saying that he's my best friend or anything. But he offered to play Santa, and he's doing it for free. It shows that the guy has a heart."

"Why are you defending him?" Ruthie demanded. "What's he doing—giving you free coffee for the next year? Or did you win it in his contest?"

Everyone in the room laughed, except for Tyler and Bruce. Ruthie's mouth had no filter, but despite her bluntness, I liked her. She reveled in filling the town with lovely arrangements, and her only wish was to make the world a little more beautiful.

"I'm not defending the guy," Bruce said hotly. "I just think that we shouldn't be so quick to condemn him. It's Christmas, for goodness' sake. The season to do unto others."

"Then how come you raised the price on ground sirloin

again?" Ruthie wanted to know. "To pay for that brand new meat cooler? It had to cost you at least ten grand."

Bruce flushed and stared down at the floor.

"Guilty as charged," Wendy whispered.

Tyler pursed his lips together. "Does anyone else have complaints about Mario that we should know about?"

To my surprise, Matt raised his hand. He'd always been on the quiet side and still looked much the same as he had in high school, with the round, baby-like cheeks, dirty blond hair that fell into his eyes, and a dimple that showed on the left side of his mouth whenever he smiled. "Russo's threatening me with a lawsuit."

Shouts of outrage went up from the crowd, and Tyler rapped the gavel again. "What happened, Matt?"

Matt stood and shoved his hands deep into the pockets of his jeans. "He claimed that his brakes failed after I worked on his car. Said he got into an accident and swears that he's lucky to be alive." Matt owned and operated The Car Doctor, an auto repair shop.

"Unlucky for us, you mean," Ruthie grumbled.

"That's enough!" Tyler never raised his voice, so this sudden outburst took everyone by surprise, including Ruthie. She wasn't used to being told to keep her opinion to herself.

The room fell silent, and after a slight pause, Tyler spoke again in a more reserved tone. "Sounds like you might need to get a lawyer."

"I know he's lying," Matt said. "I went over every inch of that car. You all know me; I do good work. Trouble is, I can't prove that's he's lying. He told me that he's going to take legal action. If I want to settle out of court, he'll be satisfied with five grand. I wouldn't be surprised if he cut his brake lines himself."

Tyler glanced in my direction. "Have you talked to Detective Mancusi or anyone else at the police department? Maybe the so-called accident was caught on camera?"

Matt looked over his shoulder to see who Tyler was staring at. When our eyes met, he turned away, as if embarrassed, and then stammered, "No, I haven't."

It was obvious—to me at least—why he hadn't. Gino had been a member of the local police force for over ten years. He was two years older than Gabby and me and had never cared for Matt, especially when we were dating. The fact that Matt had been a bit possessive after we first broke up didn't help. Gabby was not a fan of Matt's either. Still, I knew that Gino would have taken the claim seriously.

"Mario's behavior is not one that I condone," Tyler addressed the room. "This is a close-knit community and we're here to help our neighbors, not sabotage one another. If you are attending the festival tonight, please refrain from making any trouble. Think of the children. They're what Christmas is all about, after all."

"Come along," Ruthie ordered Claire. "I've heard enough of his crap."

Ever the obedient daughter, Claire rose from her chair so quickly it toppled over. Both women walked out of the room with their heads held high, with Ruthie clutching Claire's arm for support.

A muscle ticked in Tyler's jaw as he watched them leave, then he loudly rapped the gavel. "This meeting is adjourned. Thanks to all of you for donating your time, and thanks to Archie for supplying coffee and doughnuts. And a very special thank you to Tessa for all the time she's devoted to making Christmas cookies for the festival."

"Oh, I'd love to be a fly on the wall when Tyler and Mario come face to face tonight," Wendy gloated as we watched everyone file out of the room. Tyler walked right past her without a single word.

I couldn't figure Wendy out. Did she enjoy starting trouble? She'd made it clear she'd found Mario attractive, so perhaps that factored into her attitude. It wasn't the first time Wendy had complained about her boss to Gabby or me. Maybe it was a bid for attention. Wendy had been through a lot in her lifetime. She'd moved to Harvest Park at fifteen to live with her grandmother when her parents had divorced. Her mother had gone abroad to live with another man and left Wendy behind. After her grandmother passed away last year, Wendy had been stuck with the funeral bill and now lived alone in the rambling house. It was sorely in need of repairs that she couldn't afford on her present salary.

I was tempted to ask her if she knew anything about the men I'd seen Mario with yesterday but decided this wasn't the best time to bring it up.

She waited while I buttoned my wool coat. "Did you bring the cookies with you, Tessa?"

"Yes, tonight's supply is in the back of my car," I said. "There's fifteen dozen. I hope it's enough."

Her jaw dropped in amazement. "That must have taken you hours."

"It's not that bad. I prepare the dough way ahead of time and then freeze it until it's needed." I'd actually started making the dough back in October and usually ended up with about five hundred cookies for family and friends. Since I had offered to take this job on for the duration of the festival, which ran until the first week of January, the total amount of cookies would be close to four thousand. "It's all just a matter of getting organized."

"I'll walk with you to your car and get them," Wendy offered. "I need to be over to the Lake House early tonight to set up the booth for Santa. Unless you're planning to be there when the place opens?"

I shook my head. "Not until later. Justin's picking me up at seven."

Wendy grinned like a Cheshire cat. "He's awful cute, Tessa. You guys look adorable together."

My cheeks warmed. "We're not dating, Wendy." Justin Kelly had been Dylan's closest friend and was now mine. We'd always been close, but after Dylan died, Justin had become a pillar of strength for me to lean on. He'd also confessed that he'd been harboring feelings for me since the day we met ten years earlier but had never acted on it, accepting that I was happy with Dylan. When I found out, I'd been shocked and was honest with him, telling him I wasn't ready to get involved with someone else, let alone Dylan's closest friend. Justin respected that and assured me he was willing to wait for as long as it took. We continued to do the same things we'd always done—taking in an occasional movie or having dinner together. If he wasn't working, Justin would often stop by to see me when I arrived home from the restaurant for a quick chat. He was there whenever I needed him. The shock of his confession had slowly worn off, replaced with friendship, trust, and something different. A new feeling that I'd recently noticed and wasn't sure what to name.

Wendy waited as I opened the trunk and handed her the plastic totes with the cookies. I helped her place them in the back of her ancient hatchback.

"Bring me the receipt for the ingredients and I'll write you a check," she said. "It's too bad we can't reimburse you for your time as well."

I waved her off. "It's my donation to the town. Besides, I love doing it."

Wendy's smile twisted into a frown as she watched Mario's sports car zoom past the building at a speed that was at least double the 30 miles-per-hour limit. "I hope that everything goes according to plan tonight."

"It'll be fine," I assured her. "You've done a great job organizing the event."

She heaved a long sigh. "That's the problem. If something does go wrong, I'll be the first person to be blamed."

THREE

MY DOORBELL RANG AT SEVEN O'CLOCK sharp. I hurried down the stairs as Luigi leapt from the window seat in the living room and raced to the front door, easily beating me. I laughed out loud and reached down to stroke his head.

"You always think it's for you, don't you?" This year had been so lonely, and I thanked my lucky stars for my fur baby's companionship. People might argue that Luigi was only a cat, but he was so much more to me.

Justin stood at the door, dressed in jeans and a dark-blue bomber jacket that went well with his gray-blue eyes. He gave me a light peck on the cheek and then reached down to give Luigi an affectionate head rub. "How's the big guy doing today?"

Satisfied that he had not been ignored, Luigi meowed and scampered over to the Christmas tree where he began to tap a gold ball with Santa's face on it.

I clapped my hands. "Hey. Stop that."

Luigi gave me an indignant look and jumped back in the window seat. He snuggled on top of a throw pillow and quickly shut his eyes. I wasn't falling for his innocent act.

Justin stared up at the tree and grinned. "Wow. That tree is gorgeous. I wonder where it came from."

"This is the first time I've ever had one delivered to me on a fire truck," I teased. Justin worked as a firefighter for Harvest Park, and two of his co-workers had helped him set up the tree when they were off duty. Always prepared, I'd set out homemade eggnog and Christmas cookies from my pre-made supply as a thank you.

The tree had been a surprise, but a welcome one. Justin knew that I'd been dreading bringing one home by myself. Dylan and I had always picked out our Christmas tree and decorated it together, but with Justin taking the reins, I'd been spared the painful comparisons. After he'd helped me decorate, Justin and I had watched one of our favorite movies, the black and white version of *A Christmas Carol.* He made it easier for me to get into the holiday spirit.

"Are you ready to go?" Justin asked.

"All set. Do you want something to eat first?"

Justin shook his head. "Not that I'd ever willingly turn down a meal cooked by you, but I had a burger at the station earlier." He wiggled his eyebrows. "And I'm looking forward to sampling your Christmas cookies at the festival. Hope you made gingerbread. *Lots* of gingerbread."

"Hang on a sec." I laughed and went into the kitchen, returning with a bag of gingerbread I'd made. "Just in case there aren't any left—here's your own supply."

His eyes widened in delight and he immediately reached into the bag for one. "Wow, you spoil me. Every time I walk through your door, I gain five pounds."

"Oh please," I scoffed as he draped my coat around my shoulders and held the front door open for me. "You're in fantastic shape. There's not an ounce of fat on you." He had to be in top physical condition because of the rigors associated with his job.

"I don't know," he teased. "My sister always used to tell me that I had a ton of fat between my ears."

I chuckled. "I hope I get to meet her sometime."

"You will." We approached my car, which would be easier maneuvering through the single lane tunnel in the park than Justin's truck. "Do you want me to drive?" he asked.

"Please. I want to snap some pictures of the displays as we drive by them."

Justin opened the passenger door for me and went around to the driver's side while I settled myself in the seat. He started the engine and blasted the heat, then stared over at me. My teeth were chattering uncontrollably. "Cold?" he asked.

"F-freezing," I said in between my shivers. "But it doesn't matter. I'm so excited to see the lights. I missed it last year."

"I know," Justin said softly. "You missed a lot of things."

When we stopped for a red light, he reached across the seat

and took my gloved hand in his, a gesture he did often when he could sense my sadness coming on. "I want the coming year to be a good one for you, Tess. No one deserves it more."

I felt my words leave me as I stared into his beautiful eyes. My stomach did a flip-flop, that sweet feeling bubbling up, making me freeze from something other than the cold.

"You okay?" Justin's brow furrowed with concern.

"Sure." I studied his profile as he drove, trying to shake my confusing reaction. He was undoubtedly handsome, with a rugged strong face, square chin, and dark hair that was always tousled. His nose was slightly crooked from the time he broke it in a house fire when debris fell on him. But he was Justin. My friend Justin. *Dylan's* Justin. That's all.

"How's work?" I asked.

"Fine," he said shortly. Justin never talked about his job much. He was like Gino in that respect—keeping the professional face on when necessary, but there was a sensitivity about him that could not be masked.

He had recently told me in confidence that he was being considered for a lieutenant position, which was an honor and rare for someone his age. I had no doubt he would excel at it. He'd won many awards for acts of bravery that went above and beyond the call of duty. Justin was always modest about it, saying that he was only doing his job, but I secretly hated the thought that his life was constantly in jeopardy.

The last year had not only been difficult for me, but for him as well. Besides losing his best friend, Justin's father had died, and he'd taken a leave of absence to return to California and help his mother. He'd also had to straighten out some unpleasant matters with his ex-wife, Natalie.

I leaned my head back against the seat and sighed. "We're quite a pair, aren't we?"

Justin's face creased into a smile. "Meaning?"

"This year hasn't been kind to either one of us, but we don't give up. We're both trying to find our new normal. I can almost see the light at the end of the tunnel. No pun intended." I grinned over at him as we approached the display in the park.

"That's right, we never quit. Just like a chef never stops until she's fed everyone in her restaurant." His eyes twinkled at me. "Hey, did you hear how the famous Italian chef died?"

I groaned. "Um, gee, he *pasta* away?"

"Aw." He tried to look disappointed. "I thought I was being original."

We both laughed. It was amazing how comfortable I always felt with him, that I could tell him anything. Justin was a great listener and amazingly supportive, and deep down he was more sensitive than Dylan. Dylan had been quite outspoken while Justin was on the quiet side. I blinked, surprised. Why was I making comparisons between them?

I cleared my throat. "I forgot how much Christmas makes me happy. I want to carry that feeling around with me all the time. For the past year, I've only been happy when I'm cooking, or with family and friends. But I love the fact that it's snowing, we're going to the light show, and there are cookies, and I have such good company to share it all with."

"All in that order?" he teased.

I laughed. "Hey, you'll never guess who's playing Santa tonight."

Justin stopped my car at the entranceway to the park. There was a long line of vehicles in front of us. A man in a ski parka stood in a small booth, collecting admission fees. "Doesn't Ernie always do it?" he asked.

"Ernie's in bed with the flu. Guess again."

He looked at me questioningly. "It has to be Archie then."

"Nope. Archie's at Java Time tonight."

He shrugged. "I give up."

"Mario Russo. He even has his own suit."

Justin raised his eyebrows. "Seriously? That's a surprise. I'd think that he'd be more worried about his bottom line and Christmas contest than being charitable. He doesn't exactly strike me as the giving type."

I told Justin the rumor about Tyler's wife being involved with Mario. "I'm surprised that Wendy gave him the job. She must have done it to get back at Tyler for the way he treats her."

"Maybe not. I've seen her going into The Espresso Lane." Justin frowned.

"She might have an agenda. Then again, it seems that most of the town has followed suit. I wonder what's really going on over there…"

"Forget about the light display. There might be some other serious fireworks tonight. After all, Harvest Park's top chef and sleuth has just arrived." A small smile played on the corner of his lips.

I gave him a playful jab in the side. "Very funny."

Justin paid the attendant, who gave us a pamphlet and told us where to find holiday music on the radio to accompany our journey. We followed the predetermined route through the park and observed the light displays on both sides of us.

"Oh look!" I pointed excitedly at a group of reindeer in colorful red and green lights that were jumping in the air over the roadway before us. "I don't remember seeing that one before."

"They just added it last year," Justin said. "But check out the lighted candy cane display. I think that one is something else."

He was right. The red and white lights trimmed in gold sparkled in brilliance, lighting up the surrounding area. They seemed quite magical to me, which was how I'd always thought of Christmas as a child.

Each display was lovely, and the fact that it was flurrying while "Here Comes Santa Claus" played on the car radio only added to the cozy feeling. I was finally able to focus on all the good things in my life. I had a restaurant that was thriving, a warm home, good family, and friends.

"They're more beautiful than I remember." I gazed at a gingerbread house decorated with lollipops and gumdrops. It was incredible how detailed it was.

Justin smiled at me fondly. "It's always the little things in life that make you happy."

"Sometimes those turn out to be the most important ones of all," I remarked.

"I couldn't agree more."

I suddenly thought back to the first day I met Justin and, consequently enough, Dylan. They had come to Harvest Park to be groomsmen for a college friend while I'd been a bridesmaid in the same wedding. Justin and I were paired off to walk down the aisle together, but Dylan was the one who had caught my eye. Recently Justin had confided that both men had wanted to ask me out, but Dylan beat him to it.

We drove through the rest of the displays in quiet contentment. After we passed the last one, instead of exiting the park, Justin veered off to the right, which brought us to a small, red wooden cabin called the Lake House. In front of the building were Frosty the Snowman and the Grinch merrily waving at us. Elsa from *Frozen* was supervising a snowman building contest, with all the children packing snow and brandishing carrot noses while being cheered on by their parents and friends.

Justin gestured toward the kids. "How are your snowman building skills?"

"I can't remember the last time I made one," I confessed.

Justin grabbed my hand, and we ran through the snow to the side of the building, away from the crowd. He stopped and then fell onto his back in the snow.

"What are you doing?" I asked, mystified.

His eyes sparkled up at me. "Didn't you ever make snow angels when you were a kid? Come on, it's fun."

I stared down at him waving his arms and legs in the snow and couldn't stop laughing. Despite the cold, I was warmed from head to toe.

The lights from the building reflected off Justin's face as he continued to lay there in the snow. He looked perfectly happy and content. "Now the trick is to get up without ruining it." He jumped up, but one of his feet slipped and he added an extra footprint to the angel. "Oh, well, I almost made it. Come on, your turn."

I glanced around but no one seemed to be paying any attention to us. The cheering for the snowman contest grew louder. "No, some other time."

Justin put his hands on his hips. "Chickening out on me, Esposito? Scared that I've got you beat?"

I tried to look indignant, pointedly staring down at his misshapen angel. "Oh please. Anyone can make an angel with two wings and three feet."

He choked back a laugh. "Tell you what. Since you're a newbie at this, I'll help." He gave me a gentle push backward, and I giggled and shrieked when my body connected with the snow. It was powdery and brutally cold.

"I'm freezing!" I complained.

"Move your arms and legs back and forth," he said.

"I feel like an idiot." But I couldn't stop laughing and he joined in. "There's no way I can get up without ruining this."

Justin shot me a mischievous grin. "Then we'll cheat." He reached forward and held out his hands for me to grab. In one single swoop he lifted me off the ground. I stumbled against him, trying to find my footing, and he caught me before I fell.

"See? I knew you were a natural." Justin had his hands at my waist, while I clung to his arms. Our gazes met, and we continued to stare at each other for several seconds without speaking. I forgot everything except for how warm his eyes looked, realizing how easy it would be to get quite lost in them.

Justin broke the silence and linked my arm through his. "Come on. Hot chocolate is first on the agenda."

As we entered the Lake House, the smell of fried onions wafted through the air from Susie's Snack Counter. I spotted Gabby and her boyfriend, Lou Sawyer, standing in front of it, sharing an order of French fries.

"Hey you guys!" Gabby waved. She looked adorable in a red knitted hat and matching scarf. "These fries are pretty awesome. Want one?" She held the carton out to Justin.

He shook his head. "Thanks, but I'm only interested in the Christmas cookies. I hear there's a local knockout who makes them."

Gabby's mouth turned up at the corners. "Those are in a separate booth, next to Santa's station. They're going fast so you'd better hurry."

Justin turned to me. "You want to come or stay here with Gabby?"

"No, I'll wait here. I've already seen the cookies from this so-called knockout," I quipped.

He grinned as he made his way through the crowd. A couple of men called to him in greeting and he stopped to speak to them.

Gabby nudged Lou in the shoulder. "You want more of these fries, babe?"

Lou was checking out the crowd and didn't reply. Gabby nudged him again. "Did you hear me?"

He turned around and seemed to see me for the first time. "Huh? Oh, hi Tessa."

Gabby shook her head at me. "It must be something police-related. Gino does the same thing."

Lou and Gabby had been dating for about a year. It was the longest relationship Gabby had ever been in, and it was easy to see how much they cared for each other.

"What are you staring at?" Gabby asked.

Lou ran a hand over his blond brush cut. "I'm watching Russo interacting with the kids. Why he'd volunteer to play Santa I have no idea."

Gabby and I followed his gaze to the Santa booth, where Mario was sitting in a high-backed chair draped with red velvet. A little girl was wriggling on his lap as Mario tried to get her to look at the camera so Wendy could snap a picture.

"It's a wonder that Tyler lets her sleep," Gabby murmured,

guessing my thoughts. "She's pretty much on call 24 hours a day. I don't know why she doesn't quit."

"She needs the money. That house of her grandmother's is falling to bits. Plus, there's a shortage of jobs in Harvest Park right now. I've had three people come in and apply for server positions this past week." Where were they last April when my restaurant opened, and people didn't even bother to show up for interviews?

"The economy is always changing." Lou helped himself to another fry. "Gino told me about the incident at your restaurant earlier. I guess you can see for yourself that Mario's fine."

"Gino was supposed to call and let me know," I said tartly. "I realize Mario's no one's favorite person, but I was still worried."

"What about Mario?" Justin asked. He had returned holding a cardboard box between his hands, with two cups of hot chocolate piled high with whipped cream and a plate of Christmas cookies. He placed the cookies on a nearby table and helped himself to a gingerbread pizzella.

I explained the incident with Mario at my restaurant, skipping over certain parts.

"He's got a lot of nerve," Gabby fumed. "That jerk had no right to touch you."

"Gabs," I said warningly.

Justin narrowed his eyes. "Wait a second. That guy put his hands on you?"

"It was nothing," I assured him.

A vein bulged in his neck. "Tell me exactly what he did, Tessa."

His sharp tone surprised me. I wasn't used to seeing this side of him. "Mario tried to keep me from leaving his table, so he grabbed my wrist. It didn't—"

"Good thing Vince was there," Gabby commented. "Mario thinks that he's God's gift to women."

Justin fell silent, and I had a sudden urge to pinch Gabby. Vince and Justin were unfailingly polite to each other whenever their paths crossed at Anything's Pastable, which wasn't often. But neither man seemed interested in befriending the other. Thanks to Gabby, Justin had discovered that Vince had asked me out last year. He'd casually inquired last week if I intended to purchase the building outright from Vince. It was the third time he'd asked me in as many months.

I tried to change the subject. "Is Gino here?"

Gabby shook her head. "He and Lucy went to some party, and Mom's babysitting for them. They're planning to come tomorrow night. With me as designated babysitter. Lou's going to help me, aren't you, babe?"

Lou looked a bit apprehensive. "I don't know. Six-year-old twins *and* a newborn? No offense, Gabs, but your nephews are monsters. Only don't tell Gino I said so."

"They're not that bad," I protested.

Gabby went to the counter for some napkins and accidentally bumped into a man who was paying for a coffee. "Pardon me," she said politely.

"Excuse me, Gabby." Bruce Morton's tone was cool and aloof.

I hadn't recognized him before he spoke. Bruce had a dark-blue hat pulled down to his eyebrows and a muffler wrapped over his nose and mouth, revealing little of his face. He nodded curtly to the rest of us, paid for his drink, and hurried away.

"Strange behavior, even for him," Gabby noted. "Bruce has been more uptight than usual."

Lou added more ketchup to the leftover fries. "He's like the town Grinch, always upset about something."

"He defended Mario at the meeting today," I said.

We watched Bruce cross over to Santa's booth. He'd pulled the muffler down and was sipping his coffee while he observed Mario with the kids. Two little girls were left in line. Wendy put up a sign up behind them that read, *Santa needs to feed his reindeer. Will be back soon*. Bruce walked past them and exited through the back door.

"I saw the two of them having a conversation in front of Meat and Greet the other day," Lou remarked. "Maybe he's waiting for Mario to go outside so they can have another chat. New best buddies, it seems."

Justin glanced sideways at me. "All I care about is that Mario stays away from your restaurant. I don't like the idea of that guy putting his hands on you. Next time he can answer to me."

I secretly hoped that Mario would stay away too. My gaze wandered around the room, and I noticed someone resembling Archie from the back following Bruce outside. I was tempted to follow him, but Gabby began shaking my arm to get my attention.

"Look at that little girl. The one with the red hair taking the candy cane from Mario. Isn't that Stephanie's daughter?"

I stared at Santa's chair. "No, it isn't Zoe. Stephanie said they might be here if she wasn't too tired after the show."

Gabby edged closer to me. "Has she told you anything about her new boyfriend?"

"Very little. They've only been together for a few weeks, so she probably doesn't want to say anything until she knows if it's serious."

Stephanie's life had been rough since before Zoe's birth. Her ex-husband had been physically abusive, and after several years, she'd finally found the courage to leave him and start over. It had been a long fight in court, but she'd won custody of Zoe. Her ex was only allowed to see his daughter twice a month and had become so enraged when the decision was handed down that he'd been held in contempt of court. He'd then failed to show up for his visitation and Stephanie was relieved. She hoped the court would decide to suspend all of his visits in the future.

"Remember that last guy she went out with? How he forgot his wallet and she ended up paying for the entire dinner? Then he never called her again." Gabby pointed in Mario's direction. "Sounds like something Mario would do. I heard that he asked Ernie to bill him for his dry cleaning, and he still hasn't paid."

"Not surprising," Lou commented.

Gabby wasn't finished. "And he's been running a tab at the liquor store too—at least that's what Claire Dunsbach told me."

"He's making friends everywhere," Justin said sourly.

At that moment, Mario rose from his seat and went to have a word with Wendy. He pulled a packet of cigarettes from his suit pocket and disappeared outside.

"Gross." Gabby sounded like a little kid. "Who wants to sit on the lap of a Santa that smells like cigarettes?"

I'd never been a fan of smoking. "Jeez, you'd think he'd wait until he was out of sight from the kids before pulling those out."

"The more I see of that guy, the less I like him." Lou helped himself to a genetti with red and green sprinkles and passed the plate to Gabby.

I crossed over to the garbage can to throw my cup away when someone bumped into me from behind. I turned to find Matt standing at Susie's Snack Counter. He hadn't even bothered to apologize or acknowledge me, and then I realized why. He had a piece of cloth wrapped around his right hand. Spots of blood dotted the material.

"Have you got a first aid kit?" Matt asked Susie.

Susie was staring at his hand in horror. "Uh, no, only some bandages and a bottle of peroxide. Do you want to come back here and wash it in the sink?"

"Matt, what happened?" I asked.

He jumped at the sound of my voice. "Oh. Hi, Tess. It's nothing, really. I caught my hand in the car door. That's all."

"Do you want me to take a look at it?" Justin asked. In addition to being a firefighter, he was also a trained EMT.

The cloth had slipped, and I saw broken skin and blood that showed no sign of stopping. Justin tried to get a closer look, but Matt snatched his hand away.

"It's fine. A Band-Aid's all I need," he said hastily as Susie held one out to him.

"Maybe you should go to the emergency room," Justin suggested. "It looks like you might need stitches."

"I said it's fine." Matt's voice was sharp with an undercurrent of anger. His tone reminded me of the unpleasant days that had followed our breakup. I backed away from him, and Justin placed a protective arm around my shoulders, sharing my grim expression.

Matt glanced at us sheepishly. "Sorry. I didn't mean to sound like a jerk. Look, I have to get back outside. Lila's in the parking lot with the boys, waiting for me. See you guys later." He hurried off into the crowd as we stared after him.

"Good riddance," Gabby muttered.

Lou looked amused. "Not a fan?"

"Hardly. Ask Tessa about Matt sometime. Especially how I loathed him when they were dating."

I let out a groan. "Jeez, Gabs, that was thirteen years ago. I think it's time to let it go."

A blood curdling scream pierced the air. Panic and confusion flickered across the crowd. Lou stepped away from us, his hand immediately moving to the gun hidden under his shirt. Justin stepped in behind him, scanning the crowd for signs of visible distress.

From Santa's station, Wendy came peeling across the room, heading in our direction. I stepped forward, and she ran to me and clutched my arm. Her face was ghostly white. "Tessa, call 911! Quick!"

"What's wrong?" I asked in horror.

"It's Mario," she sobbed. "He's been stabbed. And—and I think he's dead."

FOUR

THE NOISE INSIDE THE LAKE HOUSE came to a sudden halt with Wendy's cry. People stared at her like frozen statues, unable to move. Then the entire place came alive and panic ensued. Parents grabbed their children and headed out the front entrance. Justin and Lou immediately sprang into action, sprinting toward the back door.

"What can we do?" Gabby shouted as she ran after them.

Lou spun around. "Stay here!" he said sharply, using a commanding voice I'd never heard before. Apparently neither had Gabby, who stopped dead in her tracks. "Call 911! And see if you can reach your brother."

As the crowd thinned inside the building, I spotted Tyler holding the back door open, trying to keep a few curious onlookers at an arm's length. Fortunately, none of them had children with them. I wanted to do something to help but was immobilized by a hysterical Wendy clinging to my arm like a life raft. As Gabby fumbled with her cell, I led Wendy behind the food counter. Susie put an arm around her and sat her down on a stool.

"Don't worry," Susie assured me. "I'll keep an eye on her."

Gabby appeared at my side. "There's an ambulance on the way. I also called Gino. Come on. Let's see if we can help."

We hurried to the rear of the building. The back door was standing open, with Tyler leaning against it. He looked resigned or bored as he watched the scenario play out, almost as if he were watching a theater production. When Gabby and I walked past him, our eyes happened to meet. His were cold and aloof and sent a chill through me. Why was he acting so nonchalant when a man might be dead?

Lou waved his arms at the crowd. "Get back! Give him air!" Behind him, I spotted the motionless body of Mario lying on the ground. Justin was bending over him. Mario's face was as white as the snow. Flakes clung to the red material of the Santa suit, the shiny black boots, and Justin's dark hair. Blood had stained the snow, and an urgency gnawed at my insides. Justin wasn't going to be able to save him.

"What's he doing?" Gabby grabbed my arm.

"Chest wound," a man next to us said. "He's applying pressure to try to stop the bleeding."

Despite the horror of it all, my heart burst with pride as I watched Justin in action. He shouted to Lou, who came over and applied pressure to Mario's chest while he began to administer CPR.

Intense emotions swept through me. Justin was a true hero in every sense of the word. I knew about this side of him, of course, but had never witnessed it in person before. While it made me proud, a new sense of dread arrived along with it.

Justin continued the CPR and felt for a pulse in Mario's neck. He swore and continued the CPR. Lou said something to him I couldn't hear, and Justin nodded grimly. His next words caused fear to lodge in my throat.

"Come on, Mario! Hang in there, man!"

Sirens screamed in the distance. The blackened sky was suddenly awash with a multitude of blue and red flashing lights. Police cars and an ambulance braked to a halt in the parking lot. Two men with a stretcher ran toward Mario. One of the EMTs said something to Justin, who rose to his feet and nodded. He helped the men load Mario onto the stretcher and spoke to Lou before jumping into the ambulance. Lou shut the doors behind him and the ambulance roared out of the parking lot, its siren blaring in my ears.

Another policeman I didn't know was talking to Lou, who then turned and gestured at the remaining crowd. "Everyone inside!" he yelled. "This is a crime scene. Please remain in the building with Officer Foster, as we will need to collect statements."

Gabby and I remained perfectly still, as if our shoes had been glued to the ground. Lou noticed us for the first time and walked over. He narrowed his green eyes at Gabby. "I thought I told you to stay inside."

Gabby stared in horror at the blood on his shirt. "Is he dead?" she whispered.

"It doesn't look good," Lou said honestly. "Justin couldn't get a pulse on him."

"Why did he go in the ambulance with the EMTs?" I asked.

"They needed his assistance. Those guys have only basic level training. Justin can do things they can't, like IVs and administer medication. They were the closet ones to Harvest Park, so they were able to get here pretty fast." His face sobered. "If Mario doesn't pull through, at least we can take comfort in the fact that we did everything possible to save him."

"What now?" Gabby asked.

Lou glanced at his watch. "When Gino gets here, we'll start questioning people to find out if they saw anything."

I swallowed hard. "What about all the others who have already left?"

His frown deepened. "We'll have to try to track them down. There's a camera inside the Lake House. Someone must have seen something. In the meantime, you two go home."

"Why don't we stay here?" Gabby suggested. "There must be something we can do to help."

Lou shot her a look of disbelief. "You never quit, do you? Please go home with Tessa. I'm going to be here for a while. I'll stop over later."

Gabby looked like she wanted to protest further, but Lou's phone buzzed, and he stepped away from us to answer it. An unmarked dark-blue sedan pulled up into the spot where the ambulance had been minutes ago. A second later, my cousin Gino emerged from the vehicle. He had classic Italian good looks with wavy dark hair, chocolate brown eyes, and olive-toned skin. I adored my cousin, even though he didn't have much of a sense of humor at times. As detective on the Harvest Park police force, he took his job seriously—sometimes too seriously.

He was dressed casually in jeans and a knit sweater that I'd never seen before. It was a mixture of vibrant blues, greens, and reds with a giant reindeer in the center eating a candy cane. I wanted to laugh, but my amusement faded quickly when I remembered Mario's body lying lifeless amidst the snow minutes ago.

"Nice sweater," Gabby snorted.

Gino glared at his sister. "Don't start. I didn't have time to change. I just came from the Hiller's ugly Christmas sweater party."

She grinned. "You must have won."

He ignored her comment. "Why are you two out here? This is a crime scene."

Lou came back over to us with his phone in hand. "Don't worry. They're leaving soon."

"What's the latest?" Gino asked him.

He shook his head grimly. "That was Randy, one of the EMTs. Justin rode with them in the ambulance." Lou paused for several seconds. "Mario didn't make it. He died on the way to the hospital."

Gino closed his eyes and cursed under his breath.

"No!" a woman's voice sobbed from behind me.

We all turned around. Wendy was standing there, a hand clamped over her mouth. I'd forgotten about her. Her face was streaked with tears. She hurled herself at my chest, and I put a comforting arm around her shoulders.

"She's the one who found Mario," I explained to Gino. "She came running into the building and alerted everyone. Justin and Lou ran outside and did their best to save him."

Lou shrugged. "We were just doing our jobs. I tried to hold back the crowd while Justin worked on him. Mario was stabbed once in the back and three times in the chest. The back wound was little more than a graze, but enough to make him fall and then have his assailant finish the job. At least that's my guess."

"Did you see who attacked him?" Gino asked Wendy.

Wendy shook her head. "There was no one else around. Mario went for a smoke break and asked me to come outside to get him after ten minutes." She wiped at her eyes. "He was lying on the ground—covered in all that blood," she sobbed.

Lou held out a plastic bag to Gino. "This was next to Mario's body on the ground. Looks like it's the weapon they used."

Gino took the bag from Lou's outstretched hand and held it up to the cabin lights. It was a knife with an olive-green handle, about six inches long. "What kind of a knife is this?"

"A bagel knife," I volunteered. "It works well on other types of bread too."

All heads turned toward me.

Gino shook the bag. "You've seen this knife before?"

A queasy feeling settled in my stomach. "Yes, I have the same one. I bought it from a vendor who came through town last fall. His name was Murray—" I drew my eyebrows together. "I can't remember his last name, but I also bought an onion slicer from him. He has a website. His card's in my desk back at the restaurant."

"Any idea if someone else in town might have bought the same knife?" Gino asked.

"Not really." I swallowed hard. Okay, that may not have been the complete truth. I'd seen that knife earlier at the town meeting and also in Java Time before and was fairly certain that other merchants in town had bought it as well. My mouth went dry when I remembered seeing the figure of a man who looked like Archie in the crowd. No, it couldn't be...

Gino watched me suspiciously and I worried that my face had betrayed me. He and Lou walked over to where Mario's body had lain in the snow, talking quietly amongst themselves.

Wendy sniffled and untangled herself from me. "Am I allowed to go home?"

"You'll have to check with Gino," I said.

She gave a small sigh and leaned against the building.

"It looks like those two are going to have their heads stuck together for quite a while," Gabby commented.

Before I could reply, Gino crooked his finger at us. Gabby

and I approached the crime tape that Lou was starting to unwrap around where Mario's body had lain. Gino lowered himself to one knee and pointed to a spot on the ground, then produced a plastic bag from his pocket. "Is forensics on their way?" he asked Lou.

"They should have been here by now. Let me try them again." Lou pulled out his phone.

Gino stood and held up another plastic bag. I squinted at it for a closer look. Inside was a key chain with a picture of a steaming mug of coffee. Underneath the mug were the words *Java Time Coffee*, with a phone number. "Does Archie give these away?"

"I don't remember seeing them before." That was the truth. The plastic of the key chain had large cracks in it and the print was faded. My guess was that the owner had been carrying it around for quite a while.

Gino gestured for Wendy to come closer. "Did you happen to notice if Mario had anything in his hands when he came outside?"

She thought for a moment, then shook her head. "No, just a pack of cigarettes and a lighter."

"Did you see Archie or Jake Fenton here tonight?" Gino pressed.

"Anyone could have dropped that key chain," I protested. "It doesn't mean that Archie was here."

Lou spoke up. "But Archie *was* here. Gabby and I saw him when we arrived. He was standing by his car in the parking lot when we pulled in. We didn't get a chance to talk to him because he was on the phone."

"That's right." Gabby nodded nervously, her lips pursing into a frown.

So, it *was* Archie that I'd seen inside. What had he been doing here? "He told me earlier that he was working at Java Time because Jake had the night off."

"I didn't see Jake here," Wendy said, "but I did see Archie. I'm sure of it. He stopped at the Santa booth with some candy canes. Mario came over to talk to him. I'm not sure what they said to each other, but Archie wasn't happy. He stormed off. Then I saw Bruce follow him outside just minutes before I found Mario— lying there." Her voice broke into a sob.

When Mario first came to town, Bruce was always griping and complaining about him. Now they were best buddies? What had changed?

"Go home, Tess," Gino demanded, "and take Gabby with you." He nodded to Lou. "Once forensics gets here, let's take a ride."

"Whatever you say," Lou replied.

"Where are you going?" Gabby wanted to know.

Gino's eyes darkened in irritation. "None of your business. Now go home."

Call me crazy, but I already had an idea of where Gino and Lou were headed. "Gino, please don't do this. There's no way Archie's involved. I'd stake my life on it."

Gino's mouth tightened into a thin, hard line. "That isn't an expression I like hearing, Tess."

FIVE

"WELL, THAT WAS A FUN EVENING," Gabby said dryly. "Tis the season for murder in Harvest Park."

"It certainly didn't turn out the way I'd expected." I started the engine and gave the car a minute to heat up.

Gabby leaned back in her seat. "I know. I figured Lou and I would go back to my house and cozy up by the fire." She shook her head in disgust. "That's what I get for dating a cop. I can't tell you how many of our dates have ended when he's had to run off on a call. You never know what's going to happen. And after a murder, I'm definitely not in the mood to get cozy anyway."

Murder. The word shook through me. Forensics had arrived, and after another admonishment from both Gino and Lou, Gabby and I had returned to my car. The parking lot was almost empty, except for the numerous police vehicles that remained and a few spectators who were still being questioned inside the Lake House.

"If this keeps up, Harvest Park is going to be known for

murder instead of apples, holiday lights, and great food." She glanced sideways at me. "Sorry, Tess. That didn't come out right."

"It's okay." Gabby was worried that I'd think she was referring to Dylan's death, not Mario's. In truth, Dylan's murder was the one that had started the disturbing trend in our town. Mario's death made four murders in Harvest Park during the past fourteen months. "Who could have done such a thing?"

Gabby rubbed her hands together. "Let's be honest. Mario wasn't very good at making friends. Apparently, the only thing he was good at was screwing over other business owners. Heck, if he'd had time, I'm sure he would have opened a bookstore in his café."

"Whoever killed him took quite a chance," I observed. "Think about it. Anyone who came out the back door could have seen what happened. Wendy just missed spotting the killer."

Gabby made a face. "Yeah, but Mario might have been smoking in that group of trees near the lake, and the person snuck up on him. Lou said he was stabbed in the back first."

"Spoken like a true detective," I teased.

"I learn from the best." Her face sobered. "Don't worry about Gino. He knows Archie isn't capable of such a crime. Maybe he just wants to ask him if he has any idea where the key chain came from."

I gave her a dubious look. Gabby was trying to cheer me up, but she knew her brother better than I did. Gino was a cop through and through. He'd say that he had to go by evidence, not personal feelings.

"Where are we going?" Gabby asked. "Want to hang out with me, at least until Justin comes back? He left his truck at your house, right?"

We both watched with interest as Gino's sedan whipped out of the parking lot. There was someone in the seat beside him—Lou, no doubt. "He texted me and said that he'd have one of the EMTs drop him off when he's done at the hospital. I think I'll head home and wait for him. Unless—"

"Unless what?"

I paused to consider. Justin wouldn't be back at my house for at least a half hour or so. We had time to make a stop first, but did I dare? "What time is it?"

"Nine thirty."

My brain was racing with ideas as I pulled out of the parking lot. "How about a hot chocolate?"

"You already had one."

"I meant one of Archie's."

Gabby frowned as I stopped for a red light. "Java Time is closed."

"Something tells me that they might make an exception tonight." I glanced sideways at my cousin, waiting for her to catch on.

Gabby's eyes gleamed with sudden understanding. "Oh! Well played, Tess. Let's do it."

If Gino and Lou had gone to Java Time as I'd suspected, they would not be happy to see either one of us. But I couldn't desert

Archie in his hour of need. He'd always done so much for me and I wanted to return the favor. Besides, I also had an urge to know what was going on. "Maybe you had better wait outside. There's no need to get Gino ticked off at you, especially since this is my idea. Lou won't be happy either."

"No way!" Gabby burst out. "I'm going with you. Besides, Gino's always ticked off at me."

Java Time was only two doors down from Gabby's bookstore and getting there was quick work. I parallel parked between Gino's sedan and a station wagon, then dashed off a quick text to Justin, saying that I would message him as soon as I arrived home. He responded immediately and said he was still at the hospital.

Passing to the front door, I was grateful that Carlita's bakery, Sweet Treats, sandwiched between the two, was closed. Although I adored Carlita, her addiction to gossip was similar to mine with cooking—a true obsession.

The sign on the front door of Java Time said *Closed*, but the lights were still on.

"Maybe someone's trying to frame Archie for the murder," Gabby said thoughtfully. "Everyone in town knows there was friction between them. Or…" She hesitated. "If Mario really was goading Archie tonight, he could make anyone lose their temper."

"And Archie just happened to have a bagel knife in his hand, ready to stab him? No. I like your first theory better. He's being set up, I'm sure of it." I quickly ran through what I knew of Mario's affair and Tyler's secret town meeting. If anything, I could give

Gino that information to help jump-start the investigation in another direction.

As expected, the front door was locked. Gabby knocked sharply on it. After what seemed like an eternity, a figure appeared on the other side of the glass. It was Jake Fenton, Archie's son. He pointed at the sign and yelled, "We're closed."

"Can you let us in?" I called. "We know Gino's inside."

"Come on," Gabby pleaded. "It's freezing out here."

Jake looked over his shoulder and said something that I couldn't understand. He unlocked the door for us and then disappeared. We stepped into the coffee shop and were greeted by Gino, blocking our path, his arms folded across his chest. As I'd surmised, he didn't look happy.

"What in God's name are you two doing here?" he barked.

"We need hot chocolate. It's cold outside." Gabby gave him an impish grin.

Gino's nostrils flared until he looked like an angry bull. "Out. *Now*."

"Please, Gino," I said. "Archie didn't do it. We have some information that might help."

Gino narrowed his eyes. "I swear, if you're making this up, I'm going to—"

"We'd never do anything like that," I promised.

He leaned against the wall. "Look. Lou and I are merely questioning him, like we did with everyone else at the Lake House. But you two are interfering with police procedures."

"I'm sorry. If you'd rather we speak to you about this later, that's fine. But I really do think it may help." Okay, I didn't have proof that Mario was fooling around with Tyler's wife, but why would Wendy lie about it? And it certainly explained the attitude Tyler had been expressing for the man. The image of his emotionless eyes after Mario's death had burned themselves into my brain.

Archie's voice carried over to us from the back of the room. "Gino, I have no problem if they'd like to stay."

Gino's cop face softened for a split second, then he let out a heavy sigh. "Fine. You can come in, but only for a minute."

We followed him to the back of the tastefully yet simply decorated room with its pine beamed ceiling and dark wood-veneered walls. The tables were empty except for a lone booth against the wall in the back that was occupied. Archie and Jake were sitting on one side with Lou across from them.

I had fond memories of coming here with Gabby as a teenager for a coffee or iced tea after school. There had been a few occasions when we were short on cash, but Archie always assured us that we could pay him next time we came in. He'd comped me free coffee for the entire summer after high school, his idea of a graduation present. To most people he was a bartender without the alcohol, always listening to everyone's problems and offering sound advice. He was more to me than that, though. Since my own father had died, he'd become a substitute one in many ways. He was always willing to lend an ear, and I greatly valued our friendship.

Jake slid out of the booth. "Can I get you ladies something to drink?"

"I'd love a peppermint hot chocolate, if it's not too much trouble," I said.

"Make that two," Gabby added.

"No trouble at all." Jake's smiled was forced and his face pinched tight with worry as he walked past us. He was about six years younger than Gabby and me. I'd seen pictures of Archie at that age, and Jake was the spitting image of his father. He had the same chocolate brown eyes and russet-colored hair before Archie's had all but disappeared. He also walked with the same proud air about him. Jake was the only family Archie had in Harvest Park. His other son, David, lived in Maine with a wife and three kids, which included Archie's granddaughter Ella.

Archie smiled warmly at us, but there was an anxious expression in his eyes. "My two favorite ladies. Tessa and Gabby, why don't you have a seat at the table next to ours."

"Be sure to drink those in record time," Gino said tartly as Jake brought the hot chocolates over to our table.

"He always has to be so difficult," Gabby grumbled in my ear.

Gino drummed his finger impatiently on the table. "All right, I'll bite. What's the information you wanted to share?"

I handed Jake a ten-dollar bill and then took a long sip of my drink. "Alexandra Randolph was having an affair with Mario."

"Who told you this?" Gino demanded.

I glanced hesitantly at Jake. "Wendy Summers."

Jake didn't even flinch. "It's probably true," he told Gino. "Wendy knows everything about their lives. She always had stories to share."

"But that's not relevant to why I'm here," Gino scowled. He sat down next to Lou and addressed Archie. "Wendy also told us that you and Mario had a confrontation. What did you talk about?"

Archie shifted in his seat. "It wasn't much of a talk. He saw me drop off the candy canes and said something like, 'Maybe you should hang on to those, old timer. You can't afford to be donating any goods right now.'"

Jake pounded his fist on the table. "The way that guy treated my father was despicable. Telling people that the health department was threatening to shut us down. And they believed him! Anything to send more business his way. Sorry, but karma always comes around."

"Show a little respect, Jacob," Archie snapped. "The man is dead, after all."

"What happened after that?" Gino asked.

Archie folded his hands on the table. "I—I should have walked away. But Mario always knew what to say to push my buttons. I told him that he didn't know anything about me, and that if he kept on spreading false rumors about my business, he would be very sorry."

Wonderful. If anyone had overheard, they would definitely get the wrong idea.

"You didn't come back to the Lake House later?" Gino asked.

Archie shook his head. "I left the building, but I got a phone call from my son David, so I stayed out in the parking lot to talk to him for a few minutes. I must have left right before Mario—" He didn't finish the sentence.

"Did you see Mario outside?" Lou interrupted.

Archie nodded. "Yes, but only from a distance. I didn't talk to him. He was over by the trees, smoking a cigarette."

Gino made a note on his tablet. "You had no contact with him at all?"

Jake glared across the table at my cousin. "What are you implying? My father didn't stab Mario. There were plenty of people in this town who wanted that guy dead. You'd be hard pressed to find anyone who *didn't* want to stab him."

"Jacob, that's enough!" Archie raised his voice, something he rarely did.

"He doesn't believe you, Dad. After all the years he's known you, been in our shop—none of that matters now." He gave Gino a scathing look and slid out of the booth. "I don't care if you're a cop, Mancusi. My father doesn't deserve to be treated like a cold-blooded killer."

Archie's expression turned to anger as he rose to his feet and gripped Jake's arm tightly, hauling him away from Gino and back down into his seat. "Gino's only doing his job."

Gino's poker face revealed nothing as he turned his attention back to Archie. "What time did you arrive at the Lake House?"

Archie scrunched his bushy, white eyebrows together. "The

place was dead, so I decided to close up early and bring over some candy canes for the kids. I meant to give them to Wendy this afternoon at Town Hall, but I forgot. I think I arrived about seven forty-five."

"What about you?" Gino asked Jake. "What time did you work until?"

Jake shot him a murderous glare. "I left about six o'clock to run some errands. I had the night off. While I was out, my girlfriend, Sarah, called me from the Lake House. She had a flat tire, so I went to get her."

Gabby kicked my boot under the table. I knew what that meant. Neither one of us had realized that Jake had a new girlfriend. "Guess there's still some secrets in Harvest Park after all," she murmured.

Gino made another note. "Why didn't you give the candy canes to Jake? He could have dropped them off at the Lake House for you."

He made it sound like Archie had intentionally lied. That didn't sit well with me, but I had no other choice than to continue listening.

Jake was quick to jump in. "I wasn't planning on going to the Lake House. Sarah stopped there to drop off some pies that she'd made. When she got back to her car, she discovered the flat. What are you trying to do, Mancusi? Trap my father into some type of confession?"

Gino reached into his coat pocket and produced the bagel knife, still inside the plastic bag. "Is this yours?" he asked Archie.

Archie peered closely at the bag, and his face turned a ghostly white. "Is that the murder weapon?"

"It was found next to Mario's body," Gino explained. "Tessa said she owns one, and I figured you might as well."

Good grief. "There's other store owners who must have the same knife," I insisted. "I'm sure Murray sold several the last time he was in town." At least I hoped so.

The look Archie cast in my direction made me feel like a Benedict Arnold. "Yes, I have the same knife," he said. "Murray's stuff is a bit on the expensive side, but they're built to last."

"Can I see the knife?" Gino asked.

"Sure, you can," Archie replied and waited until Jake moved out of the seat. He rose and lumbered behind the counter.

"I hope this is the end of your so-called questioning," Jake said to Gino. "My father's been through enough."

We watched as Archie opened a drawer under the counter. He started rifling through it, then went into the back room. He came out a minute later, shaking his head.

Jake's indignation faltered as he observed his father, glancing back and forth at Gino. Archie came out from behind the counter and slowly walked back toward us. He looked as if he'd aged years in the past few minutes. His shoulders drooped forward, and his gait was slow. His expression confirmed my worst fear before the words even tumbled out of his mouth.

"The knife's not here."

SIX

JUSTIN TOOK A SIP OF HIS beer. "Don't be so upset, Tess. It's all circumstantial. Gino can't arrest Archie without any concrete evidence."

It was after midnight, and Justin looked exhausted. We were sitting on my couch in front of a roaring fire with a view of the front window, where snowflakes continued to fall. The lights from my Christmas tree twinkled merrily in the semi-dark room, with Luigi sleeping peacefully underneath it.

It should have been a perfect evening to enjoy the season and each other's company, but Mario's death had left its mark. The Festival of Lights had been cancelled for the next couple of days, and perhaps the rest of the holiday season.

I sipped my raspberry herbal tea thoughtfully. "Maybe so, but everyone in town knows that there was no love lost between Archie and Mario. The Espresso Lane has put a huge dent in Java Time's profits, and you know how people around here think. They'll say

Archie is responsible. That he was driven to do this. When everyone finds out his knife is missing…"

Justin rubbed his eyes wearily. "Don't look at it from that angle. Instead, focus your energy on who might have committed the crime. You're smart and intuitive, and Archie needs your help right now."

I forced back a laugh. "I'm a chef, Justin. Not a detective. That's Gino's department."

He gave me a tired smile. "Don't sell yourself short. You have great instincts about people. You were the one to figure out who killed Dylan. Then there was Daphne, the publicist who died in Gabby's bookstore. You found her killer too."

"I didn't figure out who killed Dylan until right before a gun was pointed at my head. Plus, I had a lot of help from Gino and Gabby. I realize that the police are just doing their job, and they have to consider everyone who had a motive to kill Mario. But there's no way Archie did it. I will never believe that."

"Neither will I. Let's try to remember what happened right before Wendy came into the Lake House screaming for help. Who else had an axe to grind with Mario?"

I stared into the fire thoughtfully. "Well, rumor has it that Tyler's wife was having an affair with Mario, so there's two possible suspects right there."

"That's a good start," Justin agreed. "What about Matt and his bloody hand? What was he really doing outside?"

"What do you mean?"

He rolled his eyes. "Come on, Tess. I don't buy that story about how he caught his hand in the car door. First of all, there would have been bruises on both sides. And if it were true, he'd have been out of business a long time ago."

As much as I hated to admit it, Justin was right. "Okay, Matt didn't like Mario either. He told us at the town meeting that Mario threatened to bring a lawsuit against him and his shop."

"That sounds like a solid motive to me." Justin's mouth set in a firm, hard line. "If he's back to using drugs, there's a chance—"

"No," I said flatly. "Matt's been clean for several years. Plus, he's got three kids to think about. He's turned his life around."

Justin held up a hand. "Okay, I admit I don't know the guy well. He works on my truck, and that's all. But Dylan made it clear to me that he couldn't stand him, so I guess that's always put me on my guard."

"He's not the same person that he was when I dated him years ago. He's changed for the better. His divorce is final, and he's even been seeing someone else."

Justin nodded. "I know, but that doesn't matter."

My ears perked up. "What do you mean? You've seen his girlfriend?"

"Not exactly. I was in his shop last week for an oil change," he explained. "Matt picked up his cell and started grinning like a fool. I knew it had to be a woman on the other end. He said something like, 'I don't care how late it is when you get out of work. Come over. I've been thinking about you all day.'"

Well, this was interesting. Things were apparently getting cozy with his new lady friend. "So, whoever this woman is, she works evenings, and most likely lives in Harvest Park. I wonder who it could be?"

Justin finished his beer. "As long as he's not bothering you, that's all I care about."

It was sweet how he worried about me. I thought about all the things Justin did for me, and it warmed my heart. My driveway was always plowed out after a snowstorm. If Justin was working, he'd send a friend over to do it, and they never let me pay them. A few times I'd awakened in the morning to the sound of a shovel scraping against my front steps and knew that Justin hadn't even been to bed yet. Sometimes he would bring me an apple fritter from Carlita's because he knew how much I loved them, or flowers or wine if I invited him for dinner. He always knew when I was having a bad day because I'd get a phone call or a text with another one of his jokes that made me laugh.

Despite the fact that we got on so well, Justin and I were different in many ways. I liked things tidy and, from the condition of his house, he was a bit of a slob. His eating habits were deplorable, but that was another thing I chalked up to his job. We both had stubborn streaks longer than a marathon, and despite his constant heroics, he seemed to suffer from low self-esteem. I attributed that to finding his wife cheating on him with another man.

Justin's heart was enormous, his sense of humor infectious, and his generosity knew no boundaries. He would never embarrass me by stating his true feelings aloud, and he didn't have to—his eyes spoke volumes. That hesitation I had felt when Dylan first died was what had stopped me from even considering Justin as anything more than a friend. Now I was no longer sure that was true anymore.

"I should be asking if *you're* okay." Justin understood what I meant. He had tried to save a life tonight but hadn't succeeded. It must have been difficult for him.

He settled back against the pillows and closed his eyes for a moment. "I'm not going to lie to you. It's an awful feeling to watch someone die like that. I've seen it many times, but I'll never get used to it. There's a sense of responsibility that comes along with it, and I always think that maybe I could have done more to help the person, or did I do something wrong—"

"You did everything you could to try and save him."

Justin was silent for several seconds. "I took an oath when I became a firefighter. No matter who or what the circumstances, I've pledged to always try and save a life. If I ever lose sight of that, I might as well give up my job. Sure, Mario was disliked, and he did questionable things, but that part doesn't matter. He was a human being." He sighed. "There's always guilt involved when someone dies."

"Don't think like that," I said gently. "You were amazing. So calm and focused. Harvest Park is lucky to have you." I was in awe of what he and his co-workers did every day.

His cheeks flushed. "That's funny, I was going to say the same thing about you." Justin looked as if he wanted to say something else, but then he quickly rose from the couch. "I hate to leave, but I've got to be at the firehouse for a seven o'clock meeting with the chief." He hesitated. "Before I go, I'd like to ask you a favor."

"Of course."

"I know that you make dinner for your family on Christmas and spend the day with them, but I was wondering if I might be able to see you on Christmas Eve—for a few minutes. I'm sure you must have other plans," Justin added hastily.

"But I thought you were working, which was why you couldn't play Santa for my breakfast."

He frowned. "I am working, and I really wish I could do it. If I can find someone else to fill in for me, I would, but it's not looking good at this point. But I'm talking about after. I'd like to see you Christmas Eve. I promised a couple of my co-workers that I'd have Christmas dinner with them at the fire station, so I want to give you your present the night before, it that's okay."

His eyes were a smoky blue haze filled with so much hope that they made my heart melt. There was nothing wrong with two good friends spending Christmas Eve together. My gaze darted to the tree, catching Luigi adjusting his sleeping position, his eyes trained on me as if to say, *Sure, whatever you have to tell yourself*. I gave my head a shake. "Tell you what. Come over around seven and I'll make dinner, then we'll sit around and watch some holiday movies. Just you, me, and Luigi."

Justin's smile lit up the room like a little kid's on Christmas morning. "Sounds perfect. But please don't go to any special trouble on my account."

"Well, if you feel that way, I'll just take your present back to the store," I teased.

He grinned at me wickedly. "Don't you dare."

Since Anything's Pastable was closed on Monday, I had hopes of sleeping in, but instead I spent a restless night with dreams dominated by Mario's dead body. Luigi acted the part of an alarm clock, meowing and giving me several head butts until I finally gave up and rolled out of bed at eight. As soon as I went downstairs, I looked for my morning text from Justin.

Good morning. What did the fireman say to the chef?

Hope you gnocchi how wonderful you are.

Oh brother. My fingers flew over the keyboard. You're killing me.

Justin's reply contained several laugh emoticons. Have a great day off. Talk to you later.

The message warmed my heart in a way I couldn't quite understand, but before I had time to analyze it further, Luigi started yowling for his breakfast. After I'd filled his food dish and helped myself to a cup of coffee, I stood staring out the front window, watching the little girls across the street make a snowman. What a difference a year made. Although I still missed Dylan, my life was in a much better place now. My mother often said that time healed all wounds, and I was starting to believe her.

As I went back into the kitchen for a second cup of coffee, my doorbell rang. I glanced at my watch. Nine o'clock. It was still a little early for visitors unless it was Gabby. I tightened the belt on my bathrobe and peered through the peephole. Jake Fenton was standing on my porch with a young woman who looked eerily familiar. This couldn't be good. I opened the door a crack. "Hi, Jake."

Jake glanced at my bathrobe and his face colored. "Hi, Tessa. I guess we should have called first."

"Is everything all right? Your father—is he okay?"

His mouth tightened. "Do you have a minute so we could talk?"

"Of course." I opened the door and stood aside for them to enter. Luigi came scampering across the room and sniffed at Jake's sneakers. The woman immediately bent down and scratched him behind the ears. He sniffed at her black leather boots, then turned up his tail in a seal of approval and jumped into the window seat.

Jake gestured at the woman. "This is my girlfriend, Sarah Winster. Sarah, this is Tessa Esposito."

She held out her hand. "It's nice to meet you."

I studied her for a minute, trying to remember where I'd seen her before. Sarah was very pretty, with auburn hair that she wore in a blunt cut. She had a small, turned up nose and deep-set blue eyes. Then I remembered what Jake had said the night before and it clicked into place. "You work at Pie Carumba, right?"

Sarah looked surprised. "That's right. Wow, this is a first. No one ever notices me because I'm in the back room all day baking pies."

"I think I glimpsed you through the doorway once. I'm always interested in cooking and baking and people who possess the talent for it." Pie Carumba was located about a half mile from my restaurant and sold mouth-watering dessert pies, several with homemade whipped cream toppings, such as my personal favorite, deep dish strawberry. They also featured turkey and chicken pot pies for take-out dinner options.

"Do you know Stephanie Beaudry?" Stephanie had worked at Pie Carumba before I'd hired her. She'd enjoyed the place and had been fond of Greg, the owner, but more interested in learning the restaurant business. "She left in April."

Sarah shook her head. "No, I wasn't working there then."

"The pies are terrific," I smiled. "You'll have to give me your recipe for pie crust sometime. I noticed that it's flakier lately, so I'm guessing that's your doing."

She wiggled her fingers and beamed. "Thanks. I love to bake. My mother was a pastry chef, so I have her to thank for the baking gene. But you know what that's like. Jake's always raving about your restaurant. He brought me a plate of your gnocchi last week. Oh my gosh, it was so good."

Jake cleared his throat. "Tessa, I'm not sure if you've heard, but my father was arrested last night after you and Gabby left."

My eyebrows shot up. "What? Are you serious?"

"I take it that your cousin didn't tell you."

"No, he didn't." My insides were boiling with anger. As soon as Jake left, I was going to call Gino and give him an earful. "How could your father have been arrested?"

"There were fingerprints on the knife that killed Mario," Jake said. "They belonged to Dad. That was the final nail in the coffin, so to speak."

My heart sank into the pit of my stomach. "I don't believe this."

"He's already out on bail," Sarah assured me. "We took care of that."

I exhaled sharply, fighting for control. "Thank goodness. What happens now?"

Jake shrugged. "He'll have to stand trial, I guess." He rubbed his unshaven chin and then gave me a forlorn smile. "He's had no sleep, but insisted on opening the shop this morning, like nothing had happened."

Frustrated, I closed my eyes. "I feel awful about this."

"It's not your fault." Jake clenched his fists. "I know you're on his side. My dad thinks the world of you. It's your cousin who's really pissing me off. You'd think after all this time he's known my dad that Gino would cut him some slack, but no. He believes my father killed Mario."

"Hold on a second," I interrupted. "Gino's a police detective, and he's only doing his job. He may have had no choice but to arrest him. But that doesn't mean he thinks your father killed

Mario." At least I hoped not. Gino always had that unreadable cop face on, although Gabby and I could often see through it. Last night of course, had not been one of those times. I had never dreamed Archie would be arrested.

Sarah glanced from Jake to me nervously. She looked like she would rather be anywhere else, and I didn't blame her. Jake was known for his sudden outbursts, but he seemed calmer today than last night.

"My father needs you to go to bat for him. Everyone in Harvest Park knows that you figured out who killed your husband. Gino will respect your opinion. He's looking the wrong way, so I was hoping you'd point him in the right direction."

Now I understood what he meant. "Are you saying that you know who *did* kill Mario?"

Jake scoffed. "Isn't it obvious? Bruce Morton stabbed him. Sarah saw the whole thing."

SEVEN

I WAS TOO SHOCKED TO SPEAK for a minute. "Bruce Morton killed Mario?"

Sarah frowned at Jake. "I never said that he stabbed Mario. How could you say such a thing?" She cast worried eyes upon me. "He's got it all wrong. I said that I saw Bruce and Mario talking outside the Lake House. *That's all.* They had their heads close together, and I couldn't hear what they were saying."

Bruce's comments at the Town Hall meeting were still fresh in my mind. Had the two of them been involved in something shady? "Then what happened?"

She shrugged. "Nothing. Bruce took off in his car—at least I think he did. He headed off across the parking lot."

"How come I didn't see either of you in the Lake House?" I asked.

"We weren't there for long," Jake explained. "I hadn't planned on going at all until Sarah called me. Her boss had asked her to drop off some pies to the Festival on her way home that he had donated."

"Oh, that's right," I said. "You mentioned that she had a flat tire."

Sarah nodded. "I waited by my car for Jake. That's when I saw Bruce and Mario talking."

Jake put an arm around her shoulders. "It only took a couple of minutes to fix Sarah's tire. Luckily, I had a tire pump in my trunk. While I was working on it, she saw my father leaving and tried to catch him, but he must not have noticed her."

"I never would have bothered you if I'd already known your dad was there," Sarah told him and turned to me. "Then we heard the scream—" She didn't finish the sentence.

"You didn't wait to see what had happened?"

Sarah glanced sideways at Jake with huge, terrified eyes. "We—it's nothing."

"What is?"

She gulped nervously. "We were scared, or at least I was. I told Jake I just wanted to get out of there and home. It had been such a bad day, what with him and his dad fighting earlier—"

"Maybe we should get going," Jake said curtly and reached for the doorknob.

"Hang on a second." I held up a hand. "Is there something you're forgetting to mention?"

Sarah squirmed under my gaze. "No..."

Jake's face turned as red as a tomato. "Sarah, I know what you're thinking, and it didn't mean a thing."

Her lower lip trembled. "After you followed me back to my apartment that night, you told me all about the argument you had with your father earlier. So, if you want Tessa's help, you need to tell her everything."

Jake gritted his teeth. "My father never would have harmed Mario. He's being set up."

"I know that." Sarah gulped back a sob. "But you were so angry—"

I was confused. "What's going on?"

"It was nothing," Jake said. "I told my father that we should beat Mario at his own game and start a Christmas contest for Java Time. Dad refused to listen. He said he wasn't going to compete with Mario or stoop to his level. You know how proud he is. I pushed a little too hard, and then he shouted at me."

This came as a surprise. "Seriously?"

Jake nodded gravely. "He told me that since I was so smart, I could go and work for Mario for all he cared. Then a customer came in and he refused to talk about it anymore, so I left." He reached for Sarah's hand. "Sorry I lost my temper, babe."

"It's okay," she said weakly.

"Tessa, please talk to Gino for me," Jake implored. "Try to convince him that my father had nothing to do with this. Maybe you could also talk to Bruce and ask him what he and Mario were saying to each other? I can't do it. Bruce doesn't like me, and the feeling is mutual. Since when has he become such good pals with Mario? Bruce has never been chummy with anyone, except maybe my Dad."

Sarah looked at him, surprised. "You said Mario didn't have many friends either."

"Jake," I began. "I'm not sure that I should get involved."

"Please, Tessa," Sarah implored. "They really need your help."

Luigi clawed at my bathrobe, so I picked him up in my arms and absently patted his head. "I'd rather talk to your father first and see what he says. If he wants my help, then I'll do what I can."

"That's fine. I'm sure Dad will say yes." He smiled as Sarah reached past him to pet Luigi. "I appreciate it, Tessa."

"Maybe Bruce knows more than he's telling." I hadn't realized I'd spoken the words out loud until I saw Jake and Sarah both looking at me with a confused expression.

"Knows what?" Sarah asked.

"Perhaps he saw who killed Mario. Or maybe the two of them were involved in something." Another thought occurred to me. "Jake, did you happen to see Matt Smitty in the parking lot while you were working on Sarah's car?"

"Isn't he the one who owns The Car Doctor?" Sarah asked, and I nodded.

Jake shook his head. "I didn't see him, but I was busy with the tire."

"I saw him," Sarah volunteered. "He came over while I was checking the tire and introduced himself. He asked me if I wanted him to change it, but I'd already called Jake, so I told him no thanks."

Luigi started wriggling in my arms, so I set him down on the floor. "He offered to help with a bloody hand?"

Sarah studied me. "I didn't notice anything wrong with his hand. After I told him that I was waiting for Jake, he headed off across the parking lot. Then a couple of minutes later, I happened to look up and saw him going inside the Lake House."

Jake, Matt, and Tyler Randolph. Three men who all had their own reasons for not wanting Mario to see the sun rise again. Bruce wasn't exempt, either. And truthfully, as much as I hated to admit it, neither was Archie. They had all been in the vicinity of the Lake House when Mario was stabbed. Was it possible that one of these men I'd known for years was a cold-blooded killer?

After Jake and Sarah left, I showered and dressed. By then I had calmed down a bit, so I decided to call Gino.

He picked up on the first ring sounding annoyed. "What?"

"Jeez, good morning to you too."

He sighed heavily into the phone. "Sorry, Tess. It's been a bad night and I got about an hour's sleep. Anyway, what's up?"

"Why didn't you tell me that Archie was arrested last night?" Dead silence was my answer. "Hello?"

"Yeah, I'm here," Gino replied. "I wasn't aware that you were Archie's next of kin."

I bit into my lower lip, trying to control my temper. "All I'm saying is that I would have appreciated a phone call to fill me in. You know how I feel about him."

"It was late," Gino said sharply, "and I didn't want to have to deal with both you and my sister pestering me. If it makes you feel any better, I don't think Archie killed Mario."

"Then why—"

"Let me finish," he interrupted. "I didn't have much choice. My boss was coming down hard on me to make an arrest when the fingerprints checked out late last night. So, I headed over to Archie's house and brought him in."

I struggled to hold back tears. The sweetest man in town, being brought to jail like a common criminal. "I'm having a hard time with this."

Gino's voice softened. "I'm sorry, Tess. Between you and me, I had another reason for doing this."

"Which is?"

He cleared his throat. "Sometimes, when an arrest is made, it catches the killer off guard. It's possible this might help lead us to Mario's real killer."

"But Archie doesn't know that! He probably thinks he's going up the river for the rest of his life." I gulped back a sob.

"He's fine," Gino said shortly, as the sound of a baby screaming emanated in the background. "Look, I have to get dressed and go to work. Lucy was up with the baby all night, so I was trying to let her get a few hours of sleep. Can we talk about this later?"

"Sure," I managed to say before he clicked off. It was obvious that Gino was in a mood, and I wasn't going to get anywhere with him right now. I did understand the logic behind his reasoning and hoped it proved to be true.

I texted Gabby that I might be a few minutes late picking her up at the bookstore but didn't tell her about Archie. She would be upset as well, so I'd save the conversation for when I saw her in person. I drove into town, lost in thought about Mario's killer.

Java Time was unusually quiet for a Monday morning. Two elderly women I didn't know were sitting at a table, but the rest of the place was empty with the exception of Archie behind the counter. His face brightened when he saw me. "Well, now. What can I get you, honey?"

"Two peppermint hot chocolates to go, please. Gabby and I need chocolate for our shopping trip today."

"Coming right up." He turned to fill the cups from a machine behind him. When Archie rang up my order, I noticed the dark shadows underneath his eyes. I reached across the counter to pat his hand. "You look worn out. I feel terrible about what happened."

His smile faded. "Jake told you, didn't he?"

I pushed a ten-dollar bill across the counter toward him. "He and Sarah came to see me this morning."

Archie scowled. "Gosh darn it all, I told him not to. Tessa, I don't want you involved in this."

I squeezed his hand. "I want to help, but only if it's okay with you."

He sighed heavily as he adjusted the Mets ball cap over his

sparse hair. "You're like the daughter I never had, but you have enough in your life to deal with. The truth will come out sooner or later."

"I wish Gino had been the one to tell me," I fumed.

Archie shook his head. "Don't be so hard on your cousin, honey. I understand how these things work." He gave a low chuckle. "Besides, it does an old man like me good to see how the other half lives. It's been a long time since I spent the night in a holding cell."

My mouth fell open. "What are you saying?"

He grinned. "I was once arrested in the seventies, long before you were born. I went to one of those peace protests. When my parents had to come and haul me out of jail in the middle of the night, they weren't exactly jumping for joy. My father told me I was a hippie who would never amount to anything."

"Wow," I laughed. "You think you know a person."

Archie's mouth formed a thin, hard line. "Between you and me, honey, I'm worried. Not about myself, but Jake."

I winced. "Why?"

Archie glanced across the room at the two women, but they weren't paying any attention to us. "He's always had a bit of a temper, but he's off the wall lately. It's gotten worse since Wendy broke up with him two months ago."

"He seems happy with Sarah," I said.

He shook his head. "I know my son. He's on the rebound with Sarah. Don't get me wrong. She's a lovely lady, and I know he cares for her, but Jake's got Wendy on the brain. They were living together for over a year and he still loves her. A person needs time before jumping into a new relationship."

Didn't I know it. "Do you know why Wendy broke up with him?"

Archie shrugged. "She's thinking about leaving town if she can sell her house. Seems that she's had it with that dead-end job at Town Hall and catering to Tyler's every whim. She wants to go to fashion school in New York City and doesn't believe a long-distance relationship will work. Too bad because they made a nice couple."

"Sarah mentioned that you and Jake had an argument yesterday."

"Hmm." Archie waved at the women, who were on their way out the door. "My son said I was letting Mario walk all over me. That I should put up a fight for the customers in our town. Java Time's going to be his someday, you know. Maybe he worries there will be nothing left for him to inherit." His round, pinkish face grew stern. "A day later, and Mario's dead with my knife and I'm being arrested. I'm sure business will drop off even more now."

"I'm so sorry you're going through this."

Archie opened one of the drawers behind the counter and withdrew a key chain identical to the one I'd seen last night at the festival. "What really mystifies me is the Java Time key chain they found with Mario. There's only a few of those left. I haven't given any away in years." He threw it back in the drawer. "Tessa, if you're willing to ask some questions, I certainly won't refuse the help. But I don't want you to put yourself in any danger on my account."

The door slammed behind me, startling us both. I turned to see Gabby standing there, hands on her hips.

"There you are!" she said triumphantly. "I saw your car parked at the curb and wondered what you were doing." She eyed the hot chocolates on the counter. "Ooh. Is one of those for me?"

A wide grin spread across Archie's face, but his eyes held a grave, despondent look that made me anxious. "You two ladies enjoy your day. I'm off to take care of some stock while there're no customers around." With that, he disappeared into the back room.

Gabby linked an arm through mine. "I'm glad Liza didn't mind me sneaking out for a couple of hours. There's so many things I need to get."

"I thought you only had to get gifts for your nephews."

She laughed. "No, silly. I'm talking about gifts for me. I always buy myself a present for Christmas. This way, I'm assured of getting something that I like. Now, tell me why you're investigating Mario's death without me."

I told her about Archie's arrest, waiting for her to explode. She didn't disappoint.

"That's ridiculous!" Gabby fumed. "Just wait until I talk to Gino."

"I'd hold off for a while," I advised. "He's not in the best mood today."

She snorted. "Please. When is he ever? Now tell me what's our next move."

"No, Gabs. You can't get involved."

"Of course I can," she said cheerfully. "I'm your partner in crime, remember? The Watson to your Sherlock. The George and Bess to your Nancy Drew. The—"

"Okay, I get it. It's not that I don't want you to help me. But there are two big reasons why you can't. Your brother and your boyfriend."

She waved a hand in dismissal. "Please. I've been dealing with Gino my entire life, remember? And Lou is like putty in my hands."

"Oh really?" I said coyly as I pulled my car away from the curb and into traffic. "So where am I going? To Harvest Park Mall or Steinway Plaza?"

Gabby pulled a book out of her shoulder bag. "Steinway Plaza, but can we stop by Town Hall first? I got in a delivery of Stephen King's latest this morning and promised Wendy I'd save the first copy for her."

"Fine with me." I wondered if our mayor was in the office today. I'd love to hear what he had to say about Mario's murder. I proceeded down Harvest Park Lane until I reached the two-story redbrick building on the right side of the road. It was a windy, overcast day, and the flag in front of the building was whipping back and forth in the breeze. We hurried up the steps and pulled open the double glass doors. Wendy was behind the raised wooden counter, talking on the phone. Her face was pale, and she rubbed at her eyes with one hand. When she saw us, she nodded her head in greeting.

"Yes, of course. Mayor Randolph is in a meeting right now, but I'll make sure he gets the message." Wendy wrote something down on a pad. "Oh, yes. Merry Christmas to you too."

Gabby slapped the book down on the counter, and Wendy gave her a grateful look. "Thanks for bringing it by. This makes my day so much better. How much do I owe you?"

I cleared my throat noisily. "Are the Christmas trees on display in the voting room yet, Wendy?"

She turned her attention to me. "Yes, they went up a little while ago. There's a box on the table where you can drop in a vote for your favorite. The winner receives fifty dollars."

I left the two of them chatting about Stephen King and which book of his was their favorite. I didn't like horror books; cookbooks were more my speed. Besides, I loved looking at the trees that fellow townspeople decorated every year for the contest. And they were conveniently located in the vicinity of Tyler's office.

There were about twenty trees entered in this year's competition. Most of them were fake, but I did spot a few real ones. The room had a wonderful pine scent to it, reminding me of the great outdoors and the time Dylan and I had gone hiking in the Adirondacks.

The trees ranged from three to six feet in height, with the smaller ones perched on two tables. I immediately spotted the one from the local hair shop, To Dye For. It was decorated with all types of hair related ornaments, including tiny shearing scissors, a miniature hair dryer, and a hairbrush and comb. Pie Carumba's tree was filled with tiny apple, lemon, and strawberry shaped ornaments that smelled like the fruit. There were also tiny pie tins and chocolate ornaments. It was adorable, and I fervently wished that I'd done one for Anything's Pastable but had been so busy that it slipped my mind until after the deadline.

I circled the room one more time and then walked back out to the hallway. Tyler's office was to my immediate right, and the door was closed. As I walked by, a woman's angry voice called out, "You're a filthy liar!"

For a moment, I thought the voice was directed at me, and I froze in place. I glanced down the hallway, but Wendy couldn't see me from her desk. After a moment's hesitation, I pressed my ear up against the door of Tyler's office, praying it wouldn't open anytime soon.

"Keep your voice down, Alex," Tyler said angrily.

My heart leapt in my chest. It was Alexandra, Tyler's wife.

"When did you become so cruel?" Alexandra asked. "You're not the man that I married."

Tyler's voice was filled with disbelief. "I should have known you'd be pretty broken up about his death. I mean, you were sleeping with him, after all."

"It was only a couple of times," she shot back. "Look, I made a mistake. I said I was sorry. How long are you going to make me pay for it?"

His laugh filtered through the door, sounding cold and bitter. "Don't try that sympathy routine with me. You'll be lucky if I don't serve you with divorce papers for a Christmas present."

"You're not that stupid," Alexandra answered quickly. "I know the deal, remember? You need me by your side until you announce your run for Attorney General in January and then win the election in November. A wife who's stuck with you through thick and thin for fifteen miserable years. Be prepared for it to cost you."

"God, what a fool I was to marry you," he muttered. "All you've ever cared about is what you could get out of a man. What was the big attraction with Mario? Did he slip you a free Keurig machine?"

There was a long silence, and I began to creep away from the door, for fear that Alexandra would come storming out. "My God," she gasped. "You did it, didn't you?"

I paused in my retreat, holding my breath.

"Did what?" Tyler barked.

"You killed him." Alexandra's voice broke.

Her words swept over me, leaving me stunned. Tyler had a motive for killing Mario, but what about Alexandra? She'd slept with him and he had deflated her ego by dumping her. I remembered the lack of emotion on Tyler's face last night—the cold, uncaring eyes burrowing into my mind. If people in town found out about Alexandra's affair with Mario, it would bring unwanted attention to a political figure. As mayor of our town, he couldn't afford to let that happen.

I held my breath but couldn't bring myself to move away from the door. I simply had to hear Tyler's answer.

To my surprise, he laughed. "That piece of garbage wasn't worth my time. You could have run off to the Bahamas with him for all I cared."

"Maybe so, but what if he told someone about me? That might have ruined your AG bid," she said smoothly. "Did he blackmail you?"

"What?" Tyler sounded shocked.

Alexandra's high heels clicked across the floor in my direction. After a few seconds, the tap-tap came again, but her voice sounded farther away, and I allowed myself to breathe again.

"Mario used everyone, including me," Alexandra said. "He could have planned this all along—to use me to extort money from you. The day after he broke it off, he went out and got himself a new girlfriend. The man was pure scum."

"Oh please. Don't make yourself out to be the victim," Tyler sneered. "It's not going to work this time, Alex. I forgave you the last time you cheated, but not anymore. As soon as the election's over, you're out of my life. But for now, I'll settle for out of my office."

That was my cue to get the heck of out of here. I tiptoed down the hall at a run, trying to keep my low-heeled boots from making noise on the linoleum. I turned the corner and almost ran straight into Gabby, who was in midsentence when she spotted me.

Wendy's mouth dropped open. "Tessa, what's wrong? You look like you've seen a ghost."

"No, a mouse," I sputtered, the lie popping out of my mouth.

Gabby cocked her head to one side and studied me. "Oh no. Where'd you see it?"

"In one of the trees," I explained. "It scared me half to death. Nasty little rodent."

Gabby's mouth twitched at the corners. "Well, we'd better get going. I can't leave Liza alone all day."

A door slammed down the hallway. High heels clicked sharply on the linoleum, echoing louder with every step. A moment later, Alexandra came into view. She stopped when she saw us, a startled expression on her face. Alexandra's golden, shoulder-length hair was mussed and her blue eyes watery. Streaks of mascara ran down her porcelain-colored cheeks.

"Is everything okay, Alex?" Wendy rose out of her chair, her eyes as round as pepperoni slices.

"Fine," Alex managed to rasp out. "My allergies are acting up. See you later." She brushed past me and out the front door. We watched her running across the parking lot as if someone were chasing her. She got into her car and it roared down the street.

"Wonder what that was all about," Gabby mused.

"No idea," I lied.

Gabby opened the door and jogged down the front steps while I stopped to wave at Wendy. "Don't work too hard."

Wendy didn't answer. She planted her hands on her hips and stared back at me with an accusatory expression that left me uneasy. I let the door swing shut behind me and followed Gabby, sensing that Wendy's eyes were still fastened on me.

EIGHT

"OKAY, SPILL IT," GABBY SAID AS we sped off in my car. "Maybe Wendy bought your mouse story, but I know better, miss lover of all creatures great and small."

"I'm not so sure that Wendy bought it either." I told Gabby about the conversation I'd overheard between Tyler and Alexandra.

"Holy cow!" she gasped. "Well, that explains why Alexandra stormed out of there. You know what this means, right?"

"That either one of them could have killed Mario."

Gabby started counting off on her fingers. "There's two right there, plus Bruce, and—wait. Who else am I forgetting? Of course. Matt and his bloody hand. Maybe he cut himself with the knife before he stabbed Mario."

"I wonder what really did happen to his hand," I mused.

She snickered under her breath. "I wouldn't put anything past that guy, especially after all the crap he put you through."

I stopped for a red light and turned to face her. "Gabs, that was thirteen years ago. Let it go. Did you tell Gino about his bloody hand?"

Gabby shook her head. "No, but I'm sure Lou did. It was pretty late when he stopped by last night and I was tired, so he didn't stay long. But he did tell me that about thirty people were questioned, and that he and Gino would be talking to more today. Because of the camera inside the Lake House, they were able to identify who was there."

"What about outside?"

"There's one by the light display and another in front of the Lake House, but that doesn't help much."

I drove on in silence. Matt had disappeared right before Wendy screamed. Surely Lou and Gino would be questioning him soon if they hadn't already.

"You're a million miles away. What's going on inside that head of yours?" Gabby demanded.

We were approaching the parking lot of Steinway Plaza, a strip mall that held about twenty various shops. "How badly do you need to go shopping?" I asked. All of the spots were taken, and several vehicles were already circling the lot like vultures, waiting for one to open up.

Gabby looked out her window and groaned. "Well, shoot. At this rate it will take a while before we get a space and then all the things I need. I can't leave Liza alone all afternoon. Maybe I'd better shop online tonight."

"Good, because I have other plans for us." I turned the car

around and headed for the thruway, which would take me back to Harvest Park's exit.

"What are you doing?"

She wasn't going to be thrilled with what I had in mind. "I'd like to stop over at The Car Doctor and have a little chat with my favorite mechanic. Would you like to come along, or shall I drop you at the bookstore?"

"Forget it," she shot back. "I'm no fan of Matt's, but I'm not sending you into the wolf's den by yourself."

I struggled not to roll my eyes. "I am not a woolly lamb, Gabs. I can take care of myself so don't worry."

"George and Bess would never let Nancy go alone. They'd want to protect her from danger."

"I am not in any danger from Matt! You need to stop this."

She gave me a teasing grin. "We really need to get you a blue convertible."

The Car Doctor was located on the cusp between Harvest Park and the city of Albany. It was a two-bay garage repair shop that Matt had owned for about eight years. He was an excellent mechanic, and the place had a flawless reputation, until Mario and his threat of a lawsuit had entered the picture.

Matt was in one of the bays working underneath a car. It looked like he was doing an oil change. He was wearing blue coveralls and a Yankees ball cap backwards on his head. His employee, Earl, was in the adjacent bay, working on an engine repair. A radio in the background crooned Willie Nelson, and I smiled to myself. Matt had always been a huge country-western fan.

Gabby and I stood in the empty waiting room. I walked over to the door adjacent to the shop, trying to get Matt's attention. After a minute, he looked in my direction and spotted me. He seemed startled at first, then dropped his wrench under the vehicle before jogging over to me.

His face broke out into a huge grin as he pushed through the door, his bandaged hand hanging at his side. The grin immediately faded when he saw who was behind me. Matt was as fond of Gabby as she was of him. In all fairness, it was more Gabby's fault. Matt had done little things to get her attention in junior high, like putting gum in her hair and glue on her seat. He'd been somewhat shy, and now when I looked back, I suspected he'd done those things because he liked her. Unfortunately, that was not the way to win Gabby over. When Matt and I started dating in our senior year, it was too much for her to take.

Gabby was the only person in our family who didn't bring her car to Matt for service. It didn't matter that he was one of the best mechanics in the state. Her stubborn gene was off the chart at times.

"Well, well." Matt smiled at me. "This is a nice surprise." He looked at Gabby. "Who's this with you? I don't believe I've ever seen her in here before."

"And you probably never will again," she muttered.

He ignored the remark and turned back to me. "What can I do for you, Tess?"

"My car is up for inspection next month," I said. "I was wondering if I could make an appointment."

Matt walked behind the counter and typed something into the computer, then studied the screen for a moment. "You know you don't have to make an appointment. There's never any trouble fitting you in."

"I'll bet," Gabby said snidely.

Matt rolled his eyes just as his desk phone rang, and he held up a finger, indicating we should wait. "Car Doctor." He listened for a moment, then grabbed an invoice off a rack on the wall, giving me plenty of time to take in his damaged hand. "Yep, it's all ready. The total's one hundred and fifty-six dollars." He paused. "Okay, see you then." He looked up and noticed my gaze. "What are you staring at?"

This was a good time to lead into what happened last night. "I was just wondering about your hand. Did you need to get stitches?"

Matt's smiled disappeared as he stared down at it. The gauze wrapped around his palm was covered with black oil stains. He wiggled his fingers. "Nah. It's fine. I can't believe I was so clumsy."

Gabby raised her eyebrows at me and then walked across the room, pretending to be interested in a soap opera that was playing on the television.

"You heard about Mario, right?" I asked.

He nodded. "Yeah, that's awful. Does Gino have any leads yet?"

"No idea. He never tells me anything. Were your boys waiting to see Santa last night?"

Matt shook his head. "Thankfully, no. Lila already had them in my car, waiting for me. I heard the scream when I'd reached the car but thought maybe someone was fooling around. I hope there weren't any kids that witnessed what happened?"

"We don't think so."

"Well, I'm glad to hear that." Matt wound the gauze around his hand tighter. "It's a shame the guy is dead, but to be honest, I'm not losing any sleep over it. Mario was out to get me. Then again, he was busy making a lot of enemies in Harvest Park."

I couldn't argue with that philosophy. "Mario's been a huge problem for Java Time ever since he opened The Espresso Lane."

Matt pushed his bangs out of his eyes. "Yeah, it pissed me off that he was trying to run Archie's business into the ground. There's not a nicer guy around than Arch. I never went to The Espresso Lane for coffee, and it ticked Mario off when he saw me in Java Time last week. Maybe that's when he decided to concoct his made-up car accident story."

"You saw Mario in Java Time last week?" I asked.

Matt's forehead creased into a giant wrinkle. "I was getting coffee for Earl and me when he walked in, strutting about like he owned the place. He started right in on Archie, saying condescending things like, 'Oh, it's too bad you have no customers' and 'Maybe I should give you a lesson in how to run a business, Arch.'"

Ouch. "What a rotten thing to do. I've never heard Archie say a bad thing about anyone—not even him."

Matt took his ball cap off and scratched the top of his head thoughtfully. "Too bad his son doesn't take after him."

"What do you mean?" This came from Gabby, who was now standing beside me.

"I'm sorry, can I help you? In need of a brake job on your car?" he taunted.

"Thanks, but I'd rather do it myself."

"Oh, stop it," I scolded. "You're acting like a couple of five-year-olds. Go on with what you were saying, Matt."

He shot Gabby a dirty look, which she returned with a sarcastic smile. "Jake was in the back room at the time, but when he heard Mario, he came storming out. Mario just stood there, smiling, like he had all the time in the world. Archie tried to hold Jake back, but he went over and shoved Mario against the wall. Archie shouted at him, and then the two of them started arguing. Jake told Mario to get out and never come back, or he'd be sorry."

"Jake's a bit of a hothead at times," I admitted, "but he'd never hurt anyone."

"You might have thought differently if you were there. Mario managed to bring out the worst in everyone. I'm surprised he didn't threaten to sue Jake. Guess he had to settle the score with me first." Matt's tone became heavy with sarcasm. "After Mario left, Jake and Archie went into the back room and I could hear them shouting at one another."

Gabby and I exchanged glances. "Did you overhear what they were saying?" I asked.

Matt pondered the question for a minute. "Jake said something like, 'I'm not going to stand by and let him ruin this place that you've worked so hard for.' Then Archie shouted, 'You're going to mind your own business and keep your hands off him. You've only made things worse.'"

"Holy cow," Gabby murmured.

"Did you see happen to see Jake or Archie outside the Lake House that night?" I asked.

Matt shrugged. "I don't think so. But to be honest, I wasn't looking for them. I wanted to get home and—and take care of my hand."

I caught the note of hesitation in his voice. Matt was playing with the gauze and avoiding eye contact. "How did you say you hurt it again?"

He wouldn't look at me. "The hood of my car fell on it. Of all things, right? See, the oil light came on when I went to drive away, so I raised the hood up to check the engine. Then I slammed it down, forgetting that my hand was right there." He managed to give me a wry smile. "It hurt like you-know-what."

"I thought you slammed it in the car door," I said quietly.

Matt's eyes grew wide and shifted to the television, as if something interesting had caught his attention. "No, you must be mistaken."

I turned to Gabby and gestured at the television. She gave an audible sigh and moved across the room. "Matt, you can trust me. What really happened?"

"Come on, Tess," he said slowly. "I'm not stupid. We've been through this before—after Dylan died and you and the police thought I was responsible. Remember? I didn't stab Mario."

"I'm not accusing you of anything. I happen to believe you."

He looked thunderstruck. "You do?"

"Yes. I'm worried that Archie might take the blame for this." I didn't mention his arrest. "All I want to do is help him and find out if anyone saw something suspicious."

Matt ran a hand over his unshaven chin. "Okay, I'm going to level with you. I was in a real crappy mood last night. For starters, I had an argument with my girlfriend. We'd planned to meet at the festival, but at the last minute, she changed her mind about going. As soon as I drove up to the Lake House, I got a call from Lila, who was supposed to drop the kids off there." He sucked in some air. "It seems that Lila's rich fiancé got my boys tickets for Santa's Express the same night, so she said I'd have to wait and see them the next day. I kind of lost it and did something really stupid."

Uh-oh. "What happened?"

He glanced over at Gabby, who was staring intently at the television, but I knew she was hanging on every word.

Matt lowered his voice. "I walked around the parking lot, trying to blow off some steam. When I got back to my car, another one had pulled up next to mine. They were so close that I couldn't get my driver's door open. Two guys were sitting inside with the motor running. I knocked on the window to get their attention, but they ignored me. I tried again, and still nothing. Then I lost my temper and told them to move the car, or else. One of the guys rolled down his window and cussed me out, which made me even angrier. I reached inside the window to grab him and he shut the window on my hand. Then he told me to get away from the car, or I'd be sorry." Embarrassed, he stared down at the floor.

"So, the boys weren't there at all, and you lied about Lila waiting outside?" I asked gently.

Matt pursed his lips together and nodded. "Yeah. I'm sorry, Tess. It was a stupid thing to do. Anyway, the guy in the driver's seat rolled down his window and told me to find a way to get in my car and drive away, or they'd think of something."

My heart raced. "Do you remember what the vehicle looked like?"

He almost smiled. "Sorry, what's my profession again? It was a black four-door sedan. A newer model Lincoln. I've never seen it around here before."

It sounded like the same vehicle that had taken Mario for a ride earlier in the day. What did these guys want? Had they killed Mario? "What did you do then?"

Matt sighed. "My hand started bleeding, so I came inside the Lake House. When I went back out to my car, they were gone."

"This happened after you saw Sarah, right?"

He gave me a blank stare. "Who?"

"Sarah, Jake Fenton's girlfriend. She said that you offered to change a tire for her."

"Oh, right." Matt nodded. "Yeah, I didn't know her name. She was kneeling on the ground next to her car. I saw that the tire was flat and offered to help. She told me thanks, but her boyfriend was on his way. Then I said to bring the car into the shop the next day for a permanent tire, but she never came in."

"Were you still outside when Mario got stabbed?" I asked.

Matt shifted his weight from one foot to the other. "I heard some kind of commotion as I was getting in my car but didn't stick around. Honest, I only wanted to get the heck out of there, Tess. I'm embarrassed you had to see me like that."

Gabby gave a loud cough from the other side of the room, and I pretended I hadn't heard her. "There's no reason for you to be embarrassed. I'm sorry things have been so difficult for you."

He looked at me gratefully. "I appreciate you saying that. Lila's going to let me take the boys out for a sleigh ride in the park tomorrow night."

"Will your girlfriend be there?" I asked curiously.

He shook his head. "No, she's working."

I was dying to know who the mystery woman was. "Why don't you both drop by the restaurant this week for some tiramisu, on the house?"

Matt stared down at his computer screen, but not before I caught the sudden flush in his cheeks. "That's real nice of you," he stammered, "but it's a busy week. So, when did you want that inspection for?"

I'd almost forgotten about the phony inspection story. "Oh, right. I was going to make it for next week, but I just remembered that I might not be around. Why don't I call you when I know for sure?"

"No problem." Matt fumbled with the gauze on his hand again. "I'll see ya." He smiled and turned to go back into the shop.

"Hey, do I happen to know your girlfriend?"

Matt's body froze as he spoke over his shoulder. "Uh, no, I don't think so."

An awkward silence followed. Why wouldn't he tell me who the woman was? It might have been thirteen years since we'd dated, but I still knew when he was keeping something from me. "I'd love to meet her sometime."

"Sure thing, Tess." Matt's voice was low and hesitant. "We'll come by the restaurant one of these days." He let the shop door swing shut behind him, without giving me a backward glance.

NINE

"HE'S DEFINITELY HIDING SOMETHING." GABBY TOOK a bite from her plate of gnocchi. "Matt was always such a sneaky son of a gun."

I lifted a forkful of salad to my mouth and chewed, deliberately giving myself time before answering. As much as I adored my cousin, the Matt-bashing got on my nerves at times. I swallowed. "It doesn't mean he's a killer, Gabs. Maybe he wants to keep his relationship a secret for now."

She refilled her wine glass. "In this town? Good luck with that."

Since Justin and Lou were both working tonight, Gabby had come over to get my help with gift wrapping, claiming I did a better job. I'd secretly suspected she wanted dinner instead, which was fine. I was happy for the company.

"I'm more concerned about the entire town turning against Archie since the *Harvest Park Press* wasted no time printing his arrest in the paper. And even if Gino isn't sure Archie did it, he's still the main suspect and facing trial." I snapped my fingers. "What about those two guys in the Lincoln parked next to Matt? From the description he gave me, it sounds like the same guys who were talking to Mario at my restaurant. What if they came to the Lake House to hurt him?"

Gabby wiped her mouth on a linen napkin. "Do you think that Mario owed them money? Maybe they were financing his shop?"

"Gino and Vince both seemed to think it's possible."

She wrapped her hands around her wine glass. "But they didn't really do anything to Mario—not that you saw, anyway. Maybe Mario told them to meet him at the Lake House that night."

I stared at her in disbelief. "Do you honestly believe that Mario would tell them to come by while he's dressed up as Santa Claus?"

"It's possible. Look, I'm sorry to speak ill of the dead, but the man might have milked the Santa gig for all it was worth. Maybe he wanted them to feel sorry for him." Gabby raised the glass to her lips. "Wait a second. What if the person who stabbed him isn't even from Harvest Park?"

I hadn't thought about that possibility. "Meaning that Mario had enemies before he moved here."

"Exactly." Gabby brought our empty plates into the kitchen while I wiped off the table. "It makes sense. Mario was only here for a few months, and look at the list of people he managed to tick off. Imagine how many others he annoyed before he got to Harvest Park."

A loud banging commenced on my front door. Luigi trotted

toward it while I followed at a more sedate pace. Before I could reach it, Gino's voice shouted from outside. "Tess! Hurry up!"

The urgency in his tone sent a shiver of alarm down my spine. I unlocked the door, and he strode in, stomping the snow from his boots. Lou was behind him.

Gabby glanced from her brother to her boyfriend in amazement. "What's going on? Why aren't you guys working?"

Lou went to stand beside her as Gino addressed me. "Have you heard from Justin tonight?"

"No, he's working until tomorrow morning. Why?"

He swallowed hard and didn't answer right away. The troubled look in his eyes made my stomach tighten like a vice. I'd seen that same look on Gino's face before—the day that he'd come to tell me Dylan had been killed. No, it couldn't be.

My knees started to give. "What happened?"

Gino grabbed me by the arms and steadied me. "I don't have all the details yet. Maybe nothing. A massive blaze broke out at the Filler Paper Warehouse in Albany. There were people trapped inside, and they asked for backup help from Harvest Park's Fire Department." He exhaled sharply. "I heard that two people were killed, but there may be more."

A sharp cry filled the air, but it wasn't from me. *Gabby*. I was unable to turn my head and look at her. My body had gone numb. All I could do was stare into Gino's eyes, trying to understand. "Is he—" A lump formed in my throat, and I couldn't finish the sentence.

Gino patted my cheek gently. "I don't know, Tess. We learned that one was a firefighter but then the radio cut out." His mouth tightened. "Lou and I are driving over to the warehouse now. I tried calling Justin but got his voicemail. Of course, that doesn't mean anything. If he's there fighting the fire—"

"Let me get my coat." Of course he was there. Gino knew that too. It was like being caught in déjà vu. All the emotions I'd experienced from the day Dylan had died rushed back and consumed me. Helplessness, confusion, anger. Little details that I'd successfully managed to block out crept back into my mind. The lasagna I'd made for our dinner, growing cold and hard in the oven, until I'd finally remembered it a day later. Collapsing into Gino's arms when he told me the news. *No.* I couldn't go through that again. I wasn't strong enough.

"I'm going too," Gabby announced as she threw on her coat and locked the door behind me.

Lou sat in the front with Gino, talking to someone on the police radio. I stared out the window the entire trip without really seeing anything. Shivering, I drew my coat tighter around me. What was I supposed to do? Prepare myself for the worst? How did one even do that?

If Justin had been killed—*No.* I couldn't bear to think about that possibility. What would I do without him? He was always there when I needed him. Next to Gabby, he was my best friend, a source of strength in my life. He meant so much to me, perhaps more than I'd realized before. The idea that he might be gone forever was too much to bear.

Gabby squeezed my hand. "We don't know for sure that it's him, Tess," she said calmly. "Think positive. Hang on to hope."

Hope. Some days that's all there was. Justin was one of the best firefighters in Harvest Park, perhaps the entire state. He risked his life daily and thought nothing of it. "It's my job, Tess," he'd once told me. "I have to put other peoples' lives before mine. It's what I do."

Looking back, I'd never thought about Dylan dying young. I'd naturally assumed we'd grow old together, surrounded by lots of children and grandchildren. He'd worked in a safe profession—or so I'd thought—as an accountant. I'd always been secretly thankful that Dylan wasn't in law enforcement like Gino. Frankly, I didn't know how Lucy could sleep at night. Gabby had confided once too that she had misgivings about marrying a police officer.

Five years ago, when his twins were babies, Gino was called to the scene of a domestic dispute one evening. The husband had fired at the first sighting of a cop. Dylan and I had gone to the hospital, and it was the one time I'd ever glimpsed Lucy without her usual composure. The agony and pain had been transparent on her face, and she'd made no attempt to hide it. When the doctor told her that Gino would be all right, she'd broken down in tears of relief.

Dylan and I had gone home shortly afterwards and lain in bed, unable to sleep. We'd talked late into the night about Gino's near brush with death, and I'd shamefully confessed how relieved I was that something like that would never happen to him.

"Don't worry, sweetheart," Dylan had said. "You can't get rid of me that easily. You're stuck with me."

Oh, the irony.

Strobe lights flashed across the sky from several blocks away. Two police officers had their vehicles parked across the end of a one-way street that led to the warehouse. Gino stopped his car and rolled down the window.

"What's the deal, Steve?" he shouted to a tall man in uniform.

Steve came over to Gino's side of the car. "From the looks of it, they've finally got it under control."

Gino glanced over his shoulder at me, then lowered his voice. "Any word on who was killed?"

Steve shook his head. "One was a firefighter, another an employee, I think, but there may be more. They won't release all the details until the investigators have gone through the building."

"Right." Gino waved to him and was allowed to drive past. As we moved closer to the site, the noise level began to increase. Gino parked his car behind another cruiser and turned to me and Gabby. "Maybe you two should stay here. I'll let you know as soon as—"

"Forget it." I exited the car quickly, and Gabby followed. We stayed behind Gino and Lou. I'd never seen a fire close up before. It was nothing like I'd ever imagined. The roar was so deafening it made it difficult to think. Sirens blared from the responding units. Police cruisers, ambulances, EMT vehicles, and fire trucks crowded the parking lot and street. Radios crackled, engines were on idle, and commands were being shouted. Panic started to engulf me as I looked for any sign of Justin.

Smoke billowed out of a blackened building that had once been a two-story warehouse that employed over a hundred people. Gabby clutched my arm as we walked closer. My heart thundered against the wall of my chest. The air was acrid and smoky, making breathing difficult.

A giant hose that resembled a twitching snake loomed in the night sky. Two firefighters stood beside it, yelling to be heard over surrounding noise. I craned my neck for a look at them. It was difficult to glimpse who they were because of the turnout jackets and helmets, but both men were too short to be Justin.

"Stay here," Gino ordered as he and Lou walked over to the fire truck.

Gabby and I took a few steps toward an ambulance. I hated this feeling of helplessness. My stomach churned, dreading what might happen next. Two firefighters were sitting on the back of the vehicle. I'd met several of Justin's co-workers before, and there was a good chance one of them might be someone I knew. Someone who could tell me what had happened to him. But I wasn't sure if I could bear to hear the truth.

"Tess," Gabby said slowly, "maybe we should wait until—"

One of the firefighters removed something from his arm and raised his head. Our eyes met, and he came toward me.

Justin.

Air rushed out of my lungs, and I said a silent prayer of

thanks. I hurried toward him and grabbed him tightly in a hug. A sob escaped from my lips.

"I'm all right, Tess." His voice sounded gravelly and hoarse. "A little heat exhaustion, that's all. Cold packs work wonders."

There was soot all over Justin's helmet and jacket. The smell of smoke and sweat was strong around him, but I couldn't have cared less. "We heard that a firefighter had died. We were all so worried about you."

Despite the black streaks on his cheeks, Justin smiled. "It means a lot to me that you're here."

We stood there, looking at each other in silence, until Gino interrupted by clapping him on the shoulder. "Glad that you're okay. We all thought the worst when we heard a firefighter had perished in the blaze. Was it someone from Harvest Park's force?"

Justin shook his head. "No, the Albany department—Ben Parker. It's a huge loss for them. He suffered a heart attack when he came out of the building. Happens that way more often than you think. It was instantaneous. We couldn't revive him."

I gripped his hand tightly. "I'm so sorry."

"How did the fire start?" Gino asked.

"We're not positive yet, but it may have been an electrical short," Justin replied. "When we arrived on the scene, three employees had already managed to get out but said that two people were still inside. Ben and I went in together to find them. He managed to get one guy out while I helped the other."

He paused and we waited patiently for him to continue. This had to be difficult for him.

"The man that Ben found was overcome by smoke inhalation," Justin continued. "He didn't make it. As soon as Ben and I were out of the building, there was an explosion. If we'd been thirty seconds later—" He stopped to look at me and didn't finish the sentence.

Thirty seconds. The difference between life and death. It was too much to absorb, and I suddenly felt dizzy.

"Tess, why don't you and Gabby go home," Justin suggested. "It's not safe here, and I don't want to have to worry about the both of you."

I stared at him in amazement. "But what about you? You should be at the hospital. I'll go too and then—"

Justin cut me off. "I'm fine. Besides, I need to talk to the arson inspector, who should be here any minute. I'll call you in the morning." His eyes were anxious as he waited for me to answer. "You okay?"

No, I wasn't okay. The stress of the situation was consuming and had left me dazed and weak. Something had changed for me since I'd learned that Justin might have died in the blaze, that sweet feeling turning to something more solid. Tangible. Whatever it was, it drew me like a magnet to him. I didn't want to leave. What if something else happened?

Of course, I was being silly. Justin was perfectly capable of taking care of himself. He didn't need me here. But I *wanted* to be here—close to him.

"Tess?" Justin put a hand on my shoulder. "Do you need to sit down? How about some water?"

Typical Justin. He was always concerned about someone else. I forced a smile to my lips. "No, thanks, I'm okay. I was just worried about you."

"Thank you." His gaze met mine, and the tender look in his eyes told me how much my words meant to him.

I couldn't drag my gaze away from his. There were so many thing I wanted to say to him, but my brain was a jumbled mass of confusion. The noise was ear splitting, and I couldn't concentrate. There was also the fact that Gino, Lou, and Gabby were all watching us.

"I'll call you tomorrow," he said again. "Maybe we can hang out after you get home from the restaurant."

"Sure." My head was pounding, either from the noise or the panic rush I'd experienced. "Please take care of yourself."

"Hey, Kelly!" One of the firefighters was waving and shouting at him. "The arson inspector needs to talk to you."

"Be right there," Justin yelled back. He gave us all a wave. "Thanks for coming down, guys."

"Lou and I will circle back after taking the ladies home," Gino said.

Justin nodded. "We'll be here all night. There's overhaul to do."

"I'm so glad you're okay." Relief washed over me like a tidal wave, but the entire situation had hit too close to home for me.

Justin started to walk backwards and cupped his hands to his mouth so I could hear him. "You can't get rid of me that easily, Tess. You're stuck with me."

TEN

"YOU LOOK EXHAUSTED," GABBY COMMENTED AS she watched me cutting cookie dough into star and Christmas tree shapes. "Did you get any sleep at all?"

"Not much." I'd come into the restaurant at seven o'clock, earlier than usual. The ordeal with Justin last night had left me anxious and restless. To top it all off, I'd dreamed about Gino coming to tell me that Dylan was dead. That was one nightmare I never wanted to experience again.

Gabby had stopped over midmorning to see how I was doing, and Gino had joined her shortly afterward. He watched me over the rim of his coffee mug and gave a wry smile. "Maybe Tess had some late-night company she doesn't want to talk about in front of me."

I slammed the rolling pin down on the counter, and they both jumped. "Justin didn't finish his shift until six o'clock this morning, and I only know that because he sent me a text when he got home. Okay?"

There was an awkward silence in the room. I straightened up and took several deep breaths while my cousins exchanged a not-so-subtle glance between them. "Sorry. I didn't mean to snap at you. I have an awful headache."

It was a lame excuse, but my cousins didn't dispute it. I'd been obsessed with worry ever since the fire last night. I'd texted Justin this morning, before he could even send me his daily message, asking if he was okay. I'd waited on pins and needles until he'd answered me back and assured me that he was fine, just tired. I couldn't stop thinking about him all morning and how I might have lost him. It was a terrifying feeling that kept reminding me of Dylan's death.

The urge to keep my hands busy was powerful. I had already baked several trays of cookies and made a fresh supply of pasta. There was also a pot of tomato sauce simmering on the back burner. The restaurant already had enough to last for a month, but the process had helped to calm me—or at least I'd thought until now.

Gino lifted a hot chocolate cookie off a tray and bit into it. "Don't worry about it, Tess. I wish I hadn't said anything to you about the fire until I knew for sure Justin was okay. That was my fault."

"If you hadn't told me, I would have been even more upset." Why was I so short tempered today? This wasn't like me.

"See?" Gabby said to her brother. "There's no winning for you. Now tell us what you've found out about Mario's murder."

She could tell I needed a change of subject, and I appreciated that.

"We've questioned everyone who was at the Lake House that night," Gino said. "Well, everyone that we were able to track down. I'm sure there's still a few people at large. We don't have many concrete leads yet." He stared down into his coffee mug. "I know that you guys are still upset about Archie's arrest."

Gabby shot him an irritated look. "That's an understatement."

"Let's not go there again,'" I suggested.

"It is possible that Archie might be covering for someone," Gino said.

"Are you suggesting Jake had something to do with Mario's murder?" I asked incredulously.

"No way. He asked Tess to help his father," Gabby put in.

Gino narrowed his eyes. "That doesn't mean anything. And what the Fentons want is not my top priority. My job is to find a killer. It seems to me that Jake ought to spend more time worrying about himself. He's had more run-ins with Mario than any other person in town. In fact, Mario could have had him arrested for the stunt he pulled."

I placed another tray of cookies in the oven. "What stunt?"

"He went into Mario's shop a few weeks ago and refused to leave—that is, until one of my co-workers showed up to escort him out of there," Gino said. "Jake told Mario he ought to consider leaving town. Or else."

"It's a wonder the conversation didn't end up in the *Harvest Park Press*," Gabby remarked dryly.

"Did Mario file a complaint?" I asked.

Gino shook his head. "Honestly, I think he enjoyed the idea of getting under Jake's skin. There was also the other incident at Java Time that Matt overheard. He said that Jake and Archie had been arguing afterward. I'm taking a trip over to his shop today. Matt was outside when Mario was stabbed. He may know something."

I gave Gabby a warning look. It was better if Gino didn't know that we'd already been asking questions, and I hoped that Matt wouldn't mention our visit to him. "What about Tyler and Alexandra Randolph? Have you spoken to them yet? Or Bruce?"

Gino wrapped his hands around the mug. "I've spoken to Bruce and am convinced he's hiding something. I ran a background check on him, but he's as clean as a newly waxed floor. Not even a parking ticket."

"Maybe he and Mario were in on something illegal together," Gabby suggested.

Gino frowned. "Bruce wouldn't look me straight in the eye. I've known that guy for over twenty years and am willing to bet that he was lying. About what, I'm not sure. As for the Randolphs, I've talked to Tyler, and he denied seeing anything strange that night or a reason for wanting Mario dead. I appreciate how you both feel about Archie, but please let me handle this. I have enough going on right now without having to worry about you two."

The kitchen door burst open, and a little girl with curly red hair wearing a bright-green coat made a beeline for me. Stephanie shut the door behind her. "Hi, Tessa! What did you make for me today?"

"Hi, sweetheart!" I scooped Zoe up in my arms and hugged her tightly. Stephanie's little girl had stolen my heart the first day I met her, and I was always happy to see her, especially now. The more time I spent with her and Gino's baby made me wonder if I'd ever have an opportunity to have a child of my own. Dylan had wanted kids right away, but I'd insisted we wait until after the restaurant was up and running. One of my biggest regrets in life was that I'd never have a living part of him with me.

"Are you okay?" Zoe touched my face gently with her white mitten, and I was grateful for the distraction.

I gave her arm a gentle squeeze. "Sure, I'm fine. Guess what? I made a fresh batch of gingerbread men. Do you know someone who'd like to help me decorate them?"

"Me!" Zoe shrieked and couldn't wriggle out of my arms fast enough.

Stephanie tied on an apron. "Thanks for letting me bring Zoe today, Tess. The school's furnace died so classes are canceled today."

"Tell me about it." Gino placed his coffee cup in the sink. "My kids are home too." He grinned wickedly at both Gabby and me. "Makes me kind of glad that I'm working."

"Poor Lucy," Gabby lamented. "Stuck in a house full of males. No one deserves that."

Gino ruffled his sister's hair. "Remember what I said. I'm sure the two of you have enough to do this week without interfering in police business." He nodded to Stephanie and then let himself out the back door.

"What was that all about?" Stephanie asked.

"Only my brother being my brother," Gabby commented.

I helped Zoe into a child's apron I kept in the kitchen for her use. It was pink with ruffles around the edges and she loved it. "Archie's son asked me if I'd do some checking around about Mario, and who might have—" I caught myself before saying the words *stabbed him*.

Zoe stared up at me thoughtfully. "Mommy told me that Mario died. He was nice. He liked Mommy. He always talked to her when we went into his coffee shop. We went lots of times."

Stephanie's face grew so pale that the freckles stood out on her cheeks. "Honey, why don't you run out to the car and grab Mommy's phone? I forgot it on the dashboard. Watch your fingers in the door."

"Okay," Zoe agreed and pushed on the back door. Gabby helped her open it and then stood in the doorway, watching her.

Stephanie glanced at me sheepishly. "Sorry, Tess."

"For what?" I asked in surprise.

She hung her head in embarrassment. "I know how fond you are of Archie, and—well, I didn't want you to learn that I'd been to The Espresso Lane. I hoped that you'd think I was only in there once—the time I won the Keurig."

"You don't owe me any explanation." Mario's prices were cheaper, plus he had toys for kids, and that was probably a lure for her as well.

I set out paper cups with raisins, M&Ms, and colored candies for Zoe to decorate her gingerbread. "Can you grab that tray of cookies out of the oven for me, Steph? To be honest, I'm more upset that everyone is avoiding Java Time. Archie's arrest has everyone in town convinced that he's guilty."

"Thanks to my brother," Gabby muttered.

I tackled a different subject. "Steph, how does Zoe like your new boyfriend?"

The tray of cookies Stephanie was removing from the oven crashed to the floor. She covered her mouth in horror as bits of gingerbread scattered everywhere. "Oh, Tessa, I'm so sorry! I don't know what's gotten into me today."

"It happens. No worries." I pretended not to see Gabby's raised eyebrows from the doorway where she was still watching Zoe. In the past, Stephanie had always enjoyed talking about her personal life. Was there something about this new man that she didn't want us to know? I hoped he wasn't abusive like her ex.

The Christmas bells strung on my front door jingled, announcing we had a customer. Stephanie threw the cookie mess in the garbage can. "I'll seat them." She left the kitchen in a hurry.

"She's hiding something," Gabby said. "Isn't it obvious?"

I struggled not to roll my eyes. "Oh, come on. Hiding what? She's a single mother who recently went through a horrible divorce and has too much on her plate."

"It's the new boyfriend." Gabby mouthed the words until I came closer. "Mark my words. You told me that Alexandra said

Mario ended their affair and went after someone else. Zoe said that Mario liked her mother. What if she was dating him?"

"Mario liked every woman under the age of fifty in town. I think you're getting a little ahead of yourself, detective."

Zoe rushed in the back door, a triumphant smile on her face. "I've got Mommy's phone!"

"She's in the dining room, honey." Gabby shut the door and held out her hand. "I'll hang on to it while you help Tessa make cookies."

Stephanie returned with an order pad in hand. When she saw the phone, she practically snatched it out of Gabby's hand. "Thanks, Gabby. Tessa, I have two orders of lasagna here. Shall I make them up?"

"It's going to need to cool for a few minutes." I opened the oven and removed a pan of lasagna covered in my homemade tomato sauce. The warm, inviting smell always improved my mood. I looked over at Stephanie, covertly scrolling through her phone. Maybe Gabby was right about her hiding something. She certainly had taken her phone back in record time.

I turned to the little girl impatiently bouncing up and down beside me. "How about we get started on decorating that gingerbread?" I lifted three cookies off a tray and placed them on a paper plate. "They're cool enough now."

Zoe ran over with the step stool I kept in the pantry area. "Can I put extra icing on mine?"

"As much as you want," I told her. "But I think you forgot to do something first."

She looked at me, puzzled, and then her eyes widened with understanding. "Oh! Sorry, Tessa. I forgot to wash my hands!" She ran over to the sink, carrying the stool with her.

"That's a good girl." Stephanie sounded a bit distracted as she started cutting the pan of lasagna into squares.

My phone buzzed as I placed a cup of icing next to Zoe. I stared down at the screen. My mother. "Hi, Mom, what's up?"

"Hello, darling," she greeted me. "I was wondering if you had some cookies to spare for tonight? The Altar Rosary Society is holding their annual Christmas party, and I haven't had a chance to pick up anything."

My mother's words made me smile. It would never occur to her to bake anything for the party. My love of cooking and baking had come from my maternal grandmother, and Mom simply said that it skipped a generation. "You're in luck. With the Festival of Lights on hold, I have plenty to spare. How about four dozen gingerbread pizzelle and genettis?"

"Wonderful!" she exclaimed. "Now, tell me, is everything all set for your breakfast? I'll be there to help, of course. Who's playing Santa—Justin or Gino?"

I didn't want to get into this now, especially with Zoe nearby. "Justin's working and Gino said no."

"Let me talk to Gino," Mom said. "I'll get him to change his mind."

"No, he won't. The twins will be there, remember? They'd be sure to recognize him. I'll figure something out." Maybe I could ask Bruce Morton to do it. He'd say no of course, but it would give me an excuse to talk to him about his new friendship with Mario.

"Tessa, did you hear me? Would you like to join us for the party tonight? All you need to do is bring a grab bag gift. Only three steals per gift are allowed."

I stood behind Zoe, helping her position the plastic knife in her hand to apply the frosting. "No, thanks. I have other plans."

"What are you doing that's so important?" she asked. "Is Justin coming over? My friends from church want to know if anything's going on between you two. I told them that you weren't dating, but they all approve of him. It's been over a year since Dylan died so it's perfectly fine to—"

"Mom, I have to go." I hated that I was the topic of conversation at her knitting club and church functions. "Gabby will drop the cookies off to you." I clicked off before she could respond.

Gabby's face broke into a wide grin. "Aunt Marie never disappoints. What does she want to know about your life now? I'll be glad to fill her in if you want me to."

"Don't even think about it," I muttered.

Stephanie turned to Zoe. "Alice is coming to get you in an hour so don't get too comfortable, honey." Alice lived on the other side of Stephanie's duplex. She took care of Zoe after school and had a little girl, Laura, the same age.

"But I want to stay and help Tessa," Zoe whined.

I gave her shoulders a little squeeze. "You can pack up some cookies to take to Alice and Laura, okay?"

Gabby picked up the plastic container with the cookies for my mother. "Thanks for the coffee, Tess. Can you walk me to my car? I have that book you wanted."

There was no book waiting for me outside. I knew what Gabby really wanted. With a sigh, I removed my plastic gloves. "I'll be right back, Stephanie."

"Of course," she said, her manner distracted again.

We walked out the front door of the restaurant together, since Gabby's car was parked in the main lot. "Okay, out with it."

Gabby's mouth formed a thin, hard line. "You're not going to like this. I never mentioned it before, but I did see Stephanie and Mario talking in front of his shop one day. At the time I didn't think much about it, but now I'm starting to wonder if they had something going on."

"That's crazy," I protested.

"Think about it," she insisted. "What if Stephanie was dating him and found out that he had someone else on the side? Or maybe he became abusive, like her ex. Things like that can push people over the edge."

I rubbed my arms for warmth, fervently wishing I had stopped to put on my coat first. "I've worked side by side with Stephanie for the last eight months. She's been a great employee. Okay, she's a little distracted today, but that doesn't mean she killed a man. Sorry, I'm not buying it."

Gabby started the engine. "Well, I still think she's hiding something. Anyhow, what's our next move?"

She reminded me of Zoe with her unbridled enthusiasm. "I'd like to stop and have a talk with Bruce. Want to come along?"

Gabby's eyes sparkled like glitter. "I am so there. His store's open until nine, but I can't go tonight."

"Me either. I have a group of ten people who requested an eight o'clock reservation for this evening. There's no way I'll be out on time. How about tomorrow after Stephanie comes in? The restaurant will have plenty of coverage so I can sneak out for an hour."

Gabby shut the car door and rolled down her window. "All right. As long as Liza doesn't mind, and the bookstore's not busy." She examined my face closely. "You sure you're not coming down with the flu, are you? No offense, but you don't look well."

"No, just tired." The fire had upset me more than I thought. I'd gone to bed as soon as I'd arrived back home but was too wired to sleep. Thoughts of Justin had crowded my head when I'd awoken at five o'clock that morning. I'd gone downstairs and made myself a cup of tea and then sat in the darkened living room, waiting for the sun to rise. Why was I thinking about Justin so much lately? He was just a friend. My friend and Dylan's friend. That's all.

I tried to shake off my current mood. "So, what's Lou getting you for Christmas?"

"No idea. He never knows what to buy me." She shot me an impish grin. "But you know what? For the first time in my life, I don't even care. It's not important. I'm just looking forward to spending the holiday with him."

"Wow. You really are in love," I teased.

Gabby's cheeks became tinged with pink. "Jeez, Tess, who would have ever thought that I'd fall for a cop? Especially when I grew up with such an annoying one in the same house."

We both laughed, and she blew me a kiss. "I'll try to come by about noon tomorrow so we can talk to Bruce," she said.

"Sounds good." I waved while she drove out of the lot. As I turned to go back into the restaurant, the noise of squealing tires caught my attention. A dark sedan pulled out of a gas station across the street. Fear lodged in my throat when I realized it was the same vehicle that had picked up Mario the other day.

The passenger side window rolled down, and a dark-haired man, the same one who had been chatting with Mario shortly before his death, blew me a kiss. A shiver went down my spine. What did these men have to do with Mario's murder?

ELEVEN

THE REST OF THE DAY FLEW by. Even with an eight o'clock reservation, we still managed to close up by nine thirty, which was a relief. I longed to get home and unwind a little before bed.

My breath was visible in the frosty air as I hurried to my car. Despite the cold, it was a beautiful, clear night and the sky above was decorated with stars. Gabby and Lou had gone on a sleigh ride in the park tonight, and I envied them. Dylan and I went on one a few years back. They were glorious affairs that lasted about a half an hour in duration. The white painted carriages seated up to two adults and two small children. A pair of striking palominos pulled it through the park and a cleared path in the woods while you were tucked cozily underneath warm blankets.

As much as I would have enjoyed the romantic ride, the only thing I wanted to do right now was sleep. My brain was in overdrive, and I needed to sort some things out.

A light snow was falling when I arrived home. Luigi was

waiting for me by the door. I cradled him in my arms on the way upstairs and then set him down on my bed. I quickly changed into a pair of flannel pajamas and decided I'd make myself a cup of tea, then snuggle in bed to watch a Christmas movie before going to sleep.

When I came back down the stairs, I realized I'd forgotten to grab the mail. As I stepped onto the front porch, I noticed a package sitting near the mail slot. Curious, I brought it inside with the envelopes and closed the door. I glanced down at the address label, and my heart almost stopped. The package was addressed to Mr. Dylan Esposito.

I let the envelopes fall to the floor and sat down heavily on the couch, dropping the package onto the coffee table in front of me as if it were poisonous. Dylan had received mail for a time after he'd died, but that had stopped months ago. What could possibly be arriving for him fourteen months later? Everyone had been notified of his death by now.

My hands shook as I picked up the package again and squinted down at the return address. *The Perfect Gift* in New York City. I hadn't been to New York City since Dylan and I had gone to see the Rockettes Christmas show four years ago. Dylan had had clients in the city and traveled there a couple of times a year.

A stab of doubt shot through me. What if this package contained something secret? I'd learned several disturbing details about Dylan after his death—painful secrets that I wished I'd never discovered. I'd been down this road before and didn't wish to travel it again. After a while I'd been able to forgive him and understood his reasoning, but that still didn't make it right.

The best thing was to simply get it over with. My hands were shaking as I grabbed a pair of scissors from the kitchen and cut the packing tape around the box. Layers of red and green tissue paper were pressed tightly around a smaller box. There was an envelope attached to the top. I sucked in a sharp breath as I opened it and began to read.

Dear Mr. Esposito,

Please accept my humble apology. I am so embarrassed that this gift never shipped when you ordered it over a year ago. As a courtesy I tried to credit your charge card for the amount, but it was declined. I certainly would never dream of charging you for this. Please contact me at the number below so I can refund your money by another method, unless you would prefer store credit.

Again, my apologies. I do hope your wife enjoys the present even though it is a year late.

Most sincerely,
Pamela Worthington

My heart leaped with excitement. This was a gift for me? Dylan must have done some Christmas shopping before he had passed away. He'd always been a last-minute buyer, so never in my wildest dreams had I imagined something like this might happen. It was like getting a gift from the other side—someone no longer of the same world. My breathing became heavy with anticipation as I hurried to open the box.

Several more pieces of tissue were removed to reveal an ornament of a girl figurine in a white chef's coat with the name *Tessa* on one sleeve. She wore a red-and-white-checkered chef's hat over a head of black hair and was in the process of lifting the lid off a red cooking pot. On the cooking pot was written, *Greatest Chef Ever*. I stared at it for several minutes in wonder and awe. The figurine was standing on a small stand, which also had engraving along the bottom.

She who cooks with love is loved. With all my heart, Dylan.

One last gift from my angel. The lump in my throat grew until I was certain it would choke me, but I didn't cry. My grandmother had once told me that everything happened for a reason. Was Dylan's gift some type of sign?

Luigi meowed and jumped on my lap. I cuddled him for a moment, grateful for his comfort, then picked up my cell and dialed the number on the card. It was after nine, and the store might be closed, but I couldn't wait until morning.

A woman with a pleasant deep voice answered after two rings. "Good evening, The Perfect Gift."

"May I speak to Pamela, please?" I managed to choke out.

"This is Pamela."

I gave her my name and told her about my surprise delivery. Pamela's voice immediately became apologetic. "I am so sorry that this happened, Mrs. Esposito. You see, my mother originally owned this shop for many years. She sold the ornament to your husband last September. Sadly, she died a few weeks after your husband came into the store. She had a heart attack one night and passed away in her sleep."

I bit into my lower lip. "I'm so sorry for your loss."

"Thank you," Pamela said quietly. "My mother left the store to me in her will. She was a wonderful person, but not the most organized, I'm afraid. Things were a mess when I took over last year, and having Christmas weeks away didn't help. She'd sent the ornament out for engraving, and it must have come back in right after she died. One of the temporary employees I'd hired at the time probably put the package in the back room and forgot to tell me about it. I found it the other day when I was making room for inventory. Your husband's invoice with his name and address were inside the box. I was beyond mortified. There's simply no excuse for our poor service."

It took me a while to absorb all of this before I could respond. Pamela must have mistaken my silence for annoyance because she prattled on nervously. "I did try to refund your husband's credit card for the inconvenience. It wouldn't have been right to charge him, but when I tried to run the refund, it came up as invalid."

"That's because his credit cards were all canceled months ago," I whispered. "Dylan died last year as well."

"Oh, my dear, I am so sorry," Pamela gasped. "Maybe you'd like to pick out something online from our website? Or I'm happy to send you a check. I take that I can send it to the same address the ornament was delivered to?"

"It's all right," I assured her. "I'm not worried about the money."

Pamela paused for a moment. "I do hope that it brings you some comfort during this difficult time," she added gently.

"It does. Thank you."

After a minute I lifted the figurine out of the box again, my fingers caressing it gently, then carried it over to the tree. I placed the ornament on one of the higher branches so there was no way Luigi could reach it.

For a long time, I stood there, staring at the figurine, thinking of my husband and how much I missed him and always would. That part would never change, but I had to continue to live my life.

How would Dylan react if he knew I'd started to develop feelings for his best friend? A small anxiety crept up my spine, even though I knew the answer. Dylan would have wanted me to be happy no matter who it was with, and Justin was his favorite person. If our situations had been reversed, I would have felt the same way. When you love someone more than anything else in the world, you always put their happiness before your own.

But how did *I* feel? I'd been burying my emotions until last night—the questions and concerns and the blooming happiness in my stomach—because that had been easiest. When I was forced to think about Justin perishing in the warehouse fire, all my feelings suddenly became unavoidable. A world without Justin, as well as Dylan, was unimaginable.

Yes, I was falling for Justin. I let that fact sit with me a moment, finally admitting the truth. It felt warm and comforting, and my mouth started to tick up into a small smile until one bold question stopped me in my tracks: *What now?* Despite already knowing Justin's feelings for me, this was a huge risk to take. What if, God forbid, something happened to him at work? Could I face the worry and uncertainty every night knowing that he might not come home?

No. I wasn't strong enough to go through it again. I had to lock that warm feeling away, ignore it. I had to protect myself.

I reached up and touched the figurine lightly, watching it spin slowly around on the branch. There were certain times when Dylan's presence was especially strong around me, and this was one of those moments.

"Thank you," I whispered out loud. "I'll always love you."

I twisted the gold band on my left hand. I hadn't removed it once in almost seven years, but it still came off fairly easy. As I held the ring in my palm, I remembered everything it symbolized for me. The moment when Dylan had placed it on my finger at our wedding was one that would live forever in my heart. But the time had come for me to let go and move on. I walked up the stairs and gently laid the ring in my jewelry box. Then I shut the door of my bedroom noiselessly and went slowly back downstairs.

TWELVE

THE GRAY AND OVERCAST SKY THE next morning matched my mood perfectly. Snow was predicted for tonight but only a few inches. It would feel good to keep busy in the meantime. There was much to do before I stepped out with Gabby to talk to Bruce.

As usual, I was the first to arrive at the restaurant. Most of the time I enjoyed chatting with whoever was in the kitchen with me, but today I longed for solitude. I made eggplant parmesan and then tackled carbonara.

Stephanie wasn't due in until eleven, but she arrived at ten thirty, no doubt guilty about her tardiness yesterday. She had a performance tonight, and if I weren't stepping out later, I'd have been tempted to tell her not to come in at all. I had no desire to make small talk.

Gabby arrived at twelve o'clock sharp. "Sorry I didn't call first," she said. "Things were crazy this morning and just slowed down. I'll have to make this quick."

"No worries." I mixed the guanciale in with pappardelle for a party of six. "I'll only be a minute. Steph, can you grate parmesan cheese and add it on top? And the eggplant parmesan needs to come out of the oven in twenty minutes."

"I'm on it," Stephanie reassured me as Gabby went back outside to wait for me. "Don't worry. We'll be fine until you get back."

"Thanks." I was glad to see that she appeared to be in a better frame of mind today. I wished I could say the same for myself. As soon as I finished the carbonara, I whisked off my apron, grabbed my purse and coat, and headed out the back door.

Gabby was waiting in the driver's seat, checking messages on her phone. When I sat down and pulled my seat belt around me, she drove down the alley and out onto the main road. "I got an interesting call a little while ago," she murmured.

"From whom?" I asked.

"Justin. He said he texted you last night and this morning, but you never responded. He was worried that you were sick and wanted to make sure everything was okay."

"Oh." I gave a careless shrug. "I didn't have a chance to text him back."

Gabby shot me a disbelieving look. "This is me, remember? I know when you're lying. What's the deal?"

In frustration, I shut my eyes. "You won't understand."

She scowled. "Try me. I know how much you care about him, so what's up? Does this have something to do with Dylan?"

"No. Not in the way that you think."

Gabby stopped for a red light. "Tess, there's nothing you can't tell me."

"I got a Christmas present yesterday."

"And?"

"It was from Dylan." Her face changed from imploring to shocked concern as her mouth opened in surprise. I gave her the entire story.

Gabby's dark eyes filled with unshed tears. "Oh, Tess. That must have broken your heart."

"It was a shock," I admitted. "A gift from Dylan that I never expected. I know this sounds crazy, but it was like getting one last moment with him, so to speak. And it made me realize that I am finally ready to get on with my life, but I'm scared."

"Of what? Dating again?" Gabby looked confused.

"I'm scared to care about another man and have the same thing happen." There, I'd finally said it out loud. "After the fire, everything hit me like a brick wall. Remember when you told me that you weren't sure about marrying a cop? How you'd worry every night that Lou might never come home?"

The light turned green, and Gabby moved the car forward. "Yes, but love is all about taking risks. It took me a while to come to terms with that. And you will too."

She didn't understand. No one would unless they'd experienced the same type of loss. "Let's not talk about it anymore, okay? And please promise me that you won't tell Justin about this conversation."

Gabby pulled into the parking lot of Bruce's shop. "You're forgetting one thing. Justin won't let you avoid him forever. He's in love with you."

"You're not making this any easier for me." No, I couldn't avoid him forever, and honestly I didn't want to. But I wasn't sure how to make him understand. Sometimes when you love someone, you have to let them go. I suspected this might be one of those times. "I need to think about this for a while. But in the meantime, I still need to try and help Archie. If we act sympathetic with Bruce and say how sorry we are about Mario's death, he might open up to us."

Gabby blew out a sigh. "All right. You win. Let's go."

Meat and Greet was a small mom and pop grocery store that carried everyone's basic needs. Bruce could usually be found behind the combination meat, deli, and bread counter in the back. The store was fastidiously clean, but the prices were a bit on the high side. However, it was more convenient to shop here than drive into Albany where the larger supermarket chains were located.

Bruce was a butcher by trade, and his meat was prime cut. I usually stopped in every week for spareribs or beef when I hosted Sunday dinner for my family. I had to use a different vendor outside of Harvest Park to accommodate the restaurant since Bruce couldn't supply the quantity I needed. Still, I ordered from him whenever possible to support small businesses.

There was a decent amount of people milling about the aisles, pushing grocery carts. Bruce was behind the meat counter in the back with a Santa hat on top of his head.

"Hey, Tessa. Gabby." Jake Fenton was pushing a shopping cart up the aisle in our direction. "Isn't the restaurant open? What's the matter—did you run out of oregano and thyme?" he teased.

"Everyone's a comedian these days," Gabby mumbled.

I nudged her in the side. "No, I try to keep my place well stocked. What's going on?"

Sarah walked past us and placed two cartons of eggs in the basket. Always interested in other people's groceries, I noticed the cart already held several cans of pumpkin, a half a gallon of milk, and confectionary sugar.

Sarah must have overheard my remark. "I wish other business owners were as mindful as you, Tessa," she said indignantly. "I had to run out of Pie Carumba in the middle of a workday because I have orders for eight pumpkin pies…and guess what? No pumpkin!"

"Yeah, that sounds like Greg," Gabby agreed. "Never prepared." She held out her hand. "I'm Gabby Mancusi, Tessa's cousin."

"I'm sorry," I said, embarrassed at my oversight. "I thought you two might have met before."

"Nice to meet you," Sarah said and joked, "They don't let me out of the back room often enough to meet people. Greg's a great guy, but he can also be a ditz at times. He had to fly out to Pittsburgh for a funeral for a relative. He'd better reimburse me for this stuff."

Her voice was on edge, and I sympathized with her. "The bakery must be crazy busy."

"You have no idea. There are three women on the counter but just me in the back room to do all the baking." Sarah huffed, then gave Jake an adoring smile. "I owe this guy big time for bringing me here. He's been chauffeuring me around town."

"I want her driving her car as little as possible until she gets a permanent tire," Jake explained.

Sarah pulled some cash out of her wallet. "It was nice seeing you, Tessa, and meeting you, Gabby. But I really need to get back to the bakery."

"Of course. Good luck." We watched as the couple headed up the aisle toward the register. I was secretly glad they were leaving so they couldn't overhear our conversation with Bruce.

Gabby grabbed my arm. "Okay, here's the deal. Forget your earlier idea. I think we should pretend like we know everything."

I stared at her, puzzled. "What do you mean? We don't know *anything* yet."

"Yes, but we should act like we know that Bruce was in cahoots with Mario. He'll be sure to crack and then give us all the details of how they suddenly got so chummy. Or maybe Bruce pretended to be Mario's friend so no one would suspect him when he was killed."

I considered this for a moment. "That sounds a little far-fetched. And pretending we know everything could backfire big time."

"Gino's done it before and it always works for him," Gabby said defiantly. "What do we have to lose?"

"Well, for one thing, we're not detectives like your brother. And if he finds out, his blood pressure will go right through the roof."

Gabby frowned. "You worry too much."

Bruce was busy wrapping up a cut of beef in white paper. There was a man standing in front of the meat case waiting for his package. Gabby and I gaped when we saw who the customer was.

"Hello, ladies." Tyler greeted us with a smile. "How's everything?"

"Fine." I tried to act cheerful. Hopefully, he would leave soon and wouldn't have the chance to eavesdrop on our conversation with Bruce.

Alexandra appeared with two boxes of Christmas cookies between her leather gloved hands. "This is all I can find, dear. We'll have to go over to Sweet Treats if you want something else."

Tyler shook his head. "No, those will do. Just take them out of the box and place them on a plate." He gave us an apologetic smile. "We're having a little dinner party tonight for some members of the assembly and no time to bake. You know how it is, ladies."

Alexandra nodded at us coolly. The last time we had seen her she'd been running out of the Town Hall in tears. Her gaze met mine, and I wondered if she was thinking the same thing.

"Tessa *doesn't* know how it is, darling. She's a chef, remember? I do wish I had bought a couple dozen of your cookies at the Festival the other night," Alexandra lamented. "I could have passed them off as my own." She gave a little chuckle. "Of course, it slipped my mind when Mario—"

An uncomfortable silence followed. The four of us stood there awkwardly until Bruce stretched his arm over the case and handed Tyler his package.

"Six pounds on the dot. Best cut of ribeye roast you'll find in all of New York," Bruce said proudly.

"Appreciate it, buddy." Tyler gave us both a curt nod. Alexandra plastered a smile on her face and looped her arm through her husband's as they walked away.

"Cripes," Gabby groaned. "Why is it that everyone we *don't* want to see is here?"

"It's a small town, remember," I whispered. "These things happen."

"Well, well. If it isn't the two best-looking ladies in town." Bruce rubbed his hands together in satisfaction. "What can I get for you?"

"I'll take a three-pound rump roast, please." I already had one in my freezer at home, but there was always room for another.

"Is it for braciole?" Bruce asked. "Do you want me to slice it for you?"

"That would be great." I smiled graciously. "Love the hat, by the way."

Bruce chuckled as he set to work on the roast. "Yeah. It always helps me get in the Christmas spirit."

"I'm still looking for someone to play Santa for my breakfast on Christmas Eve," I said. "Would you be interested?"

He burst out laughing. "You're kidding, right?"

"Not at all," I lied. "I think you'd make a wonderful Santa."

"Way better than Mario," Gabby put in. "Of course, I shouldn't speak ill of the dead. It's so awful what happened to him."

A glimmer of suspicion shone through Bruce's eyes. Or maybe it was fear? He looked away and proceeded with slicing the meat.

"How are you handling Mario's death?" I asked. "We know that the two of you became close friends lately."

"Oh." Bruce shrugged. "We weren't really close. I used to see him at The Club Sandwich before he moved to Harvest Park, so he was probably happy to discover a familiar face in town."

The Club Sandwich was a popular delicatessen in Albany. "Mario worked there? What did he do?"

"Yeah, he made coffee and sandwiches." Bruce placed the rump roast on the scale. "He wasn't there for long. Mario once told me that it was the first job he could find after moving here from New Jersey."

"He couldn't have been making much money," I said thoughtfully. "How did he manage to buy The Espresso Lane so soon?"

"I heard he put a large down payment on the building," Gabby chimed in.

"How the heck am I supposed to know?" Bruce's tone became sharp and made me think that he *did* know. Had he been connected with Mario in something illegal?

The Club Sandwich was rumored to have connections with the mob. If the rumors were true, that might explain where Mario had gotten the cash for his down payment. There was also the matter of the extensive renovations he'd made and the top-notch equipment he'd added. Espresso machines like Mario's didn't come cheap.

Gabby leaned over the display case. "Who do you think killed him?"

Bruce shot her a puzzled look. "Why are you asking me? Seems that your brother would be the logical one to check with."

"We're worried about Archie," I put in. "You must have heard about his arrest."

Bruce slammed the meat down on a piece of white paper, causing both Gabby and me to jump. "Come on. I know what's really going on. You both are trying to add another notch to your sleuthing belts."

"What were you and Mario talking about before he was stabbed?" I asked.

"Did you happen to see anyone else hanging around outside?" Gabby added.

Bruce's nostrils flared. "Like I said, we were making small talk. You know, about the weather and Christmas. Stuff like that."

"That's not what we heard." This came out of Gabby's mouth, not mine, and made me cringe.

Bruce dropped the knife with a loud clatter. "Who have you been talking to?" he demanded.

"It's all right, Bruce," I said calmly. "We understand."

He glared at us, his lips pressed together stubbornly. "Drop the act. What do you know?"

Holy cow. Bruce *did* know something about Mario's death. I decided to take a chance that my hunch was right. "The same day that Mario was stabbed, I saw him talking to two men in a dark sedan. He didn't want to get into the car with them. That night, the same car was seen at the Lake House just before he was killed."

"We know they had something to do with his murder," Gabby said.

I elbowed her in the side to keep quiet. I wasn't positive, but after getting the Italian kiss of death from the same men, I was starting to think it was no coincidence they kept showing up in Harvest Park.

Bruce came around to the other side of the case with my package in one hand and the knife in the other. He glanced around the store, but we were the only three in proximity. His hand shook violently as he handed me the roast. "I can't talk about this now. It's not safe."

"It's all right," I said soothingly. "We only want to help." Like a faucet, Bruce could go from hot to cold in minutes. If we waited, he might change his mind. A light clicked on in my brain. "What if Gino would be willing to talk to you—in private? Maybe he could provide some police protection as well."

"No," he said sharply. "I'm not going to the police station."

He's really scared. We have to tread lightly. "I'm sure Gino would be happy to come to your house." God help me. When Gino found out about this, he would be cussing us out for a week. But we couldn't turn back now. Bruce was about to crack like an egg.

Beads of sweat glistened on Bruce's forehead. "No. Not at my house. My wife would freak if she knew."

Knew what? A deep chill settled in my bones. Bruce was definitely in some kind of trouble. "Okay. We'll have Gino meet you here."

"He's not working today," Gabby chimed in. "He and Lucy went to New York City to do some shopping, but they'll be back around seven tonight."

"The store closes at nine, right?" I asked, and Bruce nodded. "What if we ask Gino to stop by then?"

Bruce hesitated. "I don't know…"

"If you have an idea who might have killed Mario, you have a responsibility to tell the police," I reminded him. "The sooner they find this person, the safer we'll all be."

Bruce glanced up and down the aisle nervously. "Look. The truth is I think Mario's killer might be coming after me next. Have Gino meet me here at nine o'clock sharp, and I'll tell him everything I know." He pointed at me. "And I need you to come too. You can be a witness. I don't want my words twisted around. Cops have a way of doing that."

Gabby gritted her teeth together. "Not *my* brother. You've got a lot of nerve. I think I'd better come along too."

Bruce shook his head. "You're not invited."

Gabby's nostrils flared. "You can't stop me. I'll—"

I nudged her again, afraid that Bruce might say to forget the whole thing. "It's probably for the best. Gino wouldn't want you there anyway."

"Oh, fine," she grumbled.

A sharp thud made us all jump. Bruce cocked his head in the direction of the next aisle, where the sign, *Canned Goods & Spices,* dangled from the ceiling. "That blasted display of tomatoes must have fallen over again. Great. People really want to buy cans with dents in them."

"We'll pick it up on our way out," I offered.

A middle-aged man and woman approached the meat counter. Bruce nodded and smiled to us, but his eyes were anxious. "I'd appreciate that. Have a great day, ladies and uh—see you later."

"I told you it would work," Gabby gloated as walked into the next aisle.

There were about fifteen cans of tomatoes littering the aisle. Gabby and I picked them up and returned them to the display. "He must be awful scared if he agreed to talk to Gino. Why didn't he tell Gino this the first time he talked to him?"

"Good question," Gabby murmured. "Maybe something's happened since then. He could have gotten a threatening note or call from the person who killed Mario."

"It's possible, I guess."

"Shoot," Gabby mumbled. "I totally forgot that I wanted to grab a steak for Lou's dinner tonight. Do you mind if we head back to the counter?"

I glanced at my watch. We'd been gone about a half hour. "No, it's fine." We returned to the meat counter where Wendy was now standing. She was carrying a bottle of soda in one hand and a bag of chips in the other.

Her eyebrows shot up when she saw us. "Hi, Tessa. Gabby. What are you guys doing here in the middle of a workday?"

Jeez, I wished people would stop asking me that. "Oh, I needed a roast and Gabby wants to pick up a steak." I watched as Bruce, eyeing us suspiciously, placed a turkey breast on the deli slicer.

"Are you on your lunch hour or do you have the day off?" Gabby asked.

Wendy snorted. "Please. I'm lucky I even get a lunch hour. I ran out to grab a sandwich."

"Your boss was just here," I said, "with his wife. Did you see them?"

"No, thank goodness." Wendy wrinkled her nose as if she smelled something putrid. "They're throwing some impromptu dinner party tonight." She lowered her voice so that Bruce didn't hear. "I'm surprised they didn't send me out to pick up the groceries." She snorted and then addressed Bruce. "Can you add in a loaf of ciabatta bread? Sliced, please."

"The bread slicer's not working," Bruce said. "I'll have to do it by hand."

Wendy was checking her cell phone. "That's fine, thanks." She looked back up at me. "Might as well do my grocery shopping while I'm here. It's not like I'll be getting any more time off today, because I'm sure Tyler doesn't plan on coming back. Must be nice to come and go as you please and still get paid for it."

I nodded, barely listening to her. I was preoccupied with watching Bruce, who was in the process of cleaning the bread knife to slice the ciabatta. My eyes came to rest on the knife. It was an olive-green color. The one that Archie and I both owned. And the same kind that had been used to stab and kill Mario.

"I don't like this," Gino said as we drove toward Bruce's market later that evening. "You never should have asked Bruce if you could tag along, Tess. What if he's lying?"

"He asked me to come with you, I didn't volunteer," I reminded him. "Besides, if Bruce really is dangerous, you shouldn't be meeting him by yourself."

Gino almost smiled. "So, you're coming to watch my back, is that it?"

"Oh, stop being a smart aleck. You know what I mean."

Gino turned into Meat and Greet's parking lot. It was empty, but we could see a light on inside the store. "I can take care of myself," he said. "But if it makes you feel any better, one of my co-workers is in an unmarked vehicle down the street." He turned off the engine. "You are not to say a word when we get inside. I will handle everything. Understand?"

I knew better than to argue with him at a time like this. "Of course."

We exited the car and walked toward the entrance together. Bruce's *Closed* sign was hanging on the door. I peered inside but didn't see him anywhere. Gino knocked sharply on the glass. No answer. He rapped again.

"Maybe he's behind the meat counter and can't hear us," I suggested.

Gino's mouth tightened. "What's the deal with him? Was he joking around with you and Gabby earlier? I wouldn't put it past him."

I shivered and flipped the collar of my coat up. "No. Bruce was serious. He's scared that he might be next. I think he knows who killed Mario and is hoping you can provide some type of police protection."

"Then he shouldn't have lied to me when I questioned him yesterday," Gino said angrily. "Bruce told me that he didn't know anything. Let's see if his car is out back. I swear, if he's pulling some kind of stunt, I'll put him in handcuffs and drag his sorry butt down to the station."

I walked close to Gino as we rounded the building. The sky was starless and an inky shade of black that filled me with a deep sense of foreboding. I tried to shake off the feeling, but my gut seemed to be telling me this was not a good idea. Gino must have been thinking the same thing because when we approached the back lot, he pulled me behind him. His hand went to his belt, where I knew his gun was hidden.

The parking lot located at the rear of the building was primarily used for delivery trucks. There was a separate door for employees to use. Bruce and his co-workers parked their cars here. Sure enough, Bruce's station wagon was the only vehicle present.

Light shone from a single watt bulb over the back door. There was something lying on the cement steps in front of the door. I squinted at it in the dim light and my body went rigid. Gino drew his gun out of his jacket and sprang into action. I forced myself to move forward.

"Stay back, Tess!" Gino shouted.

I brought my hand to my mouth in horror as Gino gently turned Bruce onto his back. Bruce's unseeing eyes were open—his facial expression one of alarm. A kitchen knife was sticking out of his throat. Ringing commenced in my ears as a piercing scream filled the night air.

The scream was coming from me.

THIRTEEN

TWENTY MINUTES LATER, GINO RETURNED TO his vehicle where I was waiting. The flash of lights from the ambulance and police cars was making me dizzy, and my stomach started to churn. Gino opened the driver's side door and slid behind the wheel. He patted my cheek with his cold hand and spoke gently. "Are you all right?"

I clutched the blanket he'd placed around my shoulders earlier. "Just in shock. I'm starting to think that I'm the grim reaper or something." My voice shook. "I've seen too many dead bodies this year."

Gino's expression was grave. "This is why I didn't want you here. You shouldn't have to see things like—that. After doing this job for more than ten years, I'm still not used to it." He blew out a sigh. "Looks like Bruce was right to be worried. I wish we'd gotten here sooner. I don't think it happened long before we arrived. The blood hadn't pooled yet."

Bile rose in the back of my throat. "Do you think that the guys in the Lincoln are responsible?"

"It's possible." Gino placed the vehicle in drive. "My co-workers have this under control for now so I'm going to drive you home, then I need to talk to my boss and the coroner. It's going to be a long night."

The car was cozy warm, but I was chilled through. I squeezed my eyes shut and tried to block out the image of Bruce's face that kept entering my mind. It didn't work.

"Are you going to be okay?" Gino asked worriedly. "Where's Gabs tonight?"

"She and Lou had a date. Don't worry, I'll be fine."

He stopped for a red light. "But I do worry. What if the killer saw you go into Bruce's store today, or worse, heard you asking him questions? You and Gabs could be in danger as well. I'm not taking any chances with my family."

"Oh God." I gasped. "Gabby and I pretended that we knew what Bruce was keeping from the police. He believed us, but we didn't know anything. If we hadn't gone to his store today, he might still be alive." Tears prickled in my eyes and fell down my cheeks. I felt like a monster.

Gino exhaled sharply. "You don't know that for sure. Maybe Bruce really did know who killed Mario, and they got rid of him so he'd stay quiet. You can't blame yourself, Tess."

He pulled his car into my driveway, then came around to the other side to help me out. Gino placed an arm around my shoulders, and I leaned heavily against him as he unlocked my front door. The alarm started beeping, and I quickly shut it off.

"Let me check upstairs," Gino said.

"But the alarm was already on."

He scowled. "Don't argue. It will make me feel better."

I plugged in the Christmas tree and found Luigi napping underneath it. Three ornaments lay on the floor next to him, but I couldn't have cared less. He let out a small squeak and blinked sleepily as I scratched him under the chin, thankful I had him here to comfort me tonight.

Gino's boots clunked loudly against the stairs, and a few seconds later he reappeared. I walked with him to the front door. "Lock this right after I leave," he instructed. "Is Justin home? I'm sure he'd come over and stay with you if he's around."

"He's working." He'd texted me earlier, asking if I wanted him to stop by afterwards, but I'd told him I had plans with Gabby. I hated lying to him, especially since I did want to see him—more than anything. But how could I make him understand the way I felt without hurting him further?

Gino planted a kiss on my forehead. "If you need anything, call me, okay? And if you don't want to stay here alone, I'm sure Lucy would love some company."

"I'll be fine. And thanks—for everything." I wouldn't have blamed him if he'd chewed me out for going to Meat and Greet today, but he didn't. Then again, he might be saving that lecture for Gabby.

He smiled. "That's what family is all about."

"It's not your fault, Tess." Gabby hung her head. "It's all mine. I was the one who suggested we bluff about what we knew."

She was standing in Anything's Pastable's kitchen with Gino the following morning. They watched with great interest as I stirred another pot of my homemade tomato sauce on the burner. After Dylan had died, I'd made endless gallons of sauce to try and de-stress. The smell of fresh garlic, onions, and tomatoes always did wonders for me.

I blew out a breath. "No, this is on me. I'm the one who wanted to talk to Bruce. I feel like I killed him."

Gino's gaze drifted from Gabby to me and back to her again. He sipped his coffee in silence. For the life of me, I didn't know how he could stand there so unaffected after what we'd witnessed last night. He was as cool as a bowl of gazpacho.

"From the position of Bruce's body, forensics was able to determine that he was struck in the chest first, and then the back." Gino hesitated. "The placement of the wounds were eerily similar to Mario's."

My mouth went dry. "Then it must have been the same person."

Gabby shivered. "What kind of sicko are we talking about here? Was it the same knife that Mario was stabbed with?"

He shook his head. "No, which makes me think that Mario's death was planned, while Bruce's may not have been."

I agreed with him. "Bruce owned the same bagel knife as Archie and me. I saw him using it earlier. Was Mario's knife accounted for?"

"His inventory was checked, but it didn't turn up." Gino ran a hand through his hair. "Look, we're trying to keep Bruce's death as quiet as possible for now. People know that he died, but they don't know how it happened, and I'd like to wait a day or two before divulging it. His wife is only telling close relatives for now. That way, we may have a better chance of finding out who did this."

My heart ached for the poor woman. I knew all too well how she must be feeling. "Bruce said that he didn't want you to meet him at his house. He said his wife would freak. I'm guessing she knows nothing about his possible involvement with Mario or if he owed money."

"She has an idea of what was going on," Gino said. "Bruce just bought a very expensive meat cooler for his store along with some other items. When she questioned him about how he got the money, he refused to tell her."

"Where does this leave Archie?" I asked.

"I was getting to that," Gino replied. "He had an alibi—he was closing up Java Time. There was a customer in the café until nine o'clock so there's no way he could have done it. As far as Mario's murder goes, he's still a suspect."

My mouth dropped open. "That's crazy. Whoever killed Bruce must have killed Mario as well."

"You're forgetting that Archie's fingerprints were found on the knife that killed Mario," Gino remarked. "Jake's too."

"Because he owned the knife," Gabby said hotly. "The killer must have had gloves on. It was cold outside, you know."

Gino narrowed his eyes at her. "Regardless, all I can tell you is that Archie is still considered a suspect for Mario's murder. I'm only doing my job."

"Two spaghetti and meatball dinners for table six," my server Renee announced as she hurried into the kitchen. She blushed when she saw Gino. "Sorry, I didn't mean to interrupt."

"No worries," Gino assured her.

I took the order slip from Renee and handed her a tray with two garden salads and garlic bread. Then I hurried to remove a tray of cookies out of the oven before they burned. I stopped to inhale the rich scent of vanilla and sugar. Warm and cozy. It was how Christmas always made me feel. But with two recent murders in our town, and Archie still the number one suspect, the holiday was not turning out the way I'd envisioned.

After Renee had left the kitchen, Gino placed his hands flat on the countertop and looked directly at me. "I appreciate that you two are looking out for Archie. But this is no joke. A killer will usually strike again if they feel that someone is getting close. There's a good chance you've already talked to that person, and it worries me."

Gabby waved it aside. "That means nothing. The knife must have been stolen from Java Time. What about the Randolphs? Do we know who else Mario was involved with? According to Wendy, he moved on from Alexandra, but who with? Don't forget about Matt either. Maybe he found the bread knife in Mario's car while he was working on it."

I tried to shoot Gabby a warning look, but it was in vain. She reached for the glass tray and stole a sugar cookie shaped like a wreath. "Tess, you know I'm no fan of his, but are you actually buying that story he told us?"

"You guys talked to Matt as well?" Incredulity filled Gino's voice.

Thanks, Gabs. "I needed an inspection," I lied. "He told us the same car that picked up Mario from my lot was parked next to his at the festival. When Matt asked them to move it because they were too close, they threatened him. To be honest, I can't see him making that part up."

Gino thrust a finger at me. "He told me that same story as well, and I happen to believe him. That's another reason for you to be careful. Those guys are still hanging around town. You said you saw them at the gas station yesterday. I need to get a line on them—their license plate, anything that will help identify them. It's possible they could have killed Mario or Bruce. Or maybe both of them. "

"Don't worry. I'll take good care of our cuz," Gabby assured him. She grabbed another sugar cookie shaped like a star this time. "Why are you baking so many Christmas cookies today?"

I removed a tray of thyme cookies from the oven. They were

shortbread with a hint of the herb that added to their flavor. "Wendy needs them for the Festival of Lights. It's resuming tonight. Can you drop these off to her at Town Hall? This is the last tray."

"No problem," she said. "I didn't realize the festival was back on again. Finally, some good news."

"Yeah, but I doubt there will be a great turnout," Gino remarked. "'Tis the season to be scared. People are afraid to go back to the Lake House. Lucy and her mother are taking the kids to see Santa at the mall today."

It saddened me that the festival wasn't going to raise much money for the Humane Society. Dylan had gotten Luigi from their local shelter as a Christmas present for me five years earlier, and I had a soft spot for organizations that helped animals.

Gino dangled his car keys. "I'd love to talk about this further, but I have a job to do. I'm working late tonight so promise me you'll both be good. Go sell some books and some penne. This is a money-making time of year for your businesses. Leave Mario's killer to Lou and me, okay?"

I ladled pasta e fagioli into two bowls. The smell of the ripe, fresh tomatoes was heavenly and always made me think of summer. "Sure. Whatever you say."

"What about Jake?" Gabby asked suddenly. "Is he still a suspect?"

There was an awkward silence. "If you must know, yes," Gino said. "I know neither one of you want to believe Jake is capable of murder because he wouldn't want the blame to fall on his father. Think about this though—he may have done it with the intention of saving his father's business. After all, Mario's shop and competition would have been eliminated."

I considered this in silence as Gino gave Gabby's hair an affectionate tug. "I promise I'll keep you updated, as long as you two behave." He let the door slam closed behind him.

"Jeez, he still acts like I'm five years old sometimes," Gabby complained.

She left a few minutes later, and the rest of the afternoon and evening flew by. Without Stephanie, I was busier than usual. Renee, Judy, and I were running back and forth all night, especially since my other server, Hannah, was sick. When nine o'clock rolled around, I was exhausted, but secretly glad to have been so preoccupied. It had given me less time to think about Justin.

"Do you need any help in here, Tessa?" Renee asked as she shrugged into a turquoise colored wool coat that was striking against her blond hair.

"No, you two go ahead," I said to her and Judy. "I'm almost done anyway."

Judy clamped a hand over her gloved mouth. "Oh, Tessa, I almost forgot! Vince Falducci called earlier while you were talking to Mr. and Mrs. Simmons at their table. He said that he'll drop the wine off either later tonight or first thing in the morning so you have it for the luncheon."

This was a relief. I was afraid he might have forgotten. Vince owned a vineyard in western New York, and I always bought my wine directly from him. He in turn gave the restaurant a nice discount. "No worries, Judy. Thanks for letting me know."

Judy and Renee called good night, and I locked the kitchen door behind them. After I'd finished cleaning the counters and swept the floor, I picked up the bag of trash and opened the door. Snow had started to fall, and the ground was covered with a fine dusting. With the temperatures below freezing for the rest of the week, it was definitely going to be a white Christmas.

Shivering without my coat, I hurried to place the bag in the container. High intensity headlights appeared from out of nowhere, shining directly in my face and blinding me for several seconds. A car with an engine suited for the Indy 500 was coming toward me. Panicked, I held a hand up to shield my eyes and ran for the kitchen door. I slipped on a patch of ice and went down hard, scraping my knee in the process. The car came to a screeching stop in front of the door, successfully blocking my path. Fear coursed through my veins when I realized it was the same vehicle that had stopped to pick up Mario the other day.

Two men in dark overcoats alighted from the sedan and started walking toward me at a leisurely pace, as if they had all the time in the world. Terror seized me, and I let out a blood curdling scream as I stumbled to my feet and began to run down the darkened alley.

"Someone, help me!" I shrieked. "Please!"

"Don't let her get away!" a man shouted.

FOURTEEN

FOOTSTEPS POUNDED THE GROUND BEHIND ME. I screamed again—louder this time. At this time of night, no one was around. My restaurant was in one of the more isolated spots of Harvest Park, not where the majority of retail stores were located. I knew from the sound of the footsteps that they were gaining on me. My only hope was to circle around the building and try to get back into the kitchen again. The front entrance was locked, and my keys were inside the restaurant.

My breathing quickly became labored. I was no marathon runner. I screamed again, praying that someone would hear me. My hopes were dashed when I was grabbed from behind. One hand went around my waist while the other clamped down hard over my mouth, muffling the sound of my voice and making it more difficult for me to breathe.

"Shut up!" a gravelly voice muttered in my ear. "We won't hurt you if you cooperate. Just do as we say, okay? Nod your head once if you understand."

I nodded my head.

Both men half dragged, half carried me back to the sedan. The one with his hand against my mouth stopped by the passenger door. "Now, I'm going to remove my hand," he said quietly. "But if you scream, that face of yours isn't going to be so pretty anymore. Got it?"

My blood ran cold as I whimpered and then nodded my head again. As promised, he removed his hand. The strong scent of Aqua Velva permeated my nostrils. One man stood on either side of me. The one who had grabbed me was tall and thin to the point of being gaunt, while his partner was more on the robust side. The taller man grinned at me, and with help from the headlights, I caught a good look at his face. A crooked nose that had been broken at least a couple of times, thin, cracked lips, and a long, jagged scar running down his left cheek. I tried to shrink away, but the other man twisted my arm until I cried out.

"What should we do with her, Frankie?"

The taller man swore. "How stupid are you? I told you no names!" Frankie turned his attention back to me, gripping my arms so tightly they ached. "Okay, sweetie. All we want to know is what Russo did with the money. To be more specific, *our* money."

My body trembled, either from cold, shock, or fear. Maybe all three. "I-I don't know what you're talking about."

The robust man's hands tightened around my throat. "Don't play games with us. We know that you and Russo had something going on. He came here every day for lunch. The food can't be that good." He let out an evil-sounding laugh.

"I saw you making out with him in his shop last week." Frankie's hot breath was near my skin, making it crawl. "You're his new babe. If he told anyone about the money, it had to be you."

"No." My voice squeaked. "I wasn't involved with Mario. Honest, I don't know anything."

Frankie turned my face toward his and I didn't like what I saw. Eyes that were cold and dark as the frozen Hudson River stared into mine. Clearly, he was not someone to swindle, as Mario had obviously done.

The heavier set guy leaned in. His breath smelled of beer, and when he smiled, a gold tooth gleamed in the light. "Better come clean honey, unless you want to wind up like your boyfriend."

My teeth would not stop chattering. Terror whipped through me like the sharp wind. "I'm telling you the truth. Mario and I weren't a couple." Why wouldn't they believe me?

"He came here every day," Frankie muttered. He covered my nose and mouth with his hand. "We'll get her to talk," he said to the other man. "You drive. I'll sit in the back with the lovely lady."

My scream was muffled against his hand. It was getting more difficult to breathe. I struggled as he tried to shove me inside the car, but I was quickly losing the battle.

"Let her go!" a man shouted.

My heart leapt at the familiar voice. *Vince.* Where had he come from?

"I told you to drive!" Frankie yelled to the other guy as he kept trying to push me inside the car. I opened my mouth and brought my teeth down on his hand. Frankie screamed in agony and instantly recoiled, muttering various swear words at me. I scrambled out of his grip and slipped on the snow while Frankie jumped into the back seat and slammed the door. The tires smoked and squealed as the vehicle roared out of sight.

"Tessa!" Vince's voice grew louder, and he was by my side in seconds. He dropped to his knees and put his arms around me. "Are you all right?"

"I think so." My head hurt, my palms stung from where they'd hit the pavement, and my body was chilled through. I tried to stand but my legs shook violently.

Vince picked me up in his arms effortlessly and carried me inside. He kicked the back door shut behind us with his foot and waited until we were in the dining room to set me down in a chair. He removed his leather jacket and placed it around my shivering shoulders.

"Stay here. I'm going to call your cousin," he said. "I've got his number in my phone. I think you should go to the hospital."

"No. I'm all right." My voice broke. "I was so scared."

Vince cupped my cheek with his hand, his dark eyes filled with concern. "You're safe now. I'll be right back." He strode into the kitchen purposefully. I heard him talking on his phone, and a minute later, he returned with a glass of liquid that he lifted to my lips.

"Drink this," he ordered. "It will warm you up."

I started to protest, but the expression on Vince's face told me that wasn't a good idea. I took a small sip. How did he know where I kept the brandy in my kitchen?

A satisfied look came over his face as I gulped some more down. "Not as good as the wine from my vineyard, but it will do."

"Thank you," I said gratefully.

"Gino's on his way." He sat down in the chair next to mine and took my cold hands between his two warm ones, rubbing them gently. An electric current stirred and hummed in the air between us.

"Who were those guys?" Vince asked. "They looked like mobsters."

"That would be my guess," I said grimly. "They were asking about Mario."

He scowled. "Figures. I thought that car looked familiar. Isn't it the same one we saw the other day?"

I pulled his jacket closer around me. It smelled of his spicy cologne and the scent comforted me. "Yes. They kept asking me about money. Mario must have owed them. They think I was involved with him—you know, romantically."

Vince's dark eyes smoldered with anger. "I knew there was something off about that guy. He had *mob* written all over him."

"Do you think they killed him?" I asked.

He shrugged. "From my experience—not that I ever had connections with the mob, mind you—they're usually more concerned with getting their money back. What would be the sense of killing him if they didn't know where their cash was?"

Before I could reply, Vince leaned over and ran a finger lightly across my chin. I winced from the touch and watched as his mouth grew stern. "That's an awful bruise," he said. "Where's your first aid kit?"

"In the cabinet under the sink," I told him.

Vince quickly returned with the kit and dabbed gently at the raw spot on my chin with an alcohol pad. He then cleaned the scrapes on my hand. Vince's fingers were firm but gentle as they held mine. His tenderness surprised me. One of my palms was bleeding, and he applied a Band-Aid to it.

"Does that feel better?" His voice was low and soothing.

"Yes. Thank you," I managed to say.

Vince didn't let go of my hand. He sat there watching me until a banging rang from the kitchen. He cleared his throat gruffly. "I'll be right back. Don't go away."

I sat there shivering as a murmur of male voices floated toward me. Shortly afterward Gino appeared in the doorway, bringing with him a gust of cold air. He walked across the room in deliberate, angry strides and sat in the chair vacated by Vince. When he looked at me, his cop face melted away. He reached out and enveloped me in his arms, hugging me tightly against him. Tears welled in the corners of my eyes.

"My God. Are you all right, Tess?"

I clung to him, trying desperately not to cry. "Yes. Thanks to Vince."

Gino looked over my head at him gratefully. "I don't know

how to thank you. If you hadn't come along when you did, she might have—" He didn't finish the sentence.

Gino released me, and I turned to see Vince leaning against the doorway, arms folded across his broad chest. "I'm glad I was here," he said.

"Speaking of which, why *are* you here?" He never showed up at closing time.

Vince's gaze traveled from me to Gino and then back to me again. He let out a low chuckle. "There's the inquisitive Tessa we all know and love."

"Don't get me started on that," Gino mumbled.

"You asked me to drop off eight bottles of wine for your private party tomorrow, remember?"

"Oh, right. I forgot all about it."

Vince's eyes twinkled at me. "It so happens that I also brought along a freshly made torte I wanted you to try. While we sampled the wine, of course." He shot Gino a sheepish grin, but I knew it was an act. Vince was too self-assured and confident to ever be embarrassed about anything.

"How many times have you used the wine and chocolate routine on women before?" I teased.

Gino almost smiled. "Sounds a bit cheesy to me."

"I happen to value her professional opinion." Vince fixed his eyes on me until my face heated. "From one chef to another, right?"

"Uh-huh. Whatever you say." Gino was clearly not convinced.

Vince dangled his car keys. "I'll go grab the bottles out of my car and wait in the kitchen, so you two can talk privately. Then I'll escort you home, Tessa. Unless you'd prefer to go to the hospital first."

"Home is fine, but I don't need an escort."

Gino threw up his hands. "There she goes being stubborn again."

"Maybe your cousin would rather take you home," Vince said politely.

This seemed to amuse Gino. "We'll both go. I'll check the house and then you two can sample your wine and do whatever else chefs do. I wouldn't dream of depriving you of the honor."

A slow smile crossed Vince's face. "Good. That's what I like to hear." He disappeared into the kitchen, humming a tune under his breath.

"You're collecting admirers, I see," Gino remarked.

I put a finger to my lips. "You didn't have to encourage him."

"He doesn't need any encouragement," Gino assured me. "He's been interested in you since day one, when you came in here to apply for a job. Don't you ever see how that guy looks at you? But I'm willing to overlook it tonight since he came to your rescue. And his being Italian doesn't hurt either."

"I don't need a man to take care of me." My response had come out sharper than I intended, and I immediately regretted it. "Sorry. I didn't mean to sound like a jerk."

"It's all right," Gino assured me. "You're still shaken up. I hate to have you relive what happened, but I need details. Were those guys trying to rob you? Vince said on the phone that they attacked you. He thinks they were the same guys Mario got in the car with."

"Yes. They thought that Mario and I were an item and that I had information about money that belongs to them. That's why they were here."

"I knew it," Gino grunted. "Mario must have borrowed from them and failed to pay it back. That chump sure wasn't the brightest bulb in the box. Can you describe these guys?"

I gave Gino a quick description. "One of them was named Frankie. I think he was the leader. He said he saw me kissing Mario at The Espresso Lane last week."

Gino stroked his chin thoughtfully. "Who do you think they mistook you for?"

"No idea. The only person who comes to mind is Alexandra Randolph, since they had an affair, but she looks nothing like me."

He shook his head. "I'll say this. Mario Russo certainly got around, and I don't mean in a good way."

"Have you made any progress identifying his killer?"

"I'm still questioning people." Gino took a small notepad out of his pocket and wrote something down. "After what you told me tonight and the background check on Mario, I'm almost certain he had mob connections."

"I forgot to tell you something earlier. Bruce told Gabby and me that Mario once worked at The Club Sandwich. He pretty much said that Mario didn't have two dollars to rub together back then. That would make it seem all the more likely that he had help getting The Espresso Lane off the ground. A *lot* of help."

Gino nodded. "I checked with the real estate agent who handled the sale of the building. Mario paid the asking price. The agent said it was unusual given the condition of the market in New York this year, plus the fact that the place needed work. Of course, she claimed it was worth every penny."

"What else have you found out about his past?" I asked curiously.

"He was the top suspect in a possible murder in New Jersey a couple of years ago," Gino said. "Mario lived there before moving to New York."

I leaned forward in my chair. "He killed someone?"

Gino held up a hand. "Whoa. I never said that. Mario was arrested and then released after a mistrial. The woman who died was named Sonya Turner. Sonya and Mario had been dating for a few weeks before she was killed. One summer evening they went down to the lake with some friends. Both Sonya and Mario were intoxicated and the last two to leave. Sonya's body was found washed up on a bank the next morning by some hikers. She'd drowned. Her family said she couldn't swim a stroke."

"Were there any signs that she'd been abused?" I asked.

Gino shook his head. "None. It is possible that she might have fallen into the water. Mario claimed that they had a fight, and he left Sonya there with her car and walked the half mile back to his apartment. Sounds like a jerk for leaving her there, but you can't throw him in jail for that. Mario claimed he didn't know Sonya couldn't swim. He was still sleeping the alcohol off the next day when police arrived to question him."

"It sounds a little fishy to me. No pun intended. Do you think that Mario killed her?"

Gino shrugged. "It's possible. Mario was an egocentric and definitely a love 'em and leave 'em type of guy. What about the conversation you overheard between Alexandra and Tyler Randolph? Mario was having an affair with Alexandra, and then he left her for someone else. Now these guys think he was involved with someone who resembles you?"

"It looks that way. Or at least someone who looks like me from a distance. I think there may be a connection between Sonya's death and Mario's."

"That's what I'm wondering too." Gino was silent for a minute. "I may have been looking at this from the wrong perspective. Sure, Mario had enemies in Harvest Park, but the killer may be someone we haven't even considered yet."

FIFTEEN

AFTER GINO AND I HAD FINISHED talking, Vince escorted me to my car like a noble gentleman. Both men followed me home in their vehicles and waited on the front porch until I had parked my car in the garage.

"Guys, I'll be all right." They both meant well, and I appreciated it, but they didn't need to worry. After what happened earlier, there was no way that I would sleep. I'd be up all night, listening for every sound.

"There's no need to take chances." Gino held out his hand for my key.

He was right. The two men who'd assaulted me would undoubtedly be back, and the next time I might not be so lucky. Resigned, I handed the key over.

Vince shut the door behind us. A plaintive meow sounded from upstairs, and he watched in amusement as Luigi trotted down the stairs toward us. His back arched when he spotted Vince, and he approached him cautiously. Vince stuck out his hand. Luigi sniffed at it, then his Italian loafers. He seemed satisfied and sat back on his haunches as Vince scratched him behind the ears. "I think he likes you."

Vince grinned but backed away. "He's a cute little guy, but I'm allergic to cats."

"Oh, I'm sorry. Would you like me to put him in my bedroom?"

He shook his head. "Don't bother. A few minutes won't hurt."

Gino started up the stairs while Vince looked around admiringly. "Nice house." Then he sneezed twice.

Oh jeez. "Thank you. Would you like something to drink?"

"I never turn down wine if you have it."

"Of course. Is Cabernet okay?" I asked.

"Sounds fine."

I poured two glasses, then gave Luigi fresh water and a few treats as I heard Gino coming down the stairs. He would never accept alcohol while on duty, so I didn't offer him wine. When I went into the living room to hand Vince his glass, Gino was with him. "Do you want some coffee?"

Gino shook his head. "No thanks, I have to run." He bussed my cheek. "Call me if you need anything okay?" He turned to Vince. "Take good care of her."

Vince's mouth turned up at the corners. "Oh, don't worry. I will."

When the door closed behind Gino, Vince amused himself by examining the collages of pictures over my sofa. They were all photos of Dylan and me at various stages of our life together—while we were dating, from our wedding day, and the most recent shot from a vacation we took to Cape Cod three years ago.

Vince pointed at the vacation photo. "Who's the blond woman next to Justin?"

I'd forgotten all about that particular picture until now. *I should replace it.* "His ex-wife, Natalie."

"Ah." Vince took a sip of wine. "Why'd they break up?"

"She cheated on him." I changed the subject. "What about you? Have you ever been married?"

Vince shook his head. "Nope. I'm not sure it's in the cards for me."

His response intrigued me. "Why not?"

He stretched his arm lazily along the back of the couch. "Because I'm too selfish. I like my life the way it is. I'm not obligated to anyone, and come and go as I please. Whether it's New York City to visit my business partner or out to Buffalo to see my vineyard, I don't have to check with anyone first. My catering business is doing well, and I'm not killing myself at it, as I did with my restaurant. I like to travel, go to the theater, and occasionally have dinner or a glass of wine with a beautiful lady." His alluring gaze met mine.

Heat crept into my cheeks and I hastily took another sip of wine.

Vince glanced around the room. His sharp eyes missed nothing. The lights on the tree glittered, the fireplace's mantle was decorated with all types of Christmas novelties, and Luigi was sleeping peacefully in the window seat on top of a Santa throw pillow. "This room belongs in a holiday movie," he commented.

"I'll take that as a compliment." I grinned.

He rose to his feet. "But I need to see your kitchen. We both know that's the most important room in the house." He smiled wickedly. "Well, the second most important room, that is."

Good grief. "Careful, Mr. Falducci, your Italian heritage is showing."

He chuckled. "Yeah, I keep putting my foot in my mouth."

"The kitchen's this way."

Vince followed me into my pride and joy and gazed around with obvious approval at the spotless light-blue granite countertops, pristine stainless-steel appliances, wooden spice racks mounted on the walls, and my set of Italian cookware that hung from the pot rack chandelier.

"Immaculate, as I expected. You never disappoint, Tessa. I knew after the first day we worked together at Slice that you were one of those fastidious chefs who always picks up as she goes along. That drives me crazy."

I leaned against the counter and sipped my drink. "While you're the type who leaves all his pots and pans for someone else to clean."

"Of course." The silence stretched between us as we stood there, waiting for the other one to speak. Finally, Vince cleared his throat. "Would you like me to spend the night?"

Startled, I almost choked on my wine. "Excuse me?"

He laughed. "Sorry, that came out wrong. I'd be happy to sleep on the couch if you're worried about those guys coming back tonight."

"Thanks for the offer, but I'll be okay."

He reached for my hand. "I don't like you being here by yourself. You don't have to be so strong all the time, Tessa." His voice was rich, smooth, and tempting like the Cabernet. "Let me take care of you."

Gently I removed my hand from his. "I can't thank you enough for what you did earlier. But I'll be fine. I've got my alarm system, remember."

Vince sighed. "You certainly don't make it easy. I'm trying so hard to be a gallant knight in shining armor, and you're ruining my act." He snapped his fingers. "Maybe I can win you over another way."

I placed my wine glass in the sink. "I can't wait to hear this."

"What about your breakfast? Did you find a Santa yet?" Vince asked.

My shoulders slumped forward. "No, and I'm running out of time. I may have to ask Gabby to do it at this rate."

"There's no need. I'd be happy to play Santa," Vince said smoothly.

"*You?*" I couldn't believe my ears.

He raised an eyebrow. "What's the matter? I'm not the type?"

I tried to smother a snort. "Hardly."

Vince pretended to look insulted. "It just so happens that I played Santa at my restaurant. I still have the suit. The kids all loved me."

And the women too, I bet. No fake white beard could mask those sexy, dark, and dangerous eyes. While I appreciated his offer, it also made me sad. Justin was the one who should have been playing Santa, but even if that were possible, it probably wasn't for the best. I'd have to stop running to him every time I needed something. "I'd insist on paying you for your time."

"It's not necessary. I'd like to do this—for the kids, and you." He grinned. "It's part of my plan to convince you that I'm irresistible."

I had to laugh. It was so Vince. "You never quit."

After Vince left, I climbed the stairs to the spare bedroom Dylan had once used as an office for his accounting clients. I sat down in the swivel chair behind the desk and brought up Google on my laptop, then typed Sonya Turner's name into the search field. Several links flooded the page. *Woman dies from drowning. Murder suspected in drowning. Boyfriend of Sonya Turner to stand trial for murder.*

One of the links led me to an obituary from two years ago. I clicked on it and read:

Sonya Turner, age 25, died suddenly on Saturday, June 5th. She was born in Paramus, New Jersey, the daughter of Melanie and Roger Turner. She graduated from Paramus High School and attended Dwyer College in Troy, New York. Sonya worked as a web designer in New Jersey up until her death. She is survived by her father Dwight, who resides in Dallas, Texas, her mother Melanie, brother Brad, and sister Eva from Paramus. Funeral services will be private and held at the convenience of the family.

Unfortunately, there was no picture included. I checked the other links but found none. Of all the rotten luck. I needed to see what she looked like.

To my surprise, I noticed an obituary for Melanie Turner. So, Sonya's mother had passed on as well. I clicked on the link and read her obituary in full. She had only died six months ago, and the cause of death wasn't mentioned. *Suddenly on June 3rd...* I couldn't help wonder what might have happened to her. Melanie had owned an online and storefront bakery, Sweet Dreams. Curious, I googled the name but found nothing other than some glowing reviews.

I was more interested in the fact that Sonya had attended school in New York. Dwyer College was less than an hour's drive from Harvest Park. It was a small women's school, and the chances were excellent I could find more information about her there. I googled the college in search of yearbook photos but came up with nothing. I typed in other descriptions for the years I assumed that she might have graduated but still had no success.

I wondered if the fact Sonya had gone to college near Harvest

Park and that Mario had moved here from New Jersey after her death meant anything. It seemed too coincidental. Did they have a common friend in the area? If I could get a copy of her picture from a yearbook at the college, maybe I could pass it around to see if anyone in Harvest Park had known her. It was a long shot, but I didn't know where else to go from here.

I picked up my cell and called Gino. He answered on the first ring. "Is everything all right?"

"Fine," I assured him. "Vince just left. The doors are locked, and the alarm is on."

He cleared his throat. "Let me call Gabby. She'll come over and stay with you."

"No, don't. Besides, I told you that I'm okay. Did you know that Sonya Turner went to Dwyer College?"

A long silence followed, during which I suspected that Gino was probably cussing under his breath, wondering why I couldn't leave this investigation alone. "Yes, I knew this. And it concerns you how? Sorry, I can't remember."

"Look, I don't like this any better than you do, but I'm already involved. Frankie and his friend mistook me for Mario's girlfriend. They won't go away until they get their money. Have you checked Mario's apartment?"

"Yes, I've been inside both The Espresso Lane and Mario's apartment. We didn't find anything useful. If Mario had money that belonged to these guys, it wasn't hidden there. Of course, there's also a possibility that there is no money."

Puzzled, I stared at the phone. "What are you talking about?"

"Let's face it, Tess. Mario couldn't have been making much money at The Espresso Lane. He was undercutting Archie with his lower prices. As you're aware, it takes a while to turn a profit at a food and drink establishment. Plus, he was giving away all those prizes as part of his Twelve Days of Christmas contest. He was spending money faster than a politician on a campaign trail."

"If Frankie and his partner didn't kill him, do you think someone did it for revenge because of Sonya's murder? Maybe she was associated with someone else in Harvest Park besides Mario? If she spent a few years in our area, at a school less than an hour away, it's possible that she knew people in Harvest Park."

Gino hesitated. "Yes, that is one of the options I'm considering. Now please get back to your own life and let me handle this, okay?"

I clutched the phone tighter. "That's the trouble. My life isn't going to be normal until Frankie and his pal go away."

"By the way, I'm right across the street," Gino said. "I'll be here for a while, and then I'll round up a co-worker to watch your house. We'll take shifts all night."

I pulled the curtain back and saw his vehicle on the other side of the road. I sighed with relief. "You didn't have to do that." But I was glad that he had.

"I'm not taking any chances with your safety," Gino said. "Be sure to keep your car parked in the garage at all times. I'm going to ask Gabby about staying with you tomorrow night. Don't argue."

"Do you have any photos of Sonya?" I asked. "I'm curious what she looks like."

He hesitated before answering. "Not yet. I'm working on it."

I thought again about the woman I was mistaken for. "Who in this town looks like me?"

"Well, my sister, for starters."

"No kidding," I said with a chuckle. "Maybe our facial features are similar, but Gabby has shorter hair. That's the first thing someone would notice from a distance. And we know that she wasn't spending any quality time with Mario."

"There's a lot of women in this town with long, dark hair like yours. I can't exactly go door to door trying to find them all."

I thought about the conversation I'd overheard at Town Hall the other day. "Alexandra told Tyler that Mario had dumped her for another woman. Did Mario have any female employees?"

"No. Only George Elliott, who worked part time for him. He goes to community college. His younger sister Jackie has babysat for the twins a few times. Oh wait. Wendy worked there for a couple of weeks."

"Really? How did she find the time?"

Gino grunted. "Look, despite what you think, I don't know everyone's personal history in town, and I don't want to. From what I've heard, she needs the money. Why don't you ask her the next time you see her?"

"Boy, someone's grouchy tonight."

"I'm trying to stay awake until my relief gets here. The baby's been getting up three times a night, which means that I'm also up three times a night. To top it all off, Lucy told me that my Christmas Eve will consist of putting together about twelve hundred toys for the twins. I may have to clone myself. Stick a fork in me, I'm done."

Yikes. And I thought I had problems. "Let me know if I can help."

"You can help by keeping yourself safe and not taking any risks. My family is what matters most to me."

His words caused a lump in my throat. "Same here. Thanks again. Good night."

I clicked off and stared at the presents under the tree for Rocco, Marco, baby Lucas, and Zoe. Life was crazy for Gino, but to me it sounded wonderful. Sure, he might complain sometimes, but deep down, he knew how lucky he was. It made me a little envious.

Stephanie had admitted to me that it was rough being a single mother, but she wouldn't trade Zoe for anything in the world. I'd bought her a dollhouse for Christmas that Stephanie said she'd been wanting. I smiled when I thought about all the fun we'd had making gingerbread together. Zoe was always able to melt my heart. Thank goodness she hadn't been at the festival when Mario was killed. What had she said about him yesterday?

Mommy told me that Mario died. He liked Mommy. He always talked to her when we went into his coffee shop.

Could Stephanie have been dating Mario? Gabby had seemed

to think so. Stephanie had mentioned that he was cute. They'd chatted casually every time he came to the restaurant. What if Mario hadn't been coming to the restaurant to see me, but Stephanie instead? She was also being extra secretive about her new boyfriend. Why hadn't she told me who she was dating?

I'd have to find a time to talk to Stephanie privately. But first thing tomorrow, I needed to find out more about Sonya Turner.

SIXTEEN

THE INCESSANT BUZZING OF THE ALARM roused me from sleep. I was thankful I'd finally managed to get some shut-eye but even so, still didn't feel ready to face the day. I fumbled for the phone on the nightstand and my heart gave a jolt when I saw there was a text from Justin.

I heard about what happened last night at your restaurant. Glad you're safe. I'd like to see you today if you have time.

It had only been a couple of days, but I missed talking to him. What was I supposed to say to him? *I'm falling for you, but we can't be together. I'm scared to lose someone I care for again.* Would he understand? He might think I was trying to force him to choose between his job and me, and I would never do that. It was more likely I'd have to put my real feelings aside and tell him that we could never be more than just friends.

I typed out a quick response. Thanks, I'm fine. Gino took good care of me. I'm super busy today but maybe tomorrow.

Justin's reply came back immediately. Have I done something? I feel like you're avoiding me.

His text tore at my heart. No, of course not. We'll talk tomorrow.

As soon as I hit *Send*, my phone buzzed again—this time with a text from Wendy. Don't bake too many cookies today. Only three or four dozen. We have tons left over from last night. Hardly anyone came to the festival. I sure hope tonight's better.

Well, that was disappointing. At this rate, the town would be lucky to break even, and there would be no money left to donate to the shelter. *Merry Christmas indeed.*

Luigi followed me into the living room, eyeing the tree as I sipped my coffee in the window seat, waiting for the sunrise. This had always been my favorite time of day. I watched as the sun broke free from the ashen sky, a beautiful sight to behold, and tried to find peace within myself.

People had always told me that I was a strong person, especially after Dylan's death. I'd once overheard a mourner tell my mother, "Tessa's hurting now, but she'll be fine. She's strong. God doesn't give us more than we can handle." I wasn't so sure of that anymore. People didn't understand. I simply could not go through that type of loss again.

A rustling noise caught my attention, and out of the corner of my eye, I spotted Luigi swatting a large gold ball on the tree. "Hey," I scolded. "You know better than that."

Luigi let out a squeak and ran out of the room, obviously

upset that I'd ruined his play time. I went to adjust the ornament, and my eyes fell upon the figurine Dylan had bought. I ran my fingers lightly over the surface, comforted by the touch, as if he were here with me.

"I'm doing a great job screwing up the holiday," I said aloud. "Archie's being framed for murder, two people are already dead, and one might be my fault. If you were here, you'd set me straight." But he wasn't, and I had to rely on myself to figure things out.

There were only a couple of days until Christmas, and they would be busy ones. I still had to bake cookies for the festival, plus find time to pick up extra crafts and decorations for my breakfast event. The restaurant would be closed this afternoon for a private Christmas party. A local law firm was treating their employees to lunch, and they weren't sparing any expense. These were the type of events my restaurant needed more of. The price tag for the party came to more than what I brought in on my busiest day of the week.

After I'd showered and dressed, I gave Luigi a hug, locked up the house, and pointed my car in the direction of Dwyer College. Several times during the drive, I glanced in my rearview mirror, worried that someone might be following me. Fortunately, the dark sedan with Frankie and Company was nowhere to be seen. Traffic was light for rush hour, and I surmised many people had already started their Christmas vacations.

I found a parking spot near a directory of the campus. I studied it and located the Admissions Office a few buildings away.

There were several brownstones located along the street that served as dormitories. When I arrived at the Admissions building, I chided myself for not calling first. What if no one was here? Prepared to knock, I grasped the brass doorknob and was surprised when it turned easily in my hand.

The reception area was tastefully decorated with Victorian furniture and antique rugs. Bing Crosby's voice crooned to me from a speaker on the desk, dreaming of a white Christmas. Footsteps sounded and a woman in her midfifties came through an archway. She smiled pleasantly at me. "Good morning. Can I help you?"

I smiled in return. "Yes, please. I'm looking for some information on one of your former students."

Her brow wrinkled. "Are you a relative?"

"No." It was unlikely she'd give me personal data, but a yearbook photo might be enough for me to go on for now. "Actually, I was hoping that I could look at some of your past yearbooks."

"Oh." She brushed back a strand of chestnut hair from her face. "That's an entirely different matter. We can't give out personal information on students, but anyone is welcome to look at the yearbooks. Do you know where our library is?"

I shook my head. She went to the front door and pointed across the street, her violet perfume permeating the air around me. "See that brown building? They're open until noon. It's a good thing you came this morning, because they're closed tomorrow and most of next week for the holiday. What year are you looking for?"

For a moment, I considered her question. Sonya had been

twenty-five when she died two years ago, so I would need a year-book from at least five years back. "I believe the one for 2016 or 2015."

She gave me a puzzled look. "We have some recent ones in this office, but I'm afraid they're only for prospective students to view. Go to the library and ask for Kristin. She'll be glad to help you."

"Thank you so much. Merry Christmas." Moments later, I found myself back out on the windy street. I dug my leather gloves out of my pocket and wished that I'd worn a heavier coat. Well, at least I was getting my exercise in as I hurried toward the building the woman had indicated.

The library was quiet and almost deserted. Two women were standing behind the front counter. The younger of the two was typing something on a keyboard, while the other woman with short, snow colored hair was talking on the phone.

I glanced around the room. Bookshelves were marked with corresponding letters of the alphabet. There were rows of work-tables set up in the center of the room with desktop computers on the surface. A young woman was sitting at one, busily typing something while scanning the pages of a periodical next to her.

The gold name plate on the counter identified the woman typing as Kristin Longworth. She looked up and smiled pleasantly. "Can I help you?"

I gave her my most winning smile. "Yes, I was wondering if I could have a look at your yearbooks, please."

"Of course. Are you familiar with our layout?"

I shook my head. "It's been a few years since I was here last."

Kristin came around the counter and towered over me in height, her black leather boots sporting a three-inch heel. She led me into an adjoining room and spread her arms out wide.

"We have more than 250,000 volumes of books, serials, and microfilms," Kristin said with a note of pride in her voice. "There's also over 10,000 media items plus access to 60,000 electronic periodicals and approximately 80,000 ebooks."

I wished that I'd brought Gabby with me. She would have hyperventilated at this information. Gabby had never met a library she didn't like. "Wow. That's impressive."

Kristin pointed at a separate three shelf walnut bookcase in a corner. "Here's where we keep the yearbooks."

I gazed down at them. Most of the covers were green, which I assumed from the signs outside was the school's official color. The years were all in chronological order, starting with 1950.

"These are all the ones we have on hand at the time." Kristin gestured at a round plastic table nearby. "Feel free to browse through them. Let me know if you need anything further."

I thanked her and let my fingers do the walking through the rows of books. I pulled out 2015 and scanned through it. Unlike high school yearbooks, only the graduating class had photos taken with their name and major underneath. I flipped through the pictures of seniors, but there was no Sonya Turner listed. I thought briefly about searching the activities and sports teams, but there was always a chance she hadn't belonged to any.

Determined, I pulled out the 2016 book. I flipped through the pages of seniors. None of them wore the traditional black or white drapes popular at my school. Several had chosen to have their photos taken outside, posed around the campus. Christina Silvers, Katie Spencer, Julie Swanson...

I kept going. Cynthia Tibbetts, a nursing major, was followed by Sophia Tubbs, an English major. Eagerly I turned the page in anticipation and then froze.

The next page had been ripped out of the book.

SEVENTEEN

PUZZLED, I STARED AT THE FEW scraps of paper sticking out from the yearbook's binding. This was no coincidence. I was convinced that Sonya Turner's picture had been on that page and someone deliberately removed it from the yearbook. What were they afraid people would find?

I stuck the yearbook under my arm and went looking for Kristin. She was arranging books on a shelf near the front counter. She looked up at me and smiled. "Did you find what you were looking for?"

"Yes and no." I opened the book and showed her the missing page. "I was looking for a picture of a woman named Sonya Turner. She was a friend of mine. I know she was on this page, and it looks like someone ripped it out."

Kristin clucked her tongue in disgust as she examined the book. "This is terrible. I can't stand it when people destroy books."

Again, I wished that I had brought Gabby with me. She and

Kristin would have bonded immediately. Instead, I did my best to emulate her ways. "Me too. Is it possible you'd have another copy of this particular year?"

She studied me carefully. "You said the woman's name was Sonya Turner? Why does that sound familiar?"

I might as well tell her the truth, or at least part of it. "She drowned a couple of years ago, and it may not have been an accident. I can't help thinking that her death might be related to a recent murder in Harvest Park, since she knew that particular person."

Kristin's mouth dropped open. "Are you talking about the Santa Claus who was stabbed last week?"

"You heard about it then."

"Yes, but only because I have friends who live there. I'm relieved that the newspapers haven't said much, for the children's sake."

"I live in Harvest Park. If you don't mind my asking, who are your friends there? Perhaps I know them."

She picked up a thick, leather-bound book and placed it on the shelf. "I know the Munsons. They moved there last year. Every time I'm in Harvest Park, I stop at Java Time. The owner is such a nice man."

My face broke into a wide smile. "Archie Fenton. He's a good friend of mine."

Kristin's expression turned grave. "I heard from Gene Munson that Archie was under suspicion for the Santa stabbing. I can't believe that he'd do something like that."

I didn't know the Munson family, and it irked me that they were talking about Archie. "There's no way that he would."

She sighed. "I detest gossip. But it runs rampant in small towns, I guess."

That was an understatement. It was a long shot, but I decided to ask anyway. "Do you remember if anyone has asked to see the yearbooks recently?"

Kristin shook her head. "We have so many people that come in here every day. The library is open to the public, after all. I wish I could help you."

"It's very important that I see Sonya's yearbook picture. Her parents have been trying to find a necklace for her younger sister like the one she was wearing in the photo and can't remember the exact style." I was collecting lies like Gabby collected books. "I was over at the Admissions Office, and the woman I spoke to said that they had some recent yearbooks in their collection."

Kristin's mouth formed a thin, hard line. "You don't think that the page was ripped out by accident, do you?"

"No, I don't."

She held up a finger. "Wait here." She disappeared behind the counter into a separate room and closed the door behind her. I glanced at my watch. It was eight thirty. If I left soon, I'd be back at the restaurant before ten, which should give me plenty of time before the office party started at noon.

Kristin returned in a few minutes and drew me aside. "I called over to the Admissions Office and spoke to Jill. She's the woman you talked to earlier. She checked for the 2016 yearbook, but they don't have it. They only have from 2017 to present. They usually only keep four or five of the most recent ones on hand."

Disappointment settled in my chest. "Is there any other way to get one?"

She scrunched up her forehead. "Let's see. Another office that might have it is Annual Fund, but they're already closed for the holiday." She snapped her fingers. "Wait a second. A friend of my niece graduated that same year. If you want to give me your name and number, I'll see if she'll send me the picture and then I can text it to you."

After I had recited my name and cell phone number, Kristin held out her hand to me. "If you see Archie, please give him my best. He's the sweetest man alive. One time I went into his place and realized I didn't have my wallet with me, but he told me to take the coffee and pay him the next time I came in. There aren't many people that trusting in this world."

"He's one in a million." I thanked Kristin and told her I hoped to hear from her soon.

I left the building and hurried to my car. Blowing snow sprayed across my face. Shivering, I started the engine and waited for the car to heat up. As I drove away from the curb, I checked my rearview mirror, but there was no one following me. Since I needed to get to the restaurant, I'd have to put off my visit with Archie. Hopefully, I could sneak out after the lunch party.

I pulled into the alley behind the restaurant and parked in my usual spot. I was thinking ahead about what I needed to do first and the best way to manage the next two hours. Stephanie could make the antipasto when she arrived. I'd have plenty of time to whip up four large pans of chicken parmesan and then concentrate on the toppings for the cheesecakes. The tiramisu was already good to go. I'd wanted to make Italian pastries as well, but that would take too long.

When I unlocked the kitchen door and turned off the alarm, my brain was already in overdrive, this time thinking ahead to the Breakfast with Santa. I still needed to pick up craft projects, but fortunately the stores were open late tonight.

I turned on the lights and placed my purse on the counter. It was colder than usual and I glanced at the thermostat. Sixty degrees. Yikes. I hoped there was nothing wrong with the heating system.

I went into the dining room to decide where to set up the buffet. We hadn't moved the tables last night, but it would only take a few minutes when Stephanie arrived. I rubbed my arms for warmth. How could there be something wrong with the heating system? It had been cleaned last month, and the maintenance man assured me it was in excellent condition. At least the gas fireplace would warm everything up in a jiffy.

A car traveling by the restaurant sounded unusually loud. I stared toward the front entrance and noticed one of my lace curtains flapping in the breeze. Panic rose in my chest as I rushed over to it and then gasped out loud.

The window was shattered, and the front door had several

large cracks in it. I carefully unlocked and opened it slowly, afraid the glass might break in my hands. As I stepped onto the porch, something crunched underneath my boot. The entire front porch and walkway were covered with broken glass.

A whimper escaped my throat, and I turned to look at the building. Every windowpane was either cracked or blown out completely. I stood there, unable to move, shaking with fear.

If there were vandals in Harvest Park, they were few and far between. I'd never heard of something like this happening in my town before. This had to be the handiwork of Frankie and his buddy. They must have returned last night after I'd left with Vince.

One thing was for certain. Mario Russo was doing me more harm dead than alive.

EIGHTEEN

GABBY SET A CUP OF HERBAL tea in front of me. "Drink this, Tess. It will help relax you."

At this point, nothing was going to relax me. My stress level was at a 9.5 on the Richter scale. "Thanks. I know the bookstore will be busy today, so you don't have to stay. Gino should be here any minute."

Gabby squeezed my hand. "No worries. Liza's got things under control for now. Besides, I'm more worried about you than my sales."

I took another sip, thinking of all the glass that was still lying outside, but Gino had told me not to touch anything. "Why would someone do this?"

"It must be those two guys who grabbed you last night," Gabby remarked. "They came back to try and scare you again."

Even though the gas fireplace roared behind me, I was chilled through. "Well, they're doing a good job. But why destroy my restaurant? They could have followed me home instead." That was a more terrifying thought.

Gabby sipped her tea thoughtfully. "Well, they'd better not try it because I'll be staying with you tonight. Gino phoned me right after you called him about the damage. For once, I am in total agreement with my brother."

I sighed. "As much as I'd love to have you, I don't want to disrupt your life."

"It's fine," she assured me. "We'll have a sleepover like when we were kids. I'm totally psyched. We'll watch *White Christmas*, drink hot chocolate, and talk about boys." Her smile faded. "Ouch. Sorry about that."

A banging commenced from the kitchen. "Tess?" Gino shouted. "Let me in."

Gabby held up a hand. "I'll get it."

"Never mind, I'm coming with you. I have to keep my hands busy."

Gabby let Gino in while I measured out flour, eggs, parmesan, and ricotta cheese for gnocchi. I needed to de-stress badly and this would help.

Gino was in full cop mode as he strode into the kitchen. He placed his hands on his hips and glanced around the kitchen before his eyes met mine. "I've been out front to survey the damage and already filed a report. Do you happen to know if there's insurance?"

"Yes, thankfully. I called Vince. He's out of town today but checked with his insurance company for me. A representative is coming out to take pictures shortly, and they put me in touch with a glass company who can replace the windows today. They even happen to have the glass in stock."

"You lucked out there," Gino commented.

"Tell me about it." I should have been grateful, but instead felt outraged that this had happened. I mixed the dough together with my hands and even punched it a few times for good measure. Then I swiftly shaped it into rope-like pieces and placed them in a pot of boiling water.

My cousins watched me in silence. They knew I didn't need to be making pasta. They also knew that it was a form of therapy for me and a way to release my frustration. This was supposed to be the most wonderful time of the year, not one to live in fear.

Gino's face softened and he touched my arm. "You okay?"

I was about to say *fine* but remembered that they were family, and we had no secrets from each other. There was no need to put on an act for them. I shut my eyes. "No. I'm angry and feel violated."

"What about your luncheon today?" Gino asked.

"I called the senior partner of the firm and they're coming tomorrow instead." They'd been wonderful about switching days, and I was thankful their schedule was flexible.

"Tess is convinced it's those guys who tried to abduct her last night," Gabby put in.

I blew out a breath. "Why can't they leave me alone? I don't know anything about Mario and the money he owed them."

Gino pursed his lips. "I was getting to that. Your 'friends' from last night have been arrested."

"Thank goodness," I breathed. "What do you know about them?"

"Their names are Frankie Tomisa and Jeffrey Fisher," Gino said. "They traveled across the state line late last night and were stopped in New Jersey for going over 100 miles per hour. Further investigation revealed a stash of marijuana in their trunk."

"At least it wasn't a body," Gabby put in.

Gino went on. "Vince took down their license plate last night, so the Newark P.D. called me this morning. When they were questioned, both men insisted that they never meant to harm you. They only wanted to ask a few questions. They swore up and down that they never tried to force you into their car."

My temper flared. "Right. I guess I must have misunderstood their intentions."

"Don't tell me they're going to get away with it *and* Mario and Bruce's murder," Gabby said in disbelief.

"They insisted that they didn't have anything to with either man's death." Gino shifted his weight from one foot to the other. "I've got a friend at the Newark P.D. who filled me in a little while ago. When interrogated, Frankie and Jeffrey admitted to being at the festival the other night but claimed they only wanted to speak to Mario about money he owed them. Both have previous records and were arrested a few years back for beating a man close to death. Unfortunately, they got off on a technicality. They're also notorious loan sharks."

I could only imagine what they would have done to me if given more of a chance. "What you're really saying is that they didn't do the damage to my restaurant this morning."

Gino nodded soberly. "I don't see how they could have. Since they're not local, I can't question them right now, but I assure you that they're behind bars. Their past records turned up a few assault cases as well."

Gabby propped her hands up on her elbows. "Too bad Mario didn't take their warnings seriously. I'll bet those two goons killed him."

Gino reached into a cabinet and helped himself to a mug, which I then placed under the espresso machine for him. "He was either new to the business or clueless. I'm guessing both. But you're right, they're not off the hook yet for either murder."

"I don't know what to think anymore." I gave an involuntary shiver as I handed Gino his drink. "Either way, someone is still out to get me."

"Maybe it was a random act," Gabby suggested hopefully.

Gino placed his hands flat on the kitchen counter. "We don't get many random acts of violence around here. If you recall, the last one was also directed at Tessa when her car was covered in graffiti."

"Oh yes, I remember." I tried to keep the bitterness out of my voice. "That little not-so-random act cost me five grand for a new paint job."

Gino folded his arms over his chest. "I hate that you're on someone's radar again. At least with Frankie and Jeffrey, we know why they were targeting you. Is there anyone else who might believe you were involved with Mario? Maybe his new girlfriend thinks he was cheating on her with you."

This theory didn't exactly make me want to leap with joy either. "I don't know who he was seeing, besides Alexandra." A girlfriend with an axe to grind might be scarier than a couple of mobsters.

"The problem is that Mario had too many enemies to count," Gabby said.

"If we could find the woman he was seeing, it might fall into place, though," I mused.

Gino narrowed his eyes. "You seem to be forgetting something important here. *Again.* There's no *we.* I want the two of you to stop asking questions *now.* Tess, you've had two close calls already, and I don't want to hear about a third one. You're not planning on opening the restaurant today, right?"

"No. I've already called my staff and told them not to come in. Since the repairmen will be working on the windows all day, I didn't think customers would enjoy freezing in their seats or the noise along with their meal. It's not exactly a relaxing background. I'd like to visit Archie—but only to see how he's doing," I added quickly. Okay, that was a bit of a lie, but Gino didn't need to know.

Gino's expression soured. "Tess. Leave it to the police. This is not up for debate. I promise we'll find the persons responsible."

I believed Gino. But would he be able to find them before someone else wound up murdered?

NINETEEN

GABBY LEFT WHEN THE WINDOW CREW arrived. Pete, the owner of the repair shop, gave me a rough idea of what the cost would be, and I was relieved to learn that insurance would cover everything. He assured me there was no need for me to stay and freeze if I had other things to do. I left my cell number for him and fervently hoped that the work would be completed by tomorrow morning.

I decided to stop over at Java Time first and check in on Archie. As I emerged from the car, I stopped for a moment to breathe in the air and view the scenery around me. The beauty of Harvest Park always managed to calm me during difficult times. The wind had subsided, and the sun was peeking out through the clouds. Lampposts decorated with red garland were everywhere I turned. Fresh holiday wreaths from the local Christmas tree farm adorned merchant doors, and the sumptuous smell of apples and cinnamon drifted through the air from Carlita's bakery, which by the line out the door, was doing a booming business.

Sadly, this was not the case inside Java Time. A lone customer was at the counter, paying for his coffee. Archie's face brightened when he saw me, but sadness prevailed in his eyes. Even with The Espresso Lane gone, people were still finding other options for their hot beverages.

He leaned forward on the counter. "Well, well. I needed a ray of sunshine today. What can I get you, honey?"

"Some peppermint hot chocolate would hit the spot. Have you been selling a lot of it these days?"

Archie gave me a forlorn smile. "I haven't been selling a lot of *anything* these days. It's pretty obvious why, right?"

"But that's crazy." I handed him a five-dollar bill. "Everyone in this town knows you're no killer. You've run an honest business for years. How can people be so fickle?"

Archie placed my hot chocolate in front of me and added a large spoonful of homemade whipped cream to the top. "Well, you'd be surprised how fast it got around that I was arrested. Sure, folks have told me they don't believe for a second that I killed Mario. Of course, I've also had some who said they wouldn't blame me if I did and that anyone can lose control for a second...or worse." He hesitated and wouldn't look at me. "There's a few who even think it may be someone close to me."

My jaw dropped in amazement. "Jake? They honestly think your son would do something like that?"

His mouth pursed into a frown as he nodded. "It's no secret that Jake and I have had our differences in the past. He's a good kid, but stubborn as a mule. Like his old man. He was always closer to his mother. For a long time, he blamed me for her death."

I spooned some whipped cream into my mouth. "You never told me that."

Archie waved a hand in the air. "I try not to air my dirty laundry. Everyone has their own problems to deal with. Anyway, Jake needed someone to lash out at, and I was an easy target. A couple of years ago, he finally decided he was willing to give the business a try. Our relationship isn't the greatest, but it's come a long way."

I sipped my drink thoughtfully. Archie wanted Java Time to be his legacy—for his children and grandchildren. I knew that his other son, David, a psychologist, had never had an interest in running Java Time, and he lived too far away. The continuation of the business rested primarily on Jake's shoulders.

Archie watched me keenly, as if guessing my thoughts. "This place is all that I have to leave my family. My dream is for it to carry on, from generation to generation. With business being so bad lately, maybe I should think about closing it down for good. Some things just aren't meant to be."

My heart broke in two for him. "I don't believe that for a second. Harvest Park wouldn't be the same without Java Time."

He patted my hand. "I wish everyone in this town thought like you, honey. But it might be for the best. Jake's not focused since he and Wendy broke up. He was planning to propose to her."

"Really?" This was a surprise. I'd had no idea that things were so serious between the two.

"Wendy acted like a kid sometimes," Archie said. "But then again, so did Jake. I know that he loved her, but some days they fought like cats and dogs. Drove me crazy."

The ceiling creaked overhead and we both stopped to listen. Archie pointed upward. "Good thing they can't hear me. But yeah, Wendy and Jake were both pretty stubborn. When he found out she was dating Mario, he almost went berserk."

I almost dropped my drink. "You're kidding. She dated Mario?"

He bobbed his head up and down. "Maybe dating isn't the right word, but yeah, they went out a few times. I've been around for a lot of years and have an idea how the female mind works. Wendy knew Jake disliked Mario, so she brought his name up to make my son jealous. It worked like a charm."

Great. This was all Jake needed—another motive to want Mario dead. Did Gino know about Wendy and Mario dating? Another thought occurred to me. What about the woman Frankie had seen kissing Mario—could it have been Wendy? She must be the woman that Mario started dating after his affair with Alexandra ended. Why didn't Wendy tell me? What was she hiding?

Archie waved a hand in front of my face. "Honey, are you still with me?"

"Sorry." I didn't want to bring up Wendy again, but it might help to have a talk with her. "Jake and Sarah make a cute couple."

He nodded. "It's early yet, but maybe she's the one. I'll say this for Sarah. She can make one heck of a pie. I wish I could afford to employ her. At least Pie Carumba doesn't sell coffee, so all the more reason to like her."

Heavy boots thudded against the wooden stairs, and a minute later Jake came into view, followed by Sarah. They were both dressed in L.L. Bean jackets. Sarah wore a light-blue knit hat and scarf. Both were decorated with a pattern of black cats in different positions—playing, eating, and sleeping. It was an adorable and unusual set that made me smile, thinking of Luigi.

Sarah and Jake were laughing together at some private joke and holding hands. They looked surprised to see me.

"Hey, Tessa," Jake said.

I did a half wave. "Jake. Hi, Sarah. No work today?"

"It's my day off," Sarah explained as she sat down at a table to lace one of her boots. "Jake and I are going tobogganing in the park."

Archie beamed at them. "Have fun, you crazy kids."

Jake didn't even bother to acknowledge his father and edged toward the door. "Come on babe, let's go."

Sarah didn't appear to notice the friction between the two men, but I couldn't help wondering if they'd had another argument. "Tomorrow's going to be absolutely insane at Pie Carumba, and so is Christmas Eve," she said. "I have to be in at five o'clock in the morning, and they've already asked me about overtime. Guess that means no lunch break, either."

"They have to give you a lunch break," I said. "You can't work all day on an empty stomach." The thought horrified me.

Jake put an arm around her shoulders. "If it's quiet in here tomorrow, I'll bring you something from Tessa's restaurant."

Archie interrupted. "Jake, I have a doctor's appointment in the afternoon, so I'll need you to hold down the fort."

Jake didn't respond, so I stepped in. "I'd offer to bring you some myself, but I have a lunch party for forty people tomorrow. Maybe I can slip out afterwards."

"It's no big deal," Sarah assured me. "I've managed before."

"She's a trooper," Jake said as he kissed her.

Sarah giggled as she threw her arms around his neck. "Isn't he the cutest thing?"

Jeez, get a room.

After they broke apart, Jake cleared his throat. "Hey, Tessa, how are you hosting a luncheon tomorrow with all that damage to your building?"

You could always count on news to travel fast in Harvest Park. "How did you find out?"

There was a slight hesitation in Jake's response. "Oh, I drove by it earlier and saw all the glass on the sidewalk. Were kids playing a prank?"

Archie looked thunderstruck. "Why didn't you say something, honey? What happened?"

"It's nothing. Like Jake said, it was probably some kids fooling around." Archie already had enough to worry about without adding me to his list.

"It was nice seeing you, Tessa," Sarah said brightly. "Merry

Christmas." She waved to Archie as Jake held the door open for her. He started to follow her out but at the last second turned to meet my gaze.

"You need to be careful, Tessa." His voice was so low that I barely heard him. "There's a killer on the loose. I'd hate to see anything happen to you."

The frigid air blew through me as the door shut behind him. Unnerved, I watched as the pair got into Jake's car and started kissing again. A minute later the vehicle roared down the street in the direction of the park.

Something about Jake's demeanor was off. If he was still heartbroken about Wendy, he certainly was hiding it well. What really bothered me was how Jake hadn't even acknowledged his father. "Did you and Jake have an argument?"

Archie emptied the garbage can and tied up the bag. "Nah, we're fine. Jake and I don't always see eye to eye about the place. He keeps asking me to drop the prices and I refuse. Hang on a second while I throw this out in the dumpster."

The phone on the counter began to ring. Archie started toward it as I held out my hand for the bag. "I've got it. You grab the phone. Maybe it's an order."

He scowled. "You don't have to do that. You've got your own business to take care of."

"Never mind. I have plenty of time today." Boy, was that the truth.

I went into the back room and pushed open the steel door that led to the alley. The bag was heavier than I'd thought. As I raised it into the air, the plastic caught on the open lid and the bag burst open, scattering its contents all over the concrete and snow.

Frustrated, I cursed under my breath. What a great day this was turning out to be. I wrinkled my nose at the pile of garbage surrounding me. Paper cups, some with liquid still in them, coffee grounds, and filters littered the area. With a sigh, I went back inside. Archie was still talking on the phone, so I searched the storage room and found a broom, dustpan, more garbage bags, and a pair of plastic gloves. Armed with my supplies, I went back outside to start cleaning up.

As I picked up the ripped bag, I noticed a hand towel peeking out underneath it. I started to reach for it and then gasped, taking a quick step backwards. My heart pounded in my chest as I stood there immobilized, my feet frozen to the ground. Someone touched my arm from behind and I shrieked, jumping almost ten feet in the air. I turned to see Archie wearing a puzzled expression.

My hand went to my throat. "You scared me."

"Tessa, what's wrong? You look like you've seen a ghost."

"I—uh, had a little accident with the bag," I whispered.

Archie frowned. "I'm sorry about that. I never should have never let you bring it out—that was a heavy one. I've got to buy some sturdier trash bags."

I pointed a trembling finger at the towel. "What's that?"

Archie squinted at the towel and then bent down for a closer look. His eyes widened with horror. He snatched the towel off the ground and walked swiftly back inside the building with it.

I followed and watched him place the towel into a plastic bag. "Archie—"

"It's nothing, honey."

"That towel is covered in blood. Did you have an accident?" I asked gently.

Archie stood there with one hand on the bag, staring straight ahead. "Jake must have cut himself. Maybe while he was shaving. He does that a lot." He tried to emit a laugh, but it stuck in his throat. "Clumsy kid."

If that mess was the result of a shaving escapade, Jake should be in the hospital right about now. "The towel is from Jake's apartment?"

Archie's breathing became labored. He turned and went back outside to pick up the rest of the garbage. I noticed his hands shaking as he grasped the plastic bag between them.

I touched his arm. "Do you want to talk about it?"

He wouldn't look at me. "Maybe you should leave now, Tessa." Archie's tone was brisk and sharp, one that he'd never used with me before. "I've got a lot of work to do."

TWENTY

"WHERE'S THE TOWEL NOW?" GINO DEMANDED. "Why didn't you take it with you?"

I stared at my cell phone in disbelief. "What exactly was I supposed to say to Archie? 'Gee, Arch, I need that towel because I think your son stabbed Mario and was trying to get rid of the evidence.'"

When Gino grunted in response on the other end, I was almost sorry that I'd called him. The look of despair on Archie's face was one that I would not forget soon. Archie had never asked me to leave Java Time before. He was probably on the phone with Jake at this minute, telling him to get out of town. No, Archie wouldn't do that. He prided himself on honesty. Then again, this was his son we were talking about. Like any father, he would do what he could to protect him.

After Archie had told me to leave, I'd casually mumbled something about meeting Gabby for lunch and had hurried out of there as fast as I could. I'd used my hands free to dial Gino's number in the car before I was even down the street.

"Are you sure that it was blood?" Gino asked.

"No, I'm not sure," I said honestly. "But it looked like blood to me. There were red splotches all over the towel. Archie said that maybe Jake had cut himself shaving. It was obvious he thought it was blood too."

"But you're not positive," Gino insisted.

"No." I ground my teeth together in exasperation. "But what else could it be?"

"Maybe he was cooking and had an accident," Gino suggested.

I shook my head. "It wasn't food related." My nose never failed me.

"The towel was in the garbage, and we don't know for how long. That might affect the smell. If you really think it was blood, I'll check it out."

I felt as if I'd betrayed my best friend, but the towel did need to be examined. "Was there anything that would have told me it was blood? Any signs I should have looked for?"

"Blood will rinse out in cold water, even if it's dried," Gino explained. "Maybe not all of it but at least some. I need to get that towel. You said that Archie placed it in a bag?"

"I can't ask Archie for it," I said in desperation. "There's no way I can do that."

"No, you won't," Gino agreed. "I'll be the one to ask. If Archie knows that Jake killed Mario, he's an accessory to murder."

My jaw almost hit the floor. "He wouldn't do that. Archie was surprised when he saw it, same as me."

"Let me finish," Gino said calmly. "If he suspects his son did this and tries to withhold evidence or information, he's in trouble too. Archie could be accused of obstructing governmental administration."

I bit into my lower lip. How had this all gone so terribly wrong for my friend?

"Tess, I don't want to believe it either," Gino said. "But I have to get that towel and find out for sure."

I knew Gino was right, but that didn't make this any easier. "What are you going to do?"

"I'll head over to Java Time in a little while. I could use a good cup of coffee anyway. Archie and I will have a little talk, and I'll gradually get around to bringing up the towel. But first I have another matter to take care of at the station." There was a pause, and his voice turned more authoritative. "I don't want to see you anywhere near his building. Understood?"

"Fine," I promised.

Gino sounded relieved. "Good. There's only two days till Christmas. Go wrap something. Better yet, go cook something. I promise to let you know what I find out." With that, he clicked off.

Lost in thought, I continued to drive, unsure of where the road would take me. Was Jake capable of murder? Had it been a crime of passion? I couldn't see Jake premeditating it. The thought of him purposely bringing a bagel knife to the festival seemed ludicrous. Something about the scenario didn't make sense to me.

Since Jake was several years younger than me, we'd never run in the same circle of friends. He'd had a few girlfriends before Wendy and Sarah, but I didn't know them. He'd always seemed like a decent guy, despite his differences with his father. I didn't want to believe he'd killed Mario in a heated moment, and prayed that the red spots on the towel turned out to be something other than blood.

Frankie and his friend were behind bars. If they'd killed Mario and Bruce, someone else had done the damage to my restaurant, which didn't exactly make me feel all warm and fuzzy.

Matt? No. I'd been down this road before. I still had the sense that he was hiding something from me, but I knew he wasn't a killer.

Tyler and Alexandra Randolph. Tyler was angry at his wife for her affair, plus he had an election to win next November. Was he afraid that Mario would spill the beans? Maybe Mario was blackmailing him, looking for money in exchange to keep silent. Alexandra was no innocent bystander either. Had she been so furious about Mario throwing her over for a younger woman that she'd killed him out of anger?

All of these people had motives, some more prevalent than others. Every one of them had been at the Lake House when Mario was murdered. Was there someone else that I had overlooked?

With new determination, I turned the car around and sped

over to Town Hall. Wendy's car was in the lot, but Tyler's BMW was missing. The sky was turning gray again, and the smell of snow was in the air. Like me, the weather couldn't seem to make up its mind lately.

Wendy was at her desk but didn't see me come in. From several feet away I could hear music blaring through her headphones. "Have a Holly Jolly Christmas" seemed a bit out of character for our town these days. After a few seconds, she looked up and gasped.

"Good Lord, Tessa." She switched off the headphones. "You scared me half to death."

"Sorry about that. Is Tyler in by chance?"

Wendy shook her head. "No, he's at a lunch meeting. I don't expect him back for a while." She examined my face carefully. "What did you want to see him about?"

"It's not that important. I wanted to ask him about plans for next year's festival. I have a few ideas I'd like to run by him," I lied.

"What ideas?" she asked suspiciously. "You're not happy with the work I've been doing? Do you have a complaint?"

Good grief. "It's nothing like that." Wendy was extra sensitive, so I had to tread lightly around her. "Where are you spending Christmas this year?"

"Oh." She attempted a smile and then stared down at her hands. "I have a maternal great aunt who lives in the Adirondacks. She wants me to come there."

"That's quite a drive."

Wendy shrugged. "About three hours. If Tyler lets me out early on Christmas Eve, I can make it. The storm being predicted isn't supposed to hit until later that night." Her expression turned wistful. "It would have been nice to spend it with someone special this year, but that's not about to happen."

I was sorely tempted to ask about her relationship with Jake but decided against it. "If you can't make it to the Adirondacks, you're always welcome to have dinner at my house on Christmas Day."

Her eyes started to mist over. "Gosh, Tessa, that's really nice of you."

"Well, in all fairness, I should warn you. My entire family will be there, so you'll be lucky to get a word in edgewise."

She laughed. "I wouldn't mind that."

I pointed toward the hallway. "I'm going to go look at the trees."

Wendy's smiled faded. "You did that the other day."

"Oh, I can't help myself." I smiled so wide that my cheeks started to hurt. "It helps me get into the holiday spirit. I love looking at them."

"Suit yourself." Wendy gave me a funny look as her phone buzzed. "Good afternoon, Town Hall."

I hoped I hadn't made her suspicious, but what other excuse could I give? As I walked away, I was positive that Wendy's eyes were watching every move I made. My boots tapped against the floor as I held my head up high, trying to pretend I was more confident than I felt. After walking past Tyler's door, I glanced over my shoulder. There was no one in sight. I knocked once on the door and waited. No answer. My fingers gripped the doorknob and it turned easily in my hand. Heart thumping, I went inside and shut the door quietly behind me.

Tyler's office consisted of a built-in bookcase filled with official looking documents and binders, a large L-shaped walnut desk, two padded chairs, and a filing cabinet, which I tried first. Locked. Shoot. I slipped behind the desk and pulled at the main drawer. Also locked. This was not going according to plan.

I tried the top drawer on the right side, which was also locked. Then I stared down at the bottom drawer, which was deeper in size. A manila folder was sticking out of one side. I tugged at it and the drawer gave way. Tyler must have shut the drawer in a hurry, so it hadn't latched properly. I started scrolling through the folders while keeping my ear cocked toward the door. If I'd known I would have ended up snooping in Tyler's office, I'd have coaxed Gabby away from the bookstore to serve as lookout.

A folder in the back of the drawer was unmarked, and I drew it out. There were several receipts inside it, with the most current one dated last Sunday. Across the center of it, scrawled in Tyler's untidy handwriting were the words *Business Expense*. A red flag shot up for me when I noticed that it was from the Waldorf Astoria Hotel in New York City. There was a summary of charges from Sunday night's stay, which included dry cleaning and dinner. Stapled to the back of it was a receipt and breakdown of Tyler's dinner. Gee, he must have been hungry that night. Two prime rib dinners were listed along with Caesar salads and cherries jubilee for dessert. A bottle of Dom Perignon and a box of chocolates were also included. The entire cost of his hotel stay was over two thousand dollars.

This had to be a mistake. Sunday had been the informal meeting at Town Hall for Harvest Park merchants to talk about the festival. Sure, it had lasted less than an hour, but Tyler told me that he and his wife were hosting a dinner party at their home that night. He'd clearly lied about his whereabouts. Had Alexandra even been with him? I had my doubts. It sounded more like both Tyler and his wife were enjoying playing the field. That part was none of my concern. What did upset me was the fact that Tyler had claimed this trip as a business expense. Was Harvest Park footing the bill for Tyler's rendezvous?

The thought made my blood boil faster and hotter than a pot of pasta. What a phony he had been, going on about those who were in need at this time of the year. Tyler had access to the donations that went to the animal shelter. Last year the funds we'd raised had gone to a local food bank—or so he'd said. What if the funds had never made it there? Tyler could have easily drafted up a phony thank you letter like the one pinned to the board in the hallway. Would he really have done such a despicable thing?

As I took several shots of the papers with my cell phone, another unpleasant thought occurred to me. If Tyler had been stealing money from our town, did Mario know about it? If

Alexandra knew, she might have passed the information on to her former lover.

The sudden ring of Tyler's desk phone snapped me back to reality. Time to get out of here. I shut the desk drawer in haste, making sure to leave the exact same file positioned as it had been before. As I reach for the knob, the door opened and nearly struck me in the face. "Oh, Wendy, I was going to wait for Tyler in here but then I decided—"

I broke off when I realized that I wasn't talking to Wendy. Alexandra Randolph was standing directly in front of me.

TWENTY-ONE

ALEXANDRA'S GLOSSED LIPS PURSED TOGETHER INTO a frown. "What are you doing in my husband's office?"

I forced a smile to my face, hoping that my acting skills were up to par. "Merry Christmas, Alexandra. Wendy said it would be okay for me to wait in Tyler's office for him. I need to speak to him about the festival."

Her turquoise colored eyes scanned me up and down appraisingly. "Didn't she tell you that he won't be back for at least an hour? At least that's the story she gave me."

"Oh, I must have heard her wrong. I need to get back to the restaurant, so I'll catch him another time." I took a step forward.

Alexandra shut the door and leaned against it, blocking my escape. "What's really going on with you?"

"I don't know what you're talking about."

A smile tugged at the corners of her mouth. "What's your game? I know that you have something up your sleeve. You can't fool me. The poor little town widow… Boo hoo. Every time there's a murder in Harvest Park, you and that cousin of yours are somehow involved."

"Sorry to disappoint you, but those situations couldn't be helped. My husband was murdered, and a woman died in Gabby's bookstore. How could we *not* be involved?"

Alexandra waved a hand as if swatting at a fly. "Please. It's like you're the grim reaper. Somehow you make it a habit to snoop into matters that don't concern you. Just because your cousin is on the police force doesn't mean you have a right to include yourself as well. I've heard the truth about your husband and his shady dealings. Some people in this town think that he got exactly what was coming to him."

Her words stung like a wasp. "So, you're saying that it was okay for my husband to be murdered because he did something dishonest?" Nausea rolled through my stomach. "No one deserves to die like that." Dylan had burned to death in a car fire. How could she be so cruel? I'd never thought of Alexandra as the heartless type. Perhaps a little self-centered, yes. She was showing her true colors, and I didn't like this shade of her.

"Whatever," she shrugged. "I'm surprised that you weren't the person to find Mario after he was stabbed."

Despite the fact that she repulsed me, I decided to follow Alexandra's lead and gauge her reaction. "Frankly, I'm surprised it wasn't you since you were the one having an affair with him."

Alexandra's jaw went slack. She took a step toward me and

raised her hand in the air as if to slap me. "How dare you. Who's been spreading such vicious lies?"

It was difficult not to smirk, but I managed. "*You.* I overheard your argument with Tyler in here the other day."

Her hand trembled in the air for a second, then fell lifeless at her side. "You were listening in on a private conversation? Why am I not surprised? Typical."

"Not intentionally," I lied. "I was waiting to see Tyler and happened to overhear. Afterward, I figured it wasn't a good time to bother him, so I came back today."

"Baloney," she spat out. "You live for gossip. Little Miss Perfect. Baking hundreds of cookies for the festival. Always trying to help someone less fortunate. Giving out free meals to those who can't afford to pay. I swear, they should put you in a Hallmark movie. And you just happened to overhear a personal conversation between a married couple. Do you think you're the next Jessica Fletcher? This is not Cabot Cove, sweetie. What are you really after? Money?"

"No," I said calmly. "I'm only trying to help Archie. All I want is to find out who killed Mario." I had to catch myself before I mentioned Bruce, since no one knew how he had died yet.

Alexandra sneered. "Right. Well, I can assure you it wasn't me or my husband."

"You didn't want revenge because Mario dumped you for another woman?"

She shook her head. "No. I already got my revenge."

I cocked an eyebrow at her. "How so?"

Alexandra moved away from the door and dropped into one of the padded chairs by Tyler's desk. "I slept with Mario to get back at Tyler. It's not like I was looking to marry the guy. Mario was charming, good looking, and spending money like it was water—or in his case, coffee. We went to dinner a few times. He took me to a couple of five-star hotels. I *wanted* Tyler to find out. He's been cheating on me for years. It was time for him to get a dose of his own medicine."

My mouth opened in surprise. So, Alexandra was aware of Tyler's affairs. Did she know that he might be embezzling from the town as well? "Do you know who the woman is?"

Alexandra's smile was as brittle as a pencil. "Oh, there's more than one. My husband sometimes hires companions for the evening. Only when he's out of town, of course. His favorite place to go is New York City. Less than three hours away and he can always find someone to entertain him, if you know what I mean. To be honest, I'm more concerned about the money he shells out, but Tyler says that a fellow politician lets him use his penthouse for free whenever he likes."

Was she telling me the truth? I wasn't sure. I'd have to update Gino but first needed to make myself scarce before Tyler returned. "You must have been upset when Mario was killed." It was a statement, not a question.

Alexandra studied me intently. "It's never fun to see anyone die. Of course, on some level, Mario deserved it. He made me look like a fool."

"Are you saying that he used you as well?"

She cackled like a chicken. "You really are naive. Mario wanted Tyler to get the zoning regulations changed. He was quite insistent upon it. When I asked him why, he said it was in order to add on to The Espresso Lane's building. He claimed it wasn't his idea though, which made no sense. Anyway, our affair ended when I refused to help him."

This made sense to me. Maybe the goons Mario had borrowed money from wanted to expand the building into a headquarters. I was merely grasping at straws here. I was more concerned with Mario's murder. "Do you have any idea who might have stabbed him?"

"Look, I know what you're getting at and assure you that I had nothing to do with it." Her mouth twitched into a sly smile. "Maybe you should try asking Mario's current playmate—my replacement."

"You know who he was dating when he died?" I asked, amazed.

Alexandra laughed. "Don't look so shocked. I know her and so do you."

I sucked in some air. This was worse than I'd thought. "Are you saying that his new girlfriend might have killed him?"

Alexandra rose from the chair and gave me a cool smile that was only degrees above freezing. "Why don't you go ask her and see what she says. I'm sure Wendy will be glad to help you out."

"Wendy was dating Mario?" Given the information Archie had already relayed to me, it wasn't a surprise, but I tried to pretend I had no idea.

"I don't think they were serious," Alexandra admitted, "but she couldn't wait to flaunt their fling in my face. The day after Mario broke it off with me, he brought Wendy to work and they were slobbering all over each other in his car." Her lips pursed in distaste. "Disgusting. At least *I* was more discreet. It's so obvious why she went out with him."

"Not to me," I confessed.

She rolled her eyes toward the ceiling. "Tyler was thinking about firing Wendy. I mean, you can't blame him. The girl's an idiot and makes one mistake after another. She's also a nosy little thing like you and knew all about Mario and me. That's all the ammunition she needed. If people found out, it would ruin Tyler's bid for Attorney General next year. So instead of working, she goofs off and does whatever she pleases since she knows she's not in any danger of losing her job. As soon as the election is over, I guarantee she'll be gone."

I racked my brain, trying to make sense of this. If what Alexandra said was true, why would Wendy kill Mario? Dating him to save her job made sense, although Alexandra might be lying about that part. It never looked to me like Wendy slacked at her job, but I didn't know enough about her duties. She was certainly Tyler's beck and call girl, even on Sundays for impromptu meetings.

That was when it hit me. The hair color change. Wendy had dyed her hair from brown to red. I'd seen her a couple of days before the town hall meeting and it had still been dark brown, like mine. Her hair was about my length too. From a distance she resembled me and must have been the woman Frankie mistook me for.

Head smack. Wendy had been the first person to discover Mario's body after the stabbing. Why hadn't I thought about her as a suspect sooner? "Do you think Mario was getting ready to break up with her?"

Alexandra stifled a yawn, as if the conversation bored her. "It's possible. Like the saying goes, he enjoyed loving and leaving them. Now, if you'll excuse me, I have a little shopping to do. I need to max Tyler's credit cards out before the election."

She flung open the door and left me without another word. I watched as her stiletto heeled boots, Prada from the looks of them, clicked against the linoleum as she walked defiantly down the hall.

I closed Tyler's door behind me and headed back to Wendy's desk. She was texting someone and gave a sudden start when she saw me. "Oh, Tessa. I was wondering what happened to you. Did you run into the queen?"

"Yes, we talked." I hesitated, trying to phrase my question as delicately as possible. "Wendy, I didn't know you were dating Mario before he died."

Her eyes almost bugged out of her head. "What?"

"Alexandra told me that you were dating him." I purposely left Archie's name out. "Why didn't you ever say anything about it?"

Wendy swallowed nervously. "What's there to tell? We went out a couple of times. That's all. It wasn't like we were serious."

I brought my gaze level with hers. "It must have been a terrible shock when you discovered his body that night."

She narrowed her eyes. "What's this all about, Tessa? You're acting like I stabbed him."

"Did you?"

"No!" She jumped out of her seat like it was on fire. "I cared for Mario. Okay, I wasn't in love with him, but he was fun to be around. He was nice to me. Suave. A little stuck on himself, but I could deal with that. He paid for dinner every time we went out together. A lot of guys don't do that these days. And this time of year—" There was a catch in her voice. "It's hard to be alone."

"Yes, it is," I said gently. "Were you using him and his affair with Alexandra as some type of leverage against Tyler?"

Wendy smiled slyly. "Maybe. Anyway, what does it matter? It's no one's business except my own. After his stabbing, I decided to keep a low profile about our relationship in case the cops looked at me as a suspect."

"You were the first person to find his body," I reiterated. "Any idea who might have killed him? Did you see anyone outside?"

Her nostrils flared. "No, I didn't see anyone. Don't you think I would have told the cops if I had? Besides, what would I have to gain by his death?"

I folded my arms across my chest. "You tell me."

Wendy's jaw set in a determined lock. "Mario never said anything, but I had this feeling that he owed people money. I mean, he had the contest going on, with all those expensive prizes he was giving away. The man loved to spend. I think it made him feel powerful."

"Why do you think he owed money?"

Her cheeks became tinged with pink. "One night, about a week ago, his cell phone rang while he was in the shower. I was curious so I picked it up. There was a man on the other end who demanded I put him on the phone right away. I went to get Mario, and he was furious at me for answering his phone. He went into the bedroom and shut the door, but I could hear what he was saying. He kept telling the man, 'I'll have it soon. You're getting all worked up over nothing.' Then the man must have hung up because Mario opened the door. He was still angry at me, so I left. It was the last date we ever had."

"Did Mario tell you about his former girlfriends?"

"He didn't talk much about his personal life. He once told me that his parents were dead, and he had no siblings." Wendy drew her eyebrows together. "He said that his last girlfriend passed away suddenly, and he paid for her entire funeral." She sighed. "What a generous man."

What a creep. Mario had obviously left out the part about leaving town in a hurry when he was acquitted of Sonya's murder. "Did he tell you anything else about her, like her name or where she was from?"

Wendy shook her head. "No—oh wait. A couple of weeks ago, he came to my house after Christmas shopping and was all upset. When I asked what was wrong, Mario said he saw someone who reminded him of his girlfriend. It scared the daylights out of him. I never saw him so worked up before."

Alarm bells went off in my head. A picture of Sonya Turner would have come in handy right about now. "Where did he see this person? Was it in Harvest Park?"

Wendy stared at me, puzzled, and I realized that my voice had risen several octaves during my excitement. "He didn't say. It spooked him big time, though."

My heart started to race. I thought back to Sonya's obituary. She had a brother and a sister. Her mother was deceased, but did one of her siblings look like her? Or was her father out for revenge? Most importantly, could one of them be in Harvest Park?

"Why are you so interested?" Wendy asked. "Do you think this person had something to do with his death?"

"It's possible," I conceded, not wanting to share details. I wasn't sure that Wendy was telling me the truth. She had no money and was stuck in a dead-end job. It was possible that she did know where the money was that Mario's so-called friends had been looking for.

"Mario said he was thinking about relocating," Wendy went on. "He didn't like Harvest Park."

Of course, he didn't. Mario was afraid Frankie and Jeffrey would catch up to him. He had no plans to pay the money back and thought he'd stay ahead of them by slipping out in the middle of the night.

What Mario hadn't counted on was that someone else had been looking for him and also wanted him dead. Who was the person that reminded him of Sonya? If I found out, it might lead me to his killer.

TWENTY-TWO

AFTER I LEFT TOWN HALL, I picked up some items for the Santa breakfast and then spent the rest of the day making *sospiri* at my house. Ironically, the translation meant "sigh" in English, which customers often did after they bit into one. They were small, rich, Italian, crème-filled pastries that were fun to make, although time consuming. I enjoyed decorating them with colored holiday sprinkles, cherries, and crushed bits of chocolate as Luigi watched with interest from a kitchen stool. It was time to forget life's troubles for a while and concentrate on making the children happy. I played Christmas music on my iPhone and even indulged in a glass of wine.

I tried to phone Gino that evening to tell him about my conversations with both Alexandra and Wendy, and then remembered the twins were having their Christmas concert at school tonight. A text from the glass repairman had arrived by late afternoon, and he assured me that everything would be finished tomorrow morning. My office party would be able to go on as scheduled. What a relief.

There was a missed call from Stephanie that must have come in while my mixer hummed away. I tried calling her back, but it went directly to her voicemail. "Steph, it's Tessa. I noticed that you called so I wanted to check in and make sure all is well." It seemed strange because she always left a message. I hoped that she or Zoe wasn't sick. I desperately needed her help for the party tomorrow and the breakfast the day after.

After I finished cleaning up the kitchen, I picked up my phone again and thought about texting Justin. It had only been a couple of days, but we'd never gone this long without speaking before. I missed that. I needed to talk to him and make him understand that I wanted to stay friends. It would hurt to see him though because secretly I wanted more, while my heart was afraid to be broken again.

I typed out a message. I know you're working on Christmas Eve but would still love to see you at the Breakfast with Santa, if you can make it.

God, how pathetic I was. This wouldn't do. I started to erase the message when the doorbell rang, startling me out of my thoughts. The only person who ever came by this late besides Justin was Gabby, and I'd already told her not to come by. I set my phone down on the counter and went to see who it was.

My mother was standing on the porch, a paper bag between her hands. "Hi, Mom. What are you doing here this late?"

"Hello, darling." She bussed me on the cheek as I shut the door. Her lips were cold and smelled of the strawberry lip gloss she always wore. "It's not so late. Only nine o'clock."

"That's late for you," I quipped.

My mother laughed. "I'm not that old *yet*." She sniffed at the air. "Oh my. Something smells wonderful. What have you been baking?"

"Pastries for my Breakfast with Santa. Would you like one?" I led the way to the kitchen to proudly display the trays of *sospiri*. To my horror, Luigi was sitting on the counter next to an uncovered tray, his paw poised in the air. "Luigi, no!"

Luigi jumped off the counter, sending my phone clattering to the floor in the process. He scampered out of the room with a piteous yowl, as if I'd hurt his feelings. Fortunately, there were only four pastries on the uncovered tray, so it wasn't that great of a loss. "Well, I can't serve those now."

Mom rescued my phone from the floor and handed it to me. I turned it on and off, and it seemed to be working fine. "Thanks. I don't know what got into him. He never behaves like that."

"Maybe he's trying to get your attention," she said. "You're never home anymore. By the way, I stopped by the restaurant first. Did you close early today?"

I didn't want my mother to know about the smashed windows because she would surely freak. "Yes, I had to have some minor repairs done."

She set the paper bag on the counter. "Here's the anisette you wanted for the Christmas cake. I wasn't sure if you planned on making it tomorrow."

"Thanks. Would you like a cup of tea? Or a pastry?"

"No, I can't stay. I still have a million things to do." Mom walked back into the living room and smiled at the Christmas tree. "I'm so glad you put one up this year." She examined my face closely. "You look tired. Are you eating enough?"

I forced back a smile. Whether I were fifteen or fifty, my mother would always ask the same questions. It didn't matter to her that I worked with food all day. "Yes, I'm fine. It's been a busy week."

"You work too hard," she scolded.

I watched Luigi jump into the window seat and curl up into a ball, as if nothing had happened.

"It's not work when you really enjoy something, Mom."

"Well, perhaps not. I'm sorry I was never a good role model for you in the kitchen. Thank heavens for your grandmother, rest her soul. Your father always said that I could burn water." Mom was still watching me anxiously. "Something's bothering you. What's wrong?"

Wearily, I sank down on the sofa. "Do you have a minute to talk?"

She drew her eyebrows together and sat down next to me. "Of course. I always have time for my daughter."

I twisted my hands in my lap, not quite sure where to begin. "How come you haven't been involved with anyone since Dad died?" My mother was in her late fifties and very attractive for her age. Her dark hair was drawn back in a French twist, she had a svelte figure, and she attended yoga classes twice a week. She was warm, intelligent, and had a great sense of humor. I knew that she'd had plenty of offers but didn't remember her going out with the same man more than once.

"Where is this coming from?" she wanted to know.

I shrugged. "Just curious. Would you ever consider dating one of Dad's friends? Did he have one that he was close to?"

If my mother knew my reason for asking, she was careful not to show it. "Of course, Hal Ripley. They worked together at the factory for many years. He was the best man at our wedding. He came to the house a couple of times when you were a little girl. Last I knew he was living in Chicago. I haven't spoken to him since your father died."

"Oh right." I racked my brain, trying to remember the man. Tall and distinguished looking, and he'd always brought me candy. "Let's say that a year after Daddy died, you started to develop feelings for him."

My mother burst out laughing. "That would never happen."

I struggled not to roll my eyes. "Well, pretend for my sake that it could."

"But it's simply not possible, dear. Hal's been married and divorced five times. He likes his women young, and then younger. He's not exactly my type."

Defeated, I slumped against the pillows. My mother had

never been good at the "let's pretend" game. "Okay, say that Dad has another friend who you start to develop feelings for. It doesn't even have to be a friend, it could be anyone. Would you be afraid to date him? Worry that something would happen to him too?"

Mom was silent as she studied me. "Theresa, I think I know where you're going with this. You've started to develop deeper feelings for Justin, haven't you? There's nothing wrong with that. To be honest, I thought it would happen eventually. He's a wonderful man and he cares for you so much."

"I'm scared." The words tumbled out of my mouth before I could stop them.

She looked puzzled. "About what?"

"Everything. Did you hear about the fire at the paper warehouse in Albany the other night?" When she nodded, I continued. "Justin was there. One of the firefighters was killed. For a few minutes, I thought it was him."

"Oh, honey." She clasped my hands between hers. "That had to be horrible for you."

My voice started to shake. "Justin had a case of heat exhaustion, but he went right back to work. He acted like it was no big deal. But it *is* a big deal. I'm not sure I can live with that—worrying every day that he may not survive, may never come home. So, I've been avoiding him the last few days. I know it's hurting him, but I can't go through that again. All I kept thinking about was that day fourteen months ago, when Gino came to my door."

"Theresa don't do this to yourself," she pleaded. "You need to stop worrying that every man you care about will die."

"But I can't help the way I feel. I'd rather push him away than risk losing him like that." I should have gone to my mother sooner. She'd lost the only man she'd ever loved. She understood my feelings better than anyone else.

My mother stroked my cheek with her fingers. "You've been through a terrible loss. I know what it's like to lose your soul mate, your everything. At least your father and I were together for thirty wonderful years, while you and Dylan were only getting started. And we were blessed with you. There's a living part of Daddy in you and always will be. But you can't live your entire life in fear, because that wouldn't be living, would it?"

"Yes, I know this, but—"

"You're never going to love a man in the same exact way that you loved Dylan," she said, obviously not realizing her words were torturing me. "But you *can* and *will* love again. You're a young woman. It's natural that you'll marry again. Of course, the relationship will be different. It always is. Like snowflakes, there aren't two exactly alike."

The familiar saying made me smile. "Grandma used to tell me that." Everyone had adored my maternal grandmother, especially her own daughter. They'd had a wonderful, loving relationship.

"She had a lot of different sayings," my mother agreed. "Remember the other one she always said? 'Never regret the things you've done, only those you haven't tried.'"

"I remember."

Mom sighed. "Theresa, you are just like your father."

"In what way?"

"You keep your feelings inside too much. Daddy used to do that too. He was a bit on the timid side when we first met." The lamplight reflected off of her face, and I saw a blush rise in her cheeks. "I never told you this, but I actually asked him out first."

My eyebrows rose. "No way. I don't believe it."

"It's true," she insisted. "Hey, the worst he could have said was no, right? But it paid off big time for me. That's why you should never have regrets. Life is too short for them. In answer to your earlier question, yes, I've had offers to date since your father died. I've gone out a few times. Honestly? I haven't found a man I'm interested in. If it happens, it happens. I consider myself lucky to have had one true love in my lifetime. Remember, all that matters is how you and the other person feel about each other. Don't ever forget that."

"Thanks, Mom." I enveloped her in a warm hug. "I'm so glad that you stopped by."

She cupped my face with her hands. "I'm always here for you, darling. Never forget that."

TWENTY-THREE

WHEN I ARRIVED AT ANYTHING'S PASTABLE the next morning, Pete's white paneled van was already parked in the alley. I pulled into the vacant space next to him and then hurried around to the front of the building, where I examined each window, one by one. The glass had all been replaced, and there was no way to tell the restaurant had suffered from vandalism a day earlier.

I found Pete packing up his tools in the dining room. He smiled at me encouragingly. "Great timing, Mrs. Esposito. We're all finished."

I was so happy I could have kissed the man. After he and his co-worker departed, I quickly got busy in the kitchen. Stephanie had never responded last night, even when I had texted her again to see if she could possibly come in earlier today. I was starting to panic and phoned Gabby. Once Upon a Book didn't open until ten, so I hoped she might be able to help me out for a bit.

"I'm all alone here. Renee and Stephanie are supposed to be

serving, but Renee can't come in until eleven and Stephanie isn't answering her phone. Is there any possible chance you could come over for a little while?"

"Never fear, I'm on my way, cuz. Liza should be okay by herself for a while. If the store gets busy and she calls, I'll have to leave, though."

"That's okay. I'll take my chances."

Gabby arrived fifteen minutes later as I was putting the finishing touches on four pans of chicken parmigiana. "You're the best, do you know that?"

"Of course, I do." She grinned. "Now, what can I help with that doesn't involve any actual cooking skills?"

I pointed at the vegetables on the counter. "If you could slice those up for the salad, that would be a huge help."

Gabby went to wash her hands. "I think I can handle that."

A scratching sound was heard at the back door and Stephanie burst in a moment later, looking frazzled and all out of sorts.

"Tessa, I'm so sorry," she began. "I overslept and didn't see your text until about a half an hour ago."

"It's fine." I was just relieved that she had made it. "How did the show go last night?"

Stephanie tied on an apron. "Wonderful. We sold out. A few of us went out for drinks afterwards, and I didn't get to bed until three o'clock." She glanced at me sheepishly. "I had so much fun, but in a way I'm glad it's over with. It was taking time away from Zoe, and I feel guilty for leaving you hanging."

I smiled, relieved everything was back to normal. "No worries. It's always nice to be able to follow your dreams." I popped the pans of chicken parmigiana into the oven. "I saw you tried to call me last night. To be honest, I was worried you might be sick."

"No, I—I'm sorry. I should have told you I might be late today."

Gabby raised her eyebrows at me, and I knew what she was thinking. Stephanie had been acting strange the last few days. She was most likely worn out with the holidays coming up. I decided to let it go.

Renee arrived at eleven o'clock sharp. She and Stephanie moved the tables in the dining room together, then set up the buffet table. Vince's bottles of wine were placed on ice and ready to serve. The *sospiri* were laid out on a separate table along with tiramisu and cheesecakes.

When we were alone in the kitchen, Gabby came over to me, vegetable peeler in hand. "I waited for a call from you last night," she whispered. "What did you find out?"

"I didn't want to bother you during your date." I hastily filled her in on the visit to Dwyer College, my talks with Alexandra and Wendy, and the towel I'd found at Archie's.

"Holy cow," she breathed. "I don't see you for a few hours, and you go out on an all-day sleuth fest. Why do I always miss the good stuff? Poor Arch. He really needs to catch a break. Did Gino tell you if it was blood?"

"No. I left him a message last night, but he hasn't called me back yet."

Gabby went back to slicing tomatoes. "Don't worry. You're definitely on his radar. He'll call soon."

"I hope so." I finished slicing the loaves of Italian bread and placed the pieces in wicker baskets, covering them with red and white checkered cloths. The air smelled fresh and warm with their golden goodness.

Gabby drummed her fingertips on the counter. "I can't believe that Wendy was dating Mario! I knew she was hiding something. The other day when we were talking at Town Hall, she acted more jittery than usual."

I set salami, tomatoes, olives, provolone, and mozzarella down on the counter for Stephanie to make the antipasto. "Wendy probably figured her secret was safe since Mario was already dead. She was scared to say something because then people would think she was a suspect."

"Well, she is," Gabby remarked. "She was the first person to find Mario. That makes it awfully convenient."

I placed a cheese knife in Stephanie's workstation. "True, but what would her motive be? It sounds like she and Mario were using each other. If anything, Alexandra and Tyler are higher on the suspect list, especially if Mario found out Tyler was stealing money."

Gabby added croutons to the salad. "What a lousy snake. I never did trust him. Who knows how much money he's taken while he's been in office? Gino will find out. That jerk will be like putty in my brother's hands." There was an unmistakable note of pride in her voice. Gino and Gabby had always been famous for their bickering, but they still adored each other.

"And another thing." Gabby was on a roll now. "How are we supposed to find this person looking to avenge Sonya's death? We don't even know what she or he looks like. It's like searching for an olive pit in a bowl of your antipasto."

I laughed at her analogy. "The woman at the library is trying to help me. She's my only hope right now." It had barely been 24 hours, but I was anxious for some news.

Gabby was silent. "Tess, why don't you call Justin? Invite him to the breakfast tomorrow to play Santa."

I studied her neutral expression. "Why are you bringing that up now?"

"No reason," she said simply. "I know that you want to talk to him, and I'm sure he feels the same way."

Her tone made me suspicious. "Have you talked to him again? Tell me the truth."

Gabby looked insulted. "You know I wouldn't do something like that."

"Good. By the way, Vince is playing Santa."

Her jaw dropped. "Shut up. I don't believe it."

I still didn't believe it myself. "It's true. He offered, and I need someone, so I took him up on it. Now, if you don't mind, I'd rather not discuss this anymore."

"Okay." Her eyes were full of sympathy, and it pained me to have been so abrupt with her. Gabby wanted to see me happy, but this was out of her hands.

Her phone pinged and she glanced down at it. "Whoops. It's Liza. She said the store is getting busy. I'd better get back."

"Hang on a second." I removed the chicken parmigiana from the oven and started cutting up the tray. Steam escaped from it and rose delectably in the air. "Take some of this back for your lunch, and Liza's too. It's the least I can do for all your help."

"Tess, you don't have to feed me every time I'm here." She stared at the pan and licked her lips. "Okay, you talked me into it."

Stephanie came back into the room as I boxed up the food. "Can you start on the antipasto? I put everything out for you."

"Sure." Stephanie's voice was subdued as she went to her workstation. At first, I'd assumed she was tired from last night's events, but it was obvious that she was trying to avoid my gaze. Something else was going on.

"Tess, you'd feed the entire world if you could," Gabby murmured as she took the paper bag from my hands.

"I wish that I could. Be careful with those—they're piping hot. I have to remember to drop some gnocchi off at Pie Carumba later for Sarah, Jake's girlfriend, if there's time. Unless you want to go for me, Steph."

"Huh?" Stephanie looked up from the salami she was slicing.

"I was saying that maybe you could stop at Pie Carumba for me later and drop off a to-go order." I pointed at the provolone cheese she was starting to slice. "Don't forget, bite-size pieces on those and the basil leaves as well."

The knife started to shake in Stephanie's hand, and it made me uneasy to watch her. She looked like she was about to burst into tears at any moment. "Is everything okay?" I asked gently.

"Fine," she said hoarsely.

Gabby attempted to make small talk with her. "Come on, Steph, fill us in about that hunky new guy in your life. Are you spending Christmas with him?"

"Why are you asking me that?" Stephanie snapped, her knife poised in the air.

Gabby took a step back and held up her hands. "Whoa. I didn't mean any harm."

Silence emanated through the room. I moved closer to Stephanie. "Why don't you tell us what's bothering you?" I suggested.

She dropped the knife on the counter and tried to hold back a sob. "You know."

Panic seized me, but I attempted to keep my voice on an even keel. "Know what?"

"You know who I'm dating." Stephanie's face was full of misery. "I'm sorry, Tessa, I should have told you the truth from the beginning."

Gabby stared at me and shrugged, as if to say, *I've got nothing*. I put a hand on Stephanie's shoulder. "It's none of my business who you're dating." Why would she think that I'd be upset? Unless she'd been dating Mario, and I prayed that wasn't possible. She couldn't have had anything to do with his death. Again, I recalled Zoe's words from the other day. *He liked Mommy.*

"Please don't hate me," Stephanie whispered, "but I've been dating Matt Smitty for the past few weeks."

"*What*? But why?"

The words fell from Gabby's lips, and I almost laughed out loud at her tone of disbelief. "You and Matt are a couple?" I asked.

Stephanie bit into her lower lip and nodded. "I know that you two dated. He told me all about it." There was a pause. "He also said that he was in love with you once."

Gabby stared from me to Stephanie with disgust. "What on earth did you both ever see in that guy? I don't get it."

"Gabs," I warned, and turned my attention back to Stephanie. "I thought you might be seeing—" I stopped myself in the nick of time.

Stephanie waited for me to continue. "Who?"

Now I felt foolish. "Zoe said that Mario always talked to you when you went into The Espresso Lane. She said he liked you, so I jumped to conclusions."

To my surprise, Stephanie started to chuckle. "Are you kidding? That guy was after every woman in Harvest Park. He had more moves than Michael Jackson. I would never date somebody like him." Her tone turned serious. "I hope it doesn't bother you. Matt said that the two of you haven't dated since high school. If it had been more recent, I never would have asked him out."

"You asked *him* out?" Gabby's eyes almost popped out of their sockets. "This is crazier than I thought!"

I glared at Gabby and then gave her a little push in the direction of the back door. "Gee, Gabs, it's a shame that you have to leave so soon. Enjoy your lunch."

"Real nice," she grunted. "Okay, call me later."

"What's with her?" Stephanie asked after the door shut behind Gabby.

I shook my head. "Don't worry about it. She and Matt have never gotten along. Are things getting serious?"

Stephanie's face brightened like sunshine. "We're taking it slow. We both have our own issues to deal with—the kids, exes—although Lila seems pretty chill. When Ryan finds out that I'm dating, he's sure to go nuts."

I hoped for Stephanie's sake that her ex-husband wouldn't find out for a long time, perhaps never. Stephanie had relayed stories about the man that made my skin crawl.

"I really do like Matt," she went on. "He's kind and sweet and—" She broke off and glanced at me shyly. "I feel weird going on about him in front of you."

"Please don't. I'm happy for the both of you. We broke up thirteen years ago. He's not the same person that he was then." I winced inwardly, wishing I hadn't said anything. Stephanie might not know about his former drug addiction. Matt swore to me that he'd been clean for years, and I believed him, but this was none of my business.

Stephanie looked relieved as she nodded. "He said that he did some really stupid things back then. I do believe that people can change if they really want to. I met his boys the other night and we all got along well. Zoe seemed fine with it too. It's going to take some patience on everyone's part. We're taking it one day at a time."

"That's all any of us can do." After the initial shock, I sincerely hoped it worked out for them. Stephanie had been lonely since her separation and divorce, and I empathized with her. "So, you finally gave up on Vince, huh?" She'd been an admirer of his from day one, but then again, so were most of the women in Harvest Park. Carlita often said she was going to leave her husband for him, and Vince always went along with it. Smart man. Every time he went into the bakery for almond cookies, she never let him pay.

"He was never interested in me," Stephanie grinned. "Besides, Carlita would be furious if I took her boyfriend away."

"The wrath of Carlita is not to be taken lightly," I quipped.

TWENTY-FOUR

THE OFFICE LUNCH WAS A HUGE success. Employees of the law firm had a terrific time, and there were many compliments about the food. They were all in such great spirits that it was a joy to have them in my restaurant. Listening to their laughter and conversation while they ate did my heart good.

After the lunch, the senior partner sought me out to praise the food and the service. I presented him with the bill, which he didn't even blink at, and he in turn handed me his company credit card.

As I was wiping down the counters, I remembered Sarah's gnocchi and glanced at my watch. Three thirty. The dinner crowd would start rolling in within the hour. I sent Stephanie out to the dining room with the receipt as my cell phone buzzed. *Gino.* "Hey, what's up?"

"Tess." His voice sounded stern and immediately made me think the worst. "Sorry I never called you back last night. I have some news."

I sat down on a kitchen stool. "Is it about Archie?"

Gino cleared his throat. "I'll get to him in a second. I managed to track down Sonya Turner's father. His name is Dwight Turner and he's been living in Texas for the last few years. Sonya's mother passed away a few months ago, but they divorced shortly after Sonya died. It sounds like her death drove the whole family apart."

"How awful."

"The entire family knew that Mario was living in Albany, which to me means that someone may have come here with revenge on their mind."

My thoughts exactly. "Who? One of Sonya's siblings?"

"Tess," Gino said in disbelief. "Dwight's not going to come right out and say that one of his kids killed Mario. All he told me is that he hadn't spoken to his son or daughter in over a year. He never believed that Mario intentionally killed her, while the rest of the family was ready to hang him. He and his wife were having problems for years, but Sonya's death drove a bigger wedge between them."

My head was spinning. "Is this enough to clear Archie and Jake?"

"No. It's a theory."

I told Gino about my trip to Dwyer College. "Her picture was ripped out of the yearbook. There has to be a family resemblance the killer worried someone would notice. I need to see a picture of her."

Gino grunted in exasperation. "I figured that you'd end up going there. Look, I have a picture of Sonya that her father forwarded to me. When I have time, I'll send it over to you but can tell you that she doesn't look like anyone I've ever seen around Harvest Park. Her father mentioned that she had Facebook and Twitter accounts at one time, but someone deleted them. He has no idea who."

"That's weird," I mused. "Send me the picture as soon as you can."

"As for Archie"—he hesitated—"I was able to get the towel from him."

I cringed. "He must hate me for sure."

"Archie doesn't hate you," Gino replied. "If he hates anyone, it's me. There were tears in the old guy's eyes as he handed it over. I know it's my job, but I still felt like a first-class jerk. Turns out, there was no reason for him to worry."

"How can you say that?" I asked. "He's afraid Jake had something to do with Mario's death."

"Let me finish," Gino said. "It wasn't blood on the towel."

I clutched the phone tighter. "Really? What did the lab say it was?"

"We didn't take it to the lab. There's a basic test at the station that was used. We check the item under infrared light. It was hair dye."

"Then they're both off the hook," I said hopefully.

"I didn't say that." Gino's voice became sharp. "Both men

argued with Mario right before his death. Java Time's knife was the weapon used to kill him, remember."

It was hard to forget that fact. Archie's fingerprints and Jake's were both on the knife. Gino wouldn't tell me, but I had a sneaky suspicion that another arrest would be made soon. "Maybe someone else in town has the same knife."

"I checked with Murray Gates, the salesman. His records show that he sold four bagel knives in Harvest Park during his last visit in the fall. One to Archie, Bruce, Mario, and you. We finally found Mario's knife at The Espresso Lane. All things considered though, we're not much closer to finding the killer."

"We might be," I said innocently.

There was silence on the other end of the phone. "What are you saying? Where else did you go yesterday? Tell me the truth."

"Jeez, I wasn't planning to lie to you. In fact, that's why I called you last night, to fill you in on what happened."

"Okay," he said in a resigned tone. "Tell me what you found out."

"I was at Town Hall yesterday to talk to Wendy, and I ran into Alexandra Randolph. We had a little chat, and she told me that when Mario broke it off with her, he started dating Wendy." I didn't mention that Archie had told me this as well.

"She's the one who found Mario. Lou questioned her after you and Gabby went home that night." Gino paused, as if trying to process everything. "Was he cheating on Wendy too?"

"No idea, but I'm not sure she had a real motive for wanting

Mario dead. When I asked her about their relationship, it sounded like they were both using each other."

"Wait a second," Gino interrupted. "Why would Alexandra tell you about Wendy and Mario? Since when have you become her new best friend?"

I squeezed my eyes shut, prepared for the lecture. "She sort of found me in Tyler's office waiting for him. I think he's been embezzling from the town."

"What!" Gino's voice thundered through the phone.

"Hold on a second." I clicked on the pictures that I had taken and forwarded them to Gino's phone. "I just sent you the proof. Mario could have found out and decided to blackmail Tyler. Wendy also mentioned that Mario was thinking about moving soon. Kind of interesting since he's only been here a few months, right? Either he was afraid that Frankie and his friends would find him, or Tyler would try to even the score."

My attempt to distract Gino didn't work. "Where did you get these receipts from?" he demanded. "And don't give me some crap about Alexandra handing them over in exchange for your tomato sauce recipe."

If I hadn't felt so guilty about searching Tyler's desk, I would have been insulted. "They were lying on top of his desk. I couldn't help noticing them." Good thing my face wasn't visible to him.

"Right," he said angrily. "Was my sister with you?"

"No! I was alone, I swear."

Gino muttered several swear words as I cringed inwardly.

"This is damning information. How am I supposed to explain these receipts to my boss?"

"Tell him the truth. Someone sent them to your phone," I suggested.

Gino exhaled sharply. "All right. What's done is done." His radio went off in the background. "Look, Tess, I have to go. I've got Lucy on the other line with a crying baby plus a stack of paperwork and a robbery suspect waiting for me to question. I also have to tell Sergeant Warner that our mayor might be a thief. Do you have any more news for me?"

"Not at the moment."

"Hold on a second," Gino said in exasperation. "You are not to say one word about this conversation to anyone, especially Archie."

Puzzled, I stared at the phone. "I don't understand. You told me it wasn't blood on the towel. Why would you intentionally let Archie think that his son is still a murder suspect?"

"It doesn't concern you." Even though I couldn't see him, I knew his teeth were clenched. "Sometimes the only way to get the truth out of a person is to pretend that you know everything."

The same tactic Gabby and I had used with Bruce, although it had failed miserably. "Do you still think there's a chance Archie is guilty?"

Gino hesitated for a moment. "I have a job to do, Tess. I'm not allowed to get personally involved. See you at the breakfast tomorrow morning." He clicked off.

Furious, I stripped off my apron and threw it across the room.

Poor Archie was probably alone at Java Time right now, worried that Gino would be coming in at any second to arrest his son.

Stephanie returned to the kitchen and spotted my apron on the floor. She picked it up and handed it to me. "Are you okay?"

"Never better," I lied. "Are the tables all set for the dinner crowd?"

She nodded, her face glowing. "Mr. Jackson asked me to tell you goodbye and said that they will be back again soon. Guess what? He added two hundred dollars for a tip! What a great boss he must be to work for."

I forced a smile to my lips. "That's wonderful. You and Renee split it in half."

Stephanie looked shocked. "No, that's not right. We'll divide it three ways."

"No, I insist. It's all for you two." I started scrubbing the sink, an attempt to work out my frustration. I had half a mind to go over to Java Time and tell Archie what was really going on. No, that wouldn't be right. At the very least though, I could check on him and see how he was doing. Maybe I would, after I delivered Sarah's food.

Archie had done a lot for me over the years, as well as for Gino and Gabby. He'd once had his wife sew Gino's jacket after he'd been in a fight so that Aunt Mona wouldn't find out. There were plenty of times that he hadn't charged us full price for drinks, and on a few occasions, we'd received them for free if we didn't have the money. He'd even let Gino and Lucy use Java Time to host a baby shower for the twins and free of charge when their other venue canceled at the last minute. Archie wasn't just a town proprietor. He was practically family.

After I could see my face in the sink, I dried my hands and packed a bag with salad, gnocchi, and Italian bread for Sarah. "This is going to Pie Carumba," I told Stephanie. "I'll deliver it because I want to pick up a pie while I'm there. I should be back before the dinner rush. An hour at most."

"We'll be fine until you get back," she assured me.

I didn't mention going to see Archie. It would be like Gino to pop into the restaurant for a cappuccino—his not-so-subtle way of checking up on me.

"Be careful." Stephanie whisked a loaf of Italian bread into the oven. "The snow squalls are terrible out there, and it's already growing dark. Plus, this town isn't safe these days. Especially for you," she added.

I knew she was thinking about my broken windows. "No worries, I'll be fine. By the way, plan on leaving early tonight if we're not busy. I'm sure you could use some time to unwind."

"That would be awesome!" Stephanie said excitedly. "I wanted to pick up a Santa hat for Zoe to wear to the breakfast tomorrow morning. She's so excited."

I slipped off my loafers and pulled on a pair of boots. "Is Matt coming too?" Stephanie had taken most of the reservations by phone, so I wasn't positive he'd be there.

"Yes, he's planning to bring the boys." She paused. "I hope that's okay."

"Of course it is."

The phone at the hostess station started to ring, and Stephanie ran out to get it as I shut the door behind me and trudged to my car, feeling a bit envious. It had nothing to do with Stephanie dating Matt. It was more the fact that I was lonely and would be spending Christmas Eve by myself. My mother had already made plans to visit a sick friend in Vermont, and Aunt Mona was going with her. She assured me she'd be back in time for Christmas dinner and asked if I wanted to go with them, but I'd politely declined.

Stephanie hadn't been kidding about the wind. A huge gust of ice particles blew at me, stinging my face and taking my breath away. I hurried toward my car and slid behind the driver's seat. While I waited for the engine to warm up, I made sure the doors were locked. After the other night, I wasn't taking any more chances.

TWENTY-FIVE

AS I DROVE AWAY, I REALIZED that I'd forgotten my gloves on the kitchen counter. Shoot. Well, no matter. I'd be in and out of both places quickly. If Java Time wasn't busy, I should be able to find a parking space right in front.

The swirling snow made visibility difficult. I reduced my speed to a crawl and was starting to regret coming out in this weather. Still, it was the season to be charitable.

As I pulled in front of Pie Carumba, I wondered if Archie was still planning to leave town tomorrow night. If not, I'd invite him to Christmas dinner at my house. If Gino didn't like it, that was too bad.

Blinds were drawn over Pie Carumba's windows and front door. A sign on the door read, *Closed. Open Christmas Eve, from seven a.m. to two p.m.*

I rapped sharply on the door, afraid that the noise might be lost in the wind's howl. There was no answer. My unprotected hands were quickly growing numb from the cold, and the chill whipped through my coat. I started to bang on the door with my fist, until I worried about breaking the glass.

The blind wiggled slightly, and then the door opened. Sarah's astonished face looked out at me. "Oh my God, Tessa! It's freezing out. You didn't have to go to all that trouble for me."

"N-no trouble at all." My teeth wouldn't stop chattering as she shut the door behind me. Scents of vanilla and sugar wafted through the air and my stomach growled, reminding me that I hadn't eaten anything since this morning's cereal.

A marble veneer counter ran over the gleaming multitier glass display case that was temperature controlled. The case was almost as long as the front room itself. Four small glass topped tables were placed against the front window, each one with a poinsettia plant in the center. The window ledge contained a lifelike Santa and Mrs. Claus, who each held pies in their hands.

I stopped short when I saw that there was another customer in front of the display case and it was none other than Wendy. She was dressed in a dark wool coat and a festive red scarf decorated with cats and dogs. To my surprise, her mouth twisted into a frown as I approached.

"What are *you* doing here?" she asked stiffly. "The bakery's closed."

Someone was having a bad day. "Nice to see you too, Wendy."

"Come on in the back room," Sarah said to me. She led the

way, wearing a white apron dusted with flour. Her short hair was tucked neatly underneath a pink Pie Carumba hat.

Wendy cleared her throat noisily as we passed by. She must have thought I was getting preferential treatment over her. "Excuse me, I was here *first*."

"Your pie is in the oven. It will only be a few more minutes," Sarah assured her.

"The shop looks so pretty." I couldn't resist a backward glance at Wendy, who was texting something on her phone and tapping the toe of her boot against the floor. She happened to look up and our gazes met. Her eyes were as frigid as the temperatures outside and immediately put me on guard.

"Greg loves to decorate for all the holidays," Sarah remarked. "He's a great boss but I wish he paid a little more."

She checked on a pie that was in the oven, then stared in Wendy's direction. Convinced we were out of earshot, she whispered, "That's Jake's ex, right? I can see why he dumped her. She's a nasty thing. She came in five minutes before closing and announced that the pie she picked up this morning was wrong. She ordered blueberry cobbler, not apple cobbler. I mean, why didn't she call or come back sooner? Good thing I'd already had two in the oven for tomorrow. As soon as it's done, I can't wait to send Miss Snob on her way."

"She's not usually like that," I commented. "Maybe something happened at work." I didn't mention that Wendy was the one who had dumped Jake. Perhaps she was having second thoughts or was jealous of Sarah. Either way, I had no desire to get involved in a possible lover's triangle.

It was warm and cozy in the kitchen area, and the smells emitting from the ovens were divine. There were several freshly made pies sitting on a baker's rack. I'd always loved this place. As much as I adored Carlita and her goodies, there was something magical about Pie Carumba and the thirty different flavors of pies that they served—everything from apple to lemon meringue to chocolate cream.

I held out the bag of food. "Maybe this will help you feel better."

Sarah squealed when she peeked inside the bag. "This looks so good. I'm starving. I thought maybe you'd forgotten about bringing the food by, but I wasn't going to call and bother you. It's a crazy week for everyone." She removed the lid off the container, helped herself to a few bites of gnocchi, and then let out a moan. "Oh, this is amazing. I seriously don't know how you do it."

I was almost drooling from the smell of the pies. "I should have called in an order. Is there any chance of getting a peppermint chocolate pie?"

Sarah wiped her mouth with a napkin. "Oh sure! It's the least I can do. I made six for tomorrow. I'll grab one." She set the container down and went out to the storefront, then returned a minute later with the pie inside a white bakery box.

I lifted the lid and my mouth immediately started to water as I stared at the chocolate crust and the homemade whipped cream topping covered with crushed peppermint. My stomach had graduated from a light growl to a full-fledged roar. "I'm tempted to have a piece right now."

Sarah went over to one of the wall cupboards and pulled out a plate, fork, and serrated knife. "People always want samples, so we've learned to be prepared. Go ahead. I hate to eat alone."

The knife glided through the silk-like texture easily. I cut off a small slice and quickly forked a piece into my mouth. "Wow. This is even better than I remember. The crust is so flaky and practically melts in my mouth."

She blushed. "Thanks. My mother taught me everything I know."

"Sounds like we have something in common. My grandmother taught me everything I know about cooking. It's wonderful to have someone in your family to look up to."

"I guess." Sarah went to wash her hands and then started using the rolling pin to flatten a piece of dough. "Are the police any closer to finding Mario's killer? Has your cousin told you anything?"

"If they are, he's not sharing the information with me." I watched as she floured the table's surface. "Actually, I wanted to talk to you about that."

Her smile faded. "Because Jake is a suspect."

I said nothing.

She sighed. "It's okay. Jake knows that the police have him on their list. Of course, Archie knows too. They had a terrible fight earlier today. Jake texted me all about it. He's going out of his mind." She lowered her voice, as if afraid Wendy might hear. "Jake's been very different since—that night."

A sensation of dread filled me. "Different, how?"

"Oh, miss!" Wendy's irritated voice floated in from the front of the store.

Sarah ignored her. "I get the feeling he's trying to protect someone. Maybe a person close to him."

I stared at her in disbelief. "Like whom? His father?"

Sarah nodded solemnly. "Jake's worried that Archie did something in a fit of anger."

"That's ridiculous!" I fumed.

She looked frightened by my outburst, and I immediately regretted it. "Sorry. I have no right to take this out on you."

"Excuse me." Wendy peered into the doorway. "Sorry to interrupt your girl talk, but I really need my pie."

Sarah slipped on a pair of mitts and walked over to the oven. "It's coming out right now. It just needs to cool for a few minutes."

"The service here is really slow," Wendy bristled.

The ringing of the bakery's phone startled me. Sarah wiped her hands on her apron and spoke briskly. "Excuse me for a second. I'm sure it's another order for tomorrow. Greg should have cut people off yesterday." She wouldn't look at me as she walked out of the room.

I tried to remain calm. This wasn't Sarah's fault. She was only repeating what Jake had told her. But why would he say such a thing about his father? Was he trying to protect his own skin?

I forked another piece of pie into my mouth as my cell buzzed. I put down the plate and drew my phone out of my purse. There was a text from Kristin at Dwyer College.

Hi Tessa. Well, I did it! I got the yearbook with Sonya's picture. I'm here at the college till five if you need anything else. Hope it helps. Merry Christmas!

Yes! My fingers shook as I opened the attachment. Gino had to be wrong. The photo undoubtedly had the answers I was looking for and would lead me to Mario and Bruce's killer. I stared at the picture and my heart immediately sank. Sonya Turner was a beautiful girl with shoulder length blond hair, arresting brown eyes, and peaches and cream skin. It must have been a chilly day when she'd been photographed because she was wearing a bright-blue coat. Her scarf had somehow gotten tangled and was peeking out from underneath the coat. She looked vaguely familiar, but not enough for me to make a connection.

I was about to text Kristin a quick thank you when something on the scarf caught my eye. I increased the picture's size on my phone as large as possible and then squinted down at it again. I sucked in a sharp breath.

The scarf was beige and obviously handmade. There was a pattern running along it that I'd seen before. Black cats in different positions: playing, eating, and sleeping. It was so similar to the scarf that Sarah had been wearing the other day.

My head reeled as everything began to sink in. The woman who I'd just been talking to must be Sonya Turner's sister, Eva.

I thought about all the different pieces of information that had helped me to connect the dots. "My mother was a pastry chef. She taught me everything I know." The online obituary about Melanie Turner's bakery. The woman who had turned up in Harvest Park a few months ago that people knew little about. She conveniently worked in the back room of a bakery all day, having little contact with people. Mario had seen her once and been spooked. In all likelihood, he'd recognized Sarah and decided to leave town either because of her or his mobster friends. But Sarah had proven to be far more dangerous.

Then there was the matter of the hair dye on the towel. It had belonged to Sarah, not Archie or Jake. She'd been dying her hair red, so she must be a natural blond like her sister and worried someone would see a similarity. Sarah had been so concerned that someone would notice the resemblance that she'd gone to Dwyer College and ripped the picture of her sister out of the yearbook. But she'd forgotten about the scarf that Sonya had been wearing, half hidden by her coat. I might not have even paid much attention if it weren't for the unusual cat pattern. What had Gino once told me? Even the most careful killers managed to trip themselves up.

I started typing out a text to Gino. Footsteps approached and I looked up to find Sarah watching me. The smile she wore rapidly faded. "Something wrong?"

"No," I lied and kept typing, but my fingers started to shake. Come to Pie Carumba right away. Sarah is the one who kil–

She moved closer to me. "What are you doing?"

I wasn't finished but slid my finger over the *Send* button while not taking my eyes off of her. "I was letting Gabby know that I'd meet her at her bookstore in a few minutes."

Her eyes darkened as she watched me. I tried to shove the phone back in my purse, but she moved like lightning and knocked it out of my hand. It fell to the floor and the screen cracked. With horror, I noticed that the message was still displayed. It hadn't gone to Gino after all.

"What are you doing?" I reached down to pick the phone up, and Sarah gave me a shove that sent me flying into the baker's rack. The rack fell over with a loud clatter and barely missed landing on me.

Sarah stared down at my phone in her hand and read, "'Come to Pie Carumba right away. Sarah is the one who kil—'" She looked up at me with an unreadable expression. "You know."

"What's going on?" Wendy asked. She spotted me lying on the floor and looked alarmed. "Tessa! Did you have an accident? Are you okay?"

She stepped forward and extended a hand to me as Sarah grabbed the knife off the table. "Don't move. Either one of you."

Wendy's mouth dropped open. "Is this some kind of a joke?"

"Get down on the floor next to Tessa," Sarah commanded.

"You must be crazy," Wendy said.

"Just do it!" she screamed.

I nodded to Wendy, who immediately lowered herself to the floor. "Sarah, you don't want to hurt us. Just like you didn't mean to hurt Mario, either."

"Yes, I did." She wiped away a tear with the back of her hand. "Mario killed my sister. He's the reason my mother committed suicide. That slime didn't deserve to live." The knife trembled between her slim hands. "How did you find out?"

"The cat scarves," I said. "You both had ones with the exact same pattern. I saw Sonya's in her college photo. It doesn't look like a common one to find so I'm guessing they were handmade."

Sarah swore under her breath. "I was so careful. How the heck could I have not thought about the scarf?" She slumped against the table. "Our grandmother made those for us when we were teenagers. We had several sets. I remember how much Sonya loved hers. She was always crazy about cats." She hiccupped back a sob and blinked rapidly. "It doesn't matter anymore. Nothing matters since that scum destroyed my family."

"You don't know for sure that he killed her." I glanced toward the kitchen door, which was only a few feet away. The door opened into one side of the park. Help was not that far away, but how could I get to it?

"How can you say that?" Tears streamed down Sarah's cheeks. "Especially *you*. Jake told me that your husband was murdered. Didn't you want justice for him? My sister deserves it too. She was drunk and couldn't swim, but he left her anyway. Mario let her die all alone!"

I tried to keep my voice steady. "Yes, I did want justice for Dylan. And thankfully that person is behind bars now."

Sarah blinked. "So, you know where I'm coming from, right?"

She wrapped both hands around the knife and stared at me pleadingly. "A couple of more days and I would have been gone. Out of this town where people want to know every detail of your life. I was planning to slip away when Jake left for Maine with his father."

"You used Jake, didn't you? You thought that he and Archie would be the perfect patsies to take the fall for Mario's murder, since they owned the only other coffee shop in town." In the process, she'd also managed to come between father and son.

She smiled, obviously pleased with herself. "That was pretty smart of me, wasn't it? And it worked like a charm. The first time I went into Java Time, I could tell Jake was into me, so I started flirting with him. He ate it right up and asked me out. On our first date, he told me that he'd recently broken up with someone else." Sarah sneered at Wendy, who stared mutely back at her. "I couldn't have asked for a better opportunity—a guy on the rebound. You're right—he didn't mean anything to me. All I cared about was revenge."

"You had to get Jake to the festival that night," I continued, "so you called and told him you had a flat tire. You let the air out of it yourself, didn't you? That's why Jake was able to fix it so easily. You never took it to Matt's shop like he suggested because there was nothing wrong with it."

Sarah frowned. "That's where I messed up. I didn't think Matt would remember talking to me because he seemed so distracted that night."

I started to rise from the floor, but Sarah shook her head vehemently and held the knife out in front of her. "Don't move. I need to think." She pursed her lips together. "I'll have to tie both of you up. No one will be in here until tomorrow morning. By that time, I'll be out of the country. Yeah, that will work."

Her voice reeked of desperation and panic. For a moment, I was almost sorry for her. Our only hope was to keep her talking. Had I been gone long enough for anyone to miss me? Probably not. "What about Bruce? Why did he have to die?"

She stared at me in disbelief. "Duh. Because he knew I killed Mario. I heard you and Gabby talking to him in his store the other day. I had to run back inside when I forgot to buy cinnamon. Jake waited in the car for me."

"But how? I didn't see you—" Then it dawned on me. "You crashed into the display of canned tomatoes in the next aisle."

"What a stupid place to put them," she grumbled. "Anyway, I pretty much ran out of the aisle so no one would see me. I slipped the cinnamon into my coat and didn't even pay for it because I was in such a rush to get out of there."

Oh God. It was what I'd feared all along—someone had heard us talking. "Bruce didn't know anything about you."

The color drained from her face. "Yes, he did. He was going to tell your cousin, so I had to stop him. I went back to his store that night about eight thirty and bought a loaf of bread. Then I waited in my car until I was certain that his cashier had left. After everyone was gone, I pulled my car around back and knocked on the door. When he asked who it was, I pretended to be you, so he'd open it."

Bile rose in the back of my throat. This was almost as bad as if I had killed Bruce myself. "Bruce thought the loan sharks killed Mario. He also owed them money and figured they were coming for him next. You killed him for no reason!"

Sweat pooled on her forehead. "You're making that up."

"No. It's the truth."

Sarah's lips started to tremble, and she took some deep breaths. "He should have kept his big mouth shut. I thought he saw me kill Mario. What was I supposed to do? Bruce and Mario were friends. Jake told me so. I—I didn't have a choice."

"There's no way you can be certain that Mario killed your sister," I said.

"He took away my family. My mother was never the same after Sonya died. She was so distraught that she finally killed herself six months ago." Tears streamed out of Sarah's eyes and dropped onto the blade of the knife, where they glistened in the light. "Mario had to pay and I'm glad he's dead." Sarah sniffled and grabbed a roll of string used for the bakery boxes off the table. "You," she ordered Wendy. "Put your hands behind your back."

Wendy, who had not made a sound the entire time, whimpered and stared at me with terror in her eyes.

I nodded. "Do what she says."

Wendy's mouth shook, but she obeyed. Sarah pointed the

knife at me and held out the roll of string. "Tie her hands and her feet together. And don't try anything funny."

Heart thumping, I reached for the string. As Sarah placed it in my hand, I pushed the baker's rack toward her. She dropped the knife and it clattered to the floor. I pulled Wendy up by the arm and pushed her in the direction of the back door. She chose that particular moment to start screaming at the top of her lungs. "Run!" I told her. "Go get help! Hurry!"

"You're ruining everything!" Sarah shouted. She stepped around the rack and grabbed me by the hair, then pushed me down onto the floor. My face connected with a table leg. I reached my hand up onto the table as she came at me again and managed to throw a fistful of flour into her face. Sarah screamed and wiped frantically at her eyes. It gave me the split second I needed. I ran for the door and pulled it open before she fell on top of me, and we both tumbled outside.

The snow squalls were still intense, and the gusty wind made it difficult to breathe. My hands stung from the bitter cold as I struggled to free myself from Sarah's grip around my neck. She pushed my head into the snow until every inch of my face tingled with pain. I dug my nails into her flesh and was rewarded with a piercing scream. She abruptly released me, and I managed to roll over onto my back. Sarah charged at me like an angry bull as I made one last attempt to defend myself. I pulled back my legs to kick her in the stomach but missed, my foot connecting with her leg instead, causing her to stumble. Sarah's head collided with the metal dumpster, and she crumpled into the snow.

Breathing heavily, I got to my feet and staggered toward the next building for help. A horn blared behind me. I turned and saw a car approaching. The tires squealed to a stop and Gino rushed over to me, with Lou behind him.

Gino grabbed me around the waist in an attempt to steady me. "You look like you've been through a war. Are you all right?"

Panting, I nodded and pointed a trembling hand at Sarah, who Lou was lifting out of the snow. "She—she killed Mario. She's Sonya's sister."

Gino led me into the bakery and sat me down at one of the tables. "I know. That's why I went to the restaurant. Thank God Stephanie told me where you were."

"How did you find out?" I asked, but he held up a finger, indicating for me to wait. He rushed outside and was back in a minute with a blanket that he placed around my shoulders.

"Thanks," I said gratefully.

Gino sat down in the chair next to mine. "Lou's outside reading Sarah her rights. Wendy is sitting in my car, trying to calm herself. We have backup on the way." He ran a hand thoughtfully over his chin. "When I discovered Sonya went to Dwyer College, I started to do some digging. I found her old college roommate, and she mentioned that Sonya's sister had visited a few times. I knew her name as Eva from the obituary, so I ran a check on her. It turns out that Eva has a record. She was caught using a fake ID when she was underage. In New York, that's a felony, and it stays on her record for life."

"I bet she never thought it would come back to haunt her like this," I murmured.

He studied my face. "I don't approve of you involving yourself in police business. You know that, Tess. But I have to give credit where credit's due. How did you manage to put it together?"

I explained to him about the scarf and he seemed impressed, but worry lines creased his forehead. "You did a good job figuring it all out. But will you do me a favor in the future—please stick to cooking?" His expression softened. "I can't lose my family. When it comes down to it, they're all that matters."

His words touched me, and I pulled him into a hug. "No worries. Cooking will always be my first love. Solving murders doesn't even come close."

He shook his head. "I don't know. I'm beginning to think you can't have one without the other."

TWENTY-SIX

"I DON'T KNOW HOW YOU MANAGE it all, Tess," Gabby marveled. "Yesterday you were rolling around in flour and snow with a killer. Today you're cooking up delicious treats for every kid in town." She picked up a box filled with crayons and coloring books. "But I have to confess that I'm a little upset with you."

Bewildered, I looked up from the pancakes I was decorating. "Okay, what did I do now?"

Gabby placed her hands on her hips. "Because I'm your sidekick, remember? I should have been there. That woman could have killed you."

"It's not like I knew that Sarah—I mean Eva—was a killer when I started out to Pie Carumba. If I had, I certainly wouldn't have gone."

Gabby's mouth twisted into a pout. "I wish I could have seen Sarah's face when Lou led her away. She never even crossed my mind as a possible killer. Honestly, I was worried that Wendy had done it. Sarah thought of everything, even making sure that the college library didn't have her sister's picture."

"Almost everything," I corrected her. "Getting close to Jake was clever on her part. As soon as she knew that Jake and Archie had some issues with Mario, she saw her opportunity to pit them against each other. With access to Jake's apartment and Java Time, she was also able to steal the knife and remove one of Archie's key chains without anyone noticing."

"What about the hair dye?" Gabby asked.

"Gino said that when he questioned her, Sarah admitted that she'd spilled some in Jake's bathroom one night and blotted it up with the towel," I explained. "She'd cut and dyed her hair before she came to Harvest Park because it was originally the same color as Sonya's. She snuck downstairs with the towel and threw it in Java Time's garbage can."

"Natural blonds who dye their hair have it rough," Stephanie said. "They have to redo it more frequently than other people." She flipped a pancake and looked at me thoughtfully. "And Mario still recognized her."

"Yes, because he'd seen her before."

"She would have killed you, Tess." Gabby's eyes grew wide. "Does Gino think Mario had anything to do with Sonya's death?"

I shrugged. "He doesn't believe it was on purpose, but I guess we'll never know for sure. Mario was a lot of things, but I can't picture him as a cold-blooded killer. Sonya's father said there was no known motive, either. She may have been so intoxicated that she simply tripped and fell in the water."

Stephanie swung around from the stove, spatula in hand. "Sarah's the one who broke all your windows?"

"Yes." I finished decorating another stack of pancakes. "She confessed to Gino. She knew I was asking questions and hoped it would scare me off."

"Nothing scares Nancy Drew or Chef Esposito," Gabby teased. "Well, I'd better get back out there and set up the crafts table. Half the kids are eating, and the rest are standing in line to visit with Santa. You should go out there and say hi to him, Tess. He's doing a bang-up job."

Stephanie gave a low chuckle. "I want to see him in action myself. I can't imagine there's anything that Vince doesn't do well."

We all laughed at her insinuation.

"I'll be out in a few minutes," I told Gabby. "These pancakes are going like hotcakes."

"Oh please." Gabby rolled her eyes at Stephanie and grinned. "You know that Tess is feeling better when she starts making bad puns."

"The pancakes are so cute!" Stephanie said in an awe-struck voice. She had placed several more stacks in front of me and watched as I decorated them. Each stack held three minia-ture pancakes. The top one I'd created to look like Santa's face. Strawberries were used to make his hat and whipped cream for his beard. Chocolate chips were substituted for his eyes, and a cherry for the nose. I'd come up with the idea a few years back when I'd worked as a cook at Sunnyside Up Cafe. It had been very popular with the kids and, from the compliments I'd overheard, was still going strong today.

Stephanie carried the pancakes into the dining room while I ran out to take a quick look at the buffet table. There seemed to be enough food for now. Adults helped themselves to scrambled eggs, bacon, home fries, and toast. My *sospiri* pastries were proudly on display but getting a bit low. Next to them were chocolate chip and sugar cookies for the kids, plus orange juice and fruit cocktail. To my delight, the event had sold out over a week ago.

When Dylan and I had first talked about opening a restaurant, he'd suggested doing some themed events centered around children, such as Santa and Easter Bunny breakfasts. I'd fallen in love with the idea. After all, it was a family restaurant that we'd envisioned.

The thought of my late husband brought a smile to my lips. There was no doubt in my mind that Dylan would be playing Santa if he'd been here today. I would miss him forever, but he'd always have a permanent place in my heart.

Stephanie followed me back into the kitchen, interrupting my thoughts. "You should see all the kids gathered around Santa. If he took off that beard and hat, I'm sure plenty of women would be asking for a turn on his lap too."

I laughed, knowing this was true. "I'll go back out in a minute and see for myself."

The noise of happy children giggling and chattering filtered in from the dining room, but sadness pressed against my heart. There was one other person besides Dylan who should have been here. Nevertheless, I forced a smile on my face and re-entered the dining room, determined to make everyone happy.

It was time to stop thinking about myself. There were many things to be thankful for. The Festival of Lights was expecting a sold-out crowd tonight, and the display would run until mid-January, which should help to raise money for the animal shelter. Tyler Randolph had resigned as mayor when allegations of embezzlement were brought against him last night. The latest rumor in Harvest Park was that Ruthie Dunsbach, owner of The Flower Girl, was considering running for the vacancy when a special election was held next month. Last but not least, Gabby had stopped at Java Time for coffee this morning and reported there was standing room only.

I'd also received a text from Justin this morning. It wasn't a huge surprise. News always traveled fast in Harvest Park, and he was bound to be concerned after hearing about my confrontation with Sarah.

I heard about what happened last night. Glad you're okay. I'm here if you need anything...anything at all. Merry Christmas. J

Four hours later, I still hadn't answered him back. My mother's words from the other night came back to me. She was right, of course. I couldn't live the rest of my days in fear. Life was all about taking risks, especially when you cared about someone. Even if I could have predicted the future, I never would have changed what I had with Dylan. I needed to explain my feelings to Justin, and not in a text message. I owed him that much.

Armed with another tray of *sospiri*, I glanced around the dining room in satisfaction. There were different activities going on in each corner while several families were still enjoying breakfast. The tables were decorated with red linen cloths and hurricane candle centerpieces with surrounding wreaths. Snowflake danglers were suspended from the ceiling while Christmas music played softly in the background.

My mother was in one corner, helping a group of kids assemble gingerbread houses. Gino and Lucy were enjoying a quiet moment at their table minus the twins. Gino was holding the baby on his lap while his other arm was draped across Lucy's shoulders. Gabby was supervising crafts in another corner. Marco and Rocco were with her, and the kids seemed to be having a grand time decorating Christmas cards with construction paper, crayons, and glitter for their parents. Judy was in another corner coordinating pin the antler on the reindeer.

The gas fireplace held a roaring fire and next to it an overstuffed chair was draped in red velvet for Santa. Renee had dressed up like an elf and was taking pictures of him with the kids and handing out candy canes. Santa had his head bent down, listening intently to a little girl who was talking into his ear.

Someone tugged at my hand. I looked down to see Zoe

standing there, staring up at me with enormous green eyes like her mother's. She hugged me around the waist. "Tessa! This is the best breakfast ever. And the pancakes were so yummy. Thank you."

I knelt down and put my arms around her. She had no idea how much her words meant to me. "I'm so glad you're having a good time. Did you talk to Santa yet?"

"Yep." She grinned and held open her hands, which contained two candy canes. "He was really nice. I told him that I wanted a kitten for Christmas. One that looks like Luigi." She looked at me hopefully. "When Luigi has babies, can I have one?"

"Boy cats can't have babies," I laughed. "What did Santa say when you asked him for a kitten?"

"Santa said he'd try his best, but it has to be okay with Mommy. Then he told me a story about how he once got a kitty out of a tree." She giggled. "He was just being silly. Santa's too fat to get a kitty out of a tree."

"He did what?" She must have heard him wrong. Vince had said that he was allergic to cats. And he certainly didn't strike me as the type to go looking for one in a tree. Then, like a snowball to the face, it hit me. I turned and glanced over at Santa's chair. A little girl with blond pigtails reached up to hug Santa around the neck, then jumped off his lap. He looked up and our eyes met. Even from across the room, I could tell those weren't Vince's eyes. They were a smoky gray with a hint of blue that always reminded me of dawn breaking through the clouds in early morning.

I let go of Zoe's hand and walked toward him. Justin rose from the chair to meet me halfway. His eyes twinkled, and I knew there was a wide grin behind that snow-white beard. "Surprise. Ho, ho, ho."

"I thought you were working today." It was the first thing to tumble out of my mouth as I stared at the suit, wondering where it had come from. It looked vintage but suited him perfectly, and for some reason was strangely familiar.

"I was able to trade days with one of my co-workers at the last minute. And you did send me a text, inviting me to come. Remember?"

Puzzled, I stared at him. I hadn't sent him a text. Yes, I'd typed one out the night before last but never sent it. Wait a second. Luigi had been walking on the counter and knocked my phone to the floor. Maybe it had gone through after all.

Justin waved a hand in front of my face. "Everything okay?"

"Yes, of course." I paused. "It's good to see you."

"I stopped at Java Time last night," Justin explained. "Archie told me what happened. Then I asked if I could borrow his Santa suit." His eyes crinkled at the corners with mischief. "Someone may have told me that you needed a Santa, so here I am."

"Thank you," I said gratefully. "But where—" Then I caught myself in the nick of time. I couldn't help wondering what had happened to Vince.

Justin held up a white gloved hand. "Let me finish. I decided this shouldn't be about me. I wanted to do this for the kids—and for you."

A lump the size of a mountain formed in my throat. "Thank you. It means more than you know."

"You just missed my last customer," he joked as he patted his stomach. "Every kid has had a turn. A few of them even came through the line twice."

It was obvious he was using pillows to pad his stomach, and the thought made me want to giggle. "You're good at your job."

"Maybe I should think about changing careers," he remarked.

His comment reminded me of the fire, and anxiety grew inside my chest. I thought back to those few minutes when I wasn't sure if he had lived or died.

"What's wrong?" he asked. "Did I say something to upset you?"

I shook my head. "I'm sorry I've been distant lately." My breath hitched, and I tried again. "Justin, I've been doing some thinking about us. I don't want to lose what we have."

"What do we have, Tess?" Sorrow was prevalent in his eyes, which had turned a turbulent shade of gray. "You know how I feel about you—how I've always felt about you. A year ago, you told me that you were nowhere near ready to think about a relationship. Eight months ago, you told me you needed more time. And that's fine. I understood, and I've never tried to rush you, have I?"

"No, you haven't."

"But now I get the feeling that you don't want anything at all to do with me—that our friendship doesn't matter anymore. Something's changed the last few days, and I'm not sure why. What did I do wrong?"

He sounded hurt, and I couldn't blame him. "You haven't

done anything wrong. I was frightened by the fire. Then the next day I received a Christmas present from Dylan, and it stirred up some memories. It should have arrived a year ago. I had to sort out my feelings about—everything."

"The chef ornament," Justin said quietly.

My jaw dropped. "How did you know?"

Justin remained silent, but it didn't take a psychic to figure it out. "Gabby told you, didn't she?"

He looked sheepish as he nodded. "I was supposed to keep it a secret."

"So was she." I tried to sound irritated, but in truth, I was actually relieved. Gabby had gone ahead and done what I should have done myself.

"I wish you had told me the other night," he said. "You should know by now that you can tell me anything."

My heart sank at his words. "You're right. I should have explained it all to you." I took a deep breath, determined to tell him my true feelings. "These last few days I've come to realize that I—"

Zoe came running up and tugged at his coat. "Santa! Come sit at my table, please?"

He tore his gaze away from me. "Give me one minute, okay, Zoe?"

"Oh please!" she cried. "I want to show you my gingerbread house. I made it just for you."

Rocco, Marco, and another little girl surrounded Justin.

They all tried to push him in the direction of the table and began talking at once. Justin looked at me helplessly as he was dragged way.

I managed a smile. "It's all right, Santa. We can talk more later."

He tried to say something, but it was drowned out by the children's chatter. I stood and watched as he posed for more pictures with the kids and their gingerbread houses. Another little girl ran up to him and asked to sit on his lap. I'd been right all along. I knew that he would be perfect for the job.

With nothing else to do, I went back into the kitchen. I consoled myself with the fact that I'd have another chance shortly to explain everything to him. The kids would be getting ready to leave soon, then Justin would come in, have a coffee, and we'd talk, like old times. He'd stay on after everyone else left, and then maybe I could try asking him about coming over tonight.

My phone buzzed and I drew it out of my pocket. *Archie*. "Merry Christmas," I greeted him. "How are you?"

Archie chuckled. "Better, thanks to you, honey."

"How's Jake?" Gino had told me last night that Jake had gone to the police station, wanting to speak to Sarah. It had not gone well. He'd said Jake had looked devastated when he left but assured me that Archie had remained at his side. With his father's help, he'd come through it okay.

Archie sighed. "He's coping. It will take some time. The kid's going through all the emotions right now. Sarah used him and he feels betrayed. She had an agenda, and my son was merely collateral damage to her."

I wanted to disagree, but sadly, Archie was right. Sarah had told me so herself. She'd been driven by revenge and didn't care who she'd had to hurt in the process. She would have a long time to think about that in prison.

"The shop's been really busy today," Archie went on. "We have you to thank for that. Jake and I will be closing up a few hours early and then heading out to David's house in Maine for an extended holiday weekend. We hope to get there for a late supper."

"I'm going to miss that peppermint hot chocolate," I teased.

He chuckled. "Well, you won't have to wait long. Jake and I will be back on Tuesday to reopen." He lowered his voice. "Wendy came by this morning to see Jake. They had a long talk, and I have a good feeling about it."

"Is she still planning on moving? Maybe she would be willing to reconsider a long-distance relationship."

"She told Jake that she's thinking about staying in town. There are some classes she can take online for now until she decides what to do. Nothing wrong with that." There was a pregnant pause. "You young folks have lots of time. So, what are *you* doing for the holiday?"

I decided to skip over tonight's lack of festivities. "Everyone is coming to my house tomorrow. That means I'll be busy cooking all day." I was looking forward to it. Cooking always made me happy and managed to chase my troubles away.

"What about tonight?" Archie pressed. "Do you suppose Santa Claus will be coming for a visit?"

I knew what he was getting at. "No idea," I said softly. "But that's a great looking suit he's wearing. Thanks for loaning it to him. I hope you have a wonderful Christmas."

"Merry Christmas, honey," Archie said huskily. "You deserve to be happy. I hope Santa brings you everything you want." With that, he clicked off.

I placed the phone in my pants pocket and walked back into the dining room. Parents were starting to pack up their things while a few others already had their coats on and were standing in groups, chatting amongst themselves. I glanced around but didn't see Justin anywhere.

Gabby was picking up glitter and scissors from the craft table. I went over to her. "What happened to Justin?"

She gave me a sympathetic look. "He had to leave. Something about his boss needing to see him right away. He asked me to tell you goodbye."

Disappointment settled on my chest like a heavy boulder. Surely Justin could have spared a minute to come and tell me goodbye. I wanted to kick myself. He thought that he didn't matter to me when nothing could be further from the truth. "Did he mention what he was doing for the holiday?"

Gabby shook her head. "I'm sorry, Tess. He didn't say anything else." Her face suddenly brightened. "He made a great Santa, didn't he?"

I folded my arms around my middle. "The best. I knew he would. But what the heck happened to Vince?"

A sly smile played on the corners of her mouth. "Huh. No idea. Someone must have told him that the job was already taken."

TWENTY-SEVEN

"BREAKFAST WAS A BIG HIT, TESS," Stephanie said as we cleaned up the kitchen together. "Everyone was raving about the food and all the little extras. Will we be doing another one next year?"

Parents had left with boxes of assorted cookies including Italian rainbow, pizzelle, and genettis. There were also craft projects and several candy canes. Cries of "Merry Christmas" and "Thank you" rang out from the happy and excited children, who were all ready for Santa to visit them again tonight. They'd accepted the explanation that he'd left early to "get his reindeer ready."

"Definitely. I'm so glad that everyone had a good time, especially the kids." The event had been a lot of work, but worth the trouble. Now that it was over, a feeling of emptiness had descended upon me. I was always at my best when cooking was involved. Tomorrow would be a fun day at home with my family, but I still had to get through tonight first.

Renee and Judy came into the kitchen to grab their coats and handbags. I took them and Stephanie aside and handed them each an envelope with a cash bonus inside. They looked surprised but delighted.

Renee wiped tears from her eyes. "Thank you so much, Tessa. This will definitely come in handy."

"I'll say," Judy added. "I need to get new brakes on my car, and this will be a huge help." Her mouth twisted into a frown. "But I didn't get anything for you."

She sounded like a little kid, and I laughed. "There's nothing I want." Well, maybe one thing, but she couldn't help with that. "You're all wonderful employees, and it's my way of saying thank you."

Judy and Renee hugged me goodbye, called, "Merry Christmas," and departed. Zoe came running in from the dining room where she had been coloring a picture. Stephanie helped her put on her green coat and mittens. "Time to go, baby."

Zoe rushed over to me and wrapped her arms around my neck. "I had a lot of fun today, Tessa."

I kissed her cheek. "I'm so glad."

She held out the picture to me. "Merry Christmas."

"For me?" I studied it intently. Zoe had drawn a stick figure with long hair, holding a big spoon in one hand and something I couldn't identify in the other. "Is that me? What am I cooking?"

She gave me a cute but indignant look. "It's a turkey of course. You'll be serving it to all your friends tonight." She pointed at a small black dot in the corner. "And there's Luigi."

"I love it." I pinned it to the fridge with one of my Anything's Pastable magnets. "Thank you so much."

"Merry Christmas!" She waved a white mittened hand at me and started to open the kitchen door.

Stephanie stopped to give me a hug. "What are you doing tonight?"

I was starting to hate that question. "Oh, I've got food to fix for tomorrow's dinner." It was a lie of course. I'd do most of the cooking in the morning. But I didn't want anyone to worry about me.

She watched me carefully. "Zoe and I would love it if you'd join us for dinner."

"Thanks, but I'm way too busy."

Something in Stephanie's manner told me that she knew the truth, but she didn't press. "Well, if you change your mind, dinner's at six. It's only the two of us," she added hastily. "Matt and his kids are coming over tomorrow."

"I appreciate the invite. Have a great holiday." I gave her hand a tight squeeze. "Hopefully, it's the start of many more for you."

"Thanks, Tess. Merry Christmas." She clutched Zoe's hand and I watched as they got into her vehicle, parked next to mine. Zoe waved at me until the car was out of sight.

I locked the door and went through the dining room one last time, but there was nothing else for me to do. The decorations had all been removed, and the tables were set for Tuesday. I took my time emptying the dishwasher and then spent a few minutes at my desk paying some bills. What I was really trying to do was put off the inevitable, going home to an empty and quiet house. Still, Luigi was there, and he'd be wanting his supper, so I finally packed up and drove home. Maybe I'd make tomato sauce tonight. We'd have turkey and lasagna tomorrow, and Lucy was bringing a casserole, but pasta never went uneaten in my family. Sure, why not. It would help pass the time.

Luigi met me at the front door, but when I stooped to pet him, he flicked his tail at me and ran into the living room. I found him curled up on a pillow. He opened his eyes as if I'd disturbed him and meowed. What an actor.

"It's just you and me tonight, buddy." I stroked his soft fur, but he was having none of it. He jumped off the seat and went over to the Christmas tree where he boldly started tapping ornaments with his paw, and one fell onto the floor.

"Hey, you know better than that." Luigi looked up at me with enormous green eyes, as if waiting for my next move. I picked the tiny reindeer ornament off the floor and returned it to its branch. My eyes fell upon the chef ornament again. I sat there, under the tree, looking at it for a very long time.

I'd been wrong. So very wrong. I was pushing away a man I cared about because I was scared. Scared to love again. Scared of what the future might hold. But I couldn't prevent the future from coming. I had no control over it. My mother was right, and my way was wrong. It wasn't living.

After a minute, I reached for the phone, then stopped myself. Justin only lived a block away. It was my turn to go to him. With new determination, I shut off the television and threw on my coat. Fine snowflakes were falling slowly to the ground. The lighted decorations all along the street gave it a winter wonderland feel. I shut and locked the front door behind me as a vehicle turned into my driveway.

My heart gave a jolt when I saw who it was. I stood there on the porch, waiting to see what would happen next. Justin emerged from his truck and slowly walked towards me. He had something in his hands—a gold wrapped package. We stood there for a minute, looking at each other, until he cleared his throat.

"Hi," I said softly.

"You look like you're heading out somewhere so I won't stay," Justin said. "But I did want to give you your Christmas gift." He placed the small square package in my hands.

"Please don't go," I blurted out. "I wanted to talk to you after the breakfast, but you left before I had a chance."

Justin stuck his hands inside the pockets of his jacket. "Yeah, I'm sorry about that." He grinned sheepishly. "Guess what? I've been promoted to Lieutenant. Youngest guy in Harvest Park to ever make it."

"Wow." I brought a gloved hand to my mouth. "That's fantastic. Congratulations."

Snowflakes stuck to his dark hair and the sight mesmerized me. We continued to stand there, looking at each other for what seemed like a lifetime, until I finally spoke again. "I handled things wrong, and I'm sorry."

Justin nodded. "Gabby called me this afternoon. She apologized for interfering but thought it was time that I knew the truth. Why didn't you tell me that you were afraid something would happen to me as well? I should have thought of that, but I didn't."

A tear rolled down my cheek. "I've always loved you as a friend, but the night of the fire, something changed for me. The thought of not having you here was too much to bear. I guess I thought if I could distance myself from you, it would make everything easier. But the truth is, it only made it harder. Does that make sense?"

He took a step closer to me. "Yes. That's why I once told you that I could wait forever for you. I'd rather have you in my life as a friend than not at all."

"I'm ready to move forward—with us," I said slowly. "But there's something else I need to tell you first."

Justin swiped under my eyes with the pad of his thumb. "I'm listening."

I exhaled sharply, watching my breath cloud the air. "I loved Dylan more than anything else in this world. I'll never get him completely out of my heart, so I hope you can understand that."

A grin broke across Justin's face, and he gestured at the package I was still holding. "Are you going to open that before next Christmas?"

I gulped back a combination of a sob and laugh, then removed the top of the box. Inside was a lovely gold watch with tiny diamonds surrounding the face. "It's beautiful."

"Turn it over," Justin said. "See what's written on the back."

I did as he suggested and held the watch up to the porch light. The inscription on the back of it read: *We have lots of time. Love, J.*

The tears came again as Justin took the watch and placed it on my wrist. "I've always loved you, Tess. That's no secret. I would never try to replace Dylan in your heart." He paused, and his voice took on a husky note. "I only want a little piece of it to call my own."

I stepped forward and Justin wrapped his arms around me, pulling me close. We stood like that for a long time, the snow falling on us, listening to the sound of carolers somewhere further down the street, singing "It Came Upon a Midnight Clear." I thought I could have stayed like that forever.

Justin pulled back and stared down at me, his eyes shining with happiness. "Got any plans for tonight?" he asked, winding his fingers through my hair.

"As a matter of fact, yes. I have Christmas movies to watch and gingerbread to eat." I grinned at him teasingly. "So, what are you going to do?"

He gave me a sly wink. "That's funny. I'm doing the same exact thing."

"Talk about your coincidences." I stepped forward and placed my arms around his neck. He stood there, watching me as I leaned forward and closed my mouth over his. After we broke apart, he smiled tenderly at me.

"Merry Christmas, Tess."

"And a very Happy New Year," I whispered. "To the both of us."

RECIPES

CHRISTMAS THYME COOKIES

- 1/2 cup butter, softened, room temperature
- 5 tablespoons sugar
- 1 tablespoon minced fresh thyme
- 1 tablespoon grated lemon zest
- 1 large egg yolk, room temperature
- 1 cup all-purpose flour
- 1/4 teaspoon baking powder
- 1/4 teaspoon salt

Cream the butter, sugar, thyme, and lemon zest until light and fluffy. Beat in the egg yolk. In another bowl, whisk the flour, baking powder, and salt, then gradually beat into the creamed mixture. Roughly shape the dough into a 12-inch roll along the edge of a 12 x 12-inch sheet of waxed paper. Tightly roll the waxed paper over dough, using the waxed paper to mold the dough into a smooth roll. Securely wrap the roll in plastic and then refrigerate for 1 hour or overnight.

Preheat the oven to 350°F. Unwrap and cut the dough cross-wise into 1/2-inch slices. Place 2 inches apart on baking sheets lined with parchment paper. Bake until the edges begin to brown, 12–15 minutes. Cool in pans for about 5 minutes. Decorate with red and green or other Christmas-themed sprinkles. Remove to wire racks to finish cooling. Makes about two dozen cookies.

GINGERBREAD PIZZELLE

- 1/2 cup granulated sugar
- 1/4 cup light brown sugar
- 3 eggs
- 1/2 cup coconut oil, melted and cooled to room temperature
- 2 tablespoons molasses
- 1 teaspoon vanilla extract
- 2 teaspoons baking powder
- 2 teaspoons ground cinnamon
- 1 teaspoon ground ginger
- 1/2 teaspoon salt
- 1/4 teaspoon allspice
- 1/4 teaspoon ground cloves
- 2 cups all-purpose flour
- Confectioners' sugar—optional (for dusting)

In a large bowl, whisk together the granulated sugar, brown sugar, eggs, coconut oil, molasses, and vanilla until smooth. Whisk in the baking powder, cinnamon, ginger, salt, allspice, and cloves. Once incorporated, stir in the all-purpose flour.

Heat a pizzelle iron according to manufacturer's instructions. Spray or brush the iron with a high-temperature cooking spray or vegetable oil. Once the pizzelle iron is hot, drop the batter by tablespoon into the center of each cookie well. Close the iron and bake until cookies are golden brown after a few minutes.

Transfer the hot cookies to a wire rack to cool. Repeat with the remaining batter. If desired, dust the cookies with confectioners' sugar. These are best served within a day of making. Leftovers can be stored in an airtight container for up to a week, but the cookies will soften over time. Makes about 50 pizzelle.

Note: If you don't have a pizzelle iron, the best substitute is to heat a skillet, dollop a small amount of batter onto the surface, and then use a heated grill press to flatten while it cooks. Not quite as pretty as the pizzelle iron, but they will still be tasty.

HARVEST PARK
HOT CHOCOLATE COOKIES

- 1 cup butter, at room temperature
- 1 1/2 cups sugar
- 2 eggs
- 1 teaspoon vanilla extract
- 2 cups all-purpose flour
- 2/3 cup unsweetened cocoa powder
- 3/4 teaspoon baking soda
- 1/2 teaspoon salt
- 1 cup mini marshmallows, divided (if you can't find them, use regular-sized marshmallows and cut them into about eight pieces)
- 3/4 cup mini chocolate chips

Preheat the oven to 350°F. Line two baking sheets with parchment paper. In a mixing bowl, combine the butter and sugar and beat until light and fluffy, 1–2 minutes. Add in the eggs, one at a time,

scraping down the sides of the mixer as needed. Beat in the vanilla. In a separate bowl, combine the flour, cocoa powder, baking soda, and salt. Add the dry ingredients to the wet ingredients and mix just until combined. Add in 3/4 cup of the mini marshmallows along with the mini chocolate chips and mix until combined.

Scoop 1 tablespoon-size ball of dough and roll into a ball. The dough will be stiff and sticky. Place on the baking sheet, about 2 inches apart. With the remaining 1/4 cup mini marshmallows, press a few into the outside of each of the balls of dough. Place only one baking sheet of cookies in the oven at a time. Bake until the edges are set, but the center still seems a little bit wet, about 7 minutes. Remove from the oven and let the cookies sit on the baking sheet for a few more minutes before transferring to a baking rack or a sheet of waxed paper. Makes between 12 and 18 cookies.

TESSA'S EASY GNOCCHI

- 2 medium russet potatoes
- 1 1/2 cups all-purpose flour
- 1/2 cup whole-milk ricotta cheese
- 1/4 cup grated Parmesan cheese
- 1 large egg
- 3/4 teaspoon salt
- 1/4 teaspoon pepper

Preheat the oven to 400°F. Line a baking sheet with parchment paper. Pierce the potatoes with a fork and place onto the baking sheet. Bake until tender, about 1 hour. You can also microwave them, if you are in a hurry, for 6–7 minutes. Let cool completely. Cut in half and scoop the flesh into a medium bowl and then mash. Transfer 1 1/2 cups of the potatoes to a large bowl; stir in the flour, ricotta, Parmesan, egg, salt, and pepper. Working on a lightly floured surface, divide the dough into 6 equal pieces. Roll each piece into an 18-inch-long rope, about 1-inch in diameter, sprinkling with additional flour as needed to prevent sticking.

Using a sharp knife, cut each rope into 3/4-inch bite-size pieces. Bring a large pot of salted water to a boil and drop the pieces in separately. Cook the gnocchi until tender, stirring occasionally, 4–6 minutes. Drain well, then cover with tomato sauce and serve. Makes 2–3 decent-size portions, so if you have a large family, you will want to double the recipe.

To freeze, place the uncooked gnocchi in a single layer on a heavily floured, parchment-lined baking sheet, letting them air dry at room temperature for at least 1 hour and up to 4 hours. Transfer the baking sheet to the freezer until solid, about 1 hour. Transfer to freezer bags.

Note: Low-fat skim milk ricotta can be substituted for the whole-milk kind.

Ready for another Italian-themed
mystery in Harvest Park?
Read on for a look at the first book in
the Italian Chef Mystery series.

ONE

THE RICH AROMA FROM THE MIXTURE of tomatoes and onions cooking wafted through the air, hitting my nose with a distinct perfume. It was a soothing smell that blanketed me in its warm hold. If alone, I would have been content to stand in front of my stove all day.

I stirred the sauce and listened as my cousin Gino Mancusi flipped through the sports section of the newspaper at my breakfast counter and grumbled about his beloved Giants losing again.

"The season is pretty much over. I actually thought they might get another ring this time." He sighed and pushed the paper aside. "You shouldn't have gone to any trouble, Tessa. A sandwich would have been fine."

"It's never any trouble." I enjoyed watching others sample my creations and had vowed years ago that no one would ever leave my home hungry. Part of this obsession came from my love of cooking, but I attributed the rest to my Italian heritage. Italians are passionate about almost everything in the world, and food is at the top of the list.

"It's rare for you to go out for lunch," I said. Gino was a police detective in our hometown of Harvest Park. "Did Lucy tell you to come over and check up on me? Is it your day? Oh wait, let me grab the calendar."

"Stop being a smart aleck." He left the counter and came into the kitchen to grab ice cubes out of the freezer for his soda. On his way back, he stopped and planted an affectionate kiss on the top of my head. "That's what family is for, Tess. We're all worried about you."

I squeezed his arm and turned off the burner. "Grab the parmesan cheese out of the fridge, will you? I grated it this morning."

Gino nodded without another word. I appreciated all that he and the rest of the family were doing, but I was determined not to start crying again today.

It was still difficult to talk about my husband's death, even with loved ones. I'd spent the last five weeks in a trance—or perhaps shock was a better term. Thanks to my mother, cousins, and my friend Justin, I had finally started to come around. Whenever I thought I'd fully recovered though, a kind word or a nice gesture from anyone would make me dissolve into a puddle of tears again.

Last night, my elderly neighbor Stacia from across the street had brought me a fresh baked apple pie. "I know how much you love them, dear." She'd beamed at me from underneath a mass of pink foam hair curlers. Apple pie—anything apple, actually—had been Dylan's favorite, but I didn't have the heart to tell her so. Instead, I'd cried after she left and then devoured a huge slice.

Gino placed the cheese on the breakfast counter. He had classic Italian good looks complemented by dark hair, an olive complexion, and brown eyes that could either be sympathetic or suspicious. I suspected that the latter one was a cop thing.

"Right here at the bar is fine, Tess," he said. "Don't bother setting the table. I have to get back to work in a little while anyway."

"Okay, it's all ready." I ladled the ruby-red sauce onto his plate of penne, inhaling the rich savory smell. It was a little bit like summer, with the sweet fragrance of vine-ripe tomatoes complemented by the minty smell of fresh basil from my garden.

"It smells great," Gino said as he sat down. "Then again, I've never eaten anything of yours that wasn't top-notch. You need to give Lucy some pointers."

"Lucy's a good cook. She's too busy taking care of those devilish twins of yours to do much else. I've got a little bit of extra sauce if you want to take some home to her."

Gino's eyes widened as he swallowed a bite of pasta. "A *little*? Come on, Tess. I saw your extra sauce." He wiped his mouth on a starched white linen napkin. "When I opened the freezer, there were at least twenty ziplock bags in there. Maybe you're a bit obsessed with making sauce, huh?"

Like the rest of my family, Gino's focus was strictly on how the food tasted. For me, there was more to it. I loved the aromas, the spices, the way preparing food made me feel—relaxed, confident, and in control. I'd been cooking for twenty years, since the tender age of ten. My grandmother, a fabulous cook herself, and I had shared a special bond. Whenever we went to her house, I'd head straight to the kitchen to watch her make dinner, and we'd chat the afternoon away. My love of cooking came from her. On my thirteenth birthday, she gave me a special present—her secret tomato sauce recipe. She passed away when I was sixteen, and I took the recipe and made it my own over the years, with the help of a few special ingredients. Although I could make just about anything, tomato sauce was my passion and specialty, always bringing to mind wonderful memories of our time together.

"No, I'm not obsessed." There was silence in the room, except for the clink of Gino's fork hitting the china plate. He didn't understand. No one did. My love of cooking also helped soothe the grief of losing my husband, at least temporarily. Dylan had passed away a little over a month ago in a tragic car accident that would probably give me nightmares for the rest of my life.

This wasn't supposed to happen to us. We'd been young, in love, and trying to have a baby. Dylan and I were married for almost six wonderful years. Although by no means rich, we'd lived comfortably enough. Dylan had been employed as an accountant for a large healthcare firm, We Care, in Albany. As a certified CPA, he'd prepared taxes privately for several clients outside the firm as well. To add to our modest income, a couple of months before Dylan's death, I'd begun working as a cook for the Sunnyside Up

Café. Back then, my main goal in life—besides starting a family—had been to run my own restaurant someday.

Dylan had been extremely supportive of my passion. He'd always teased that he couldn't wait to quit his job and call me "boss," serving as my maître d'. Kidding aside, I knew he'd been as excited about the venture as I was. Still, we didn't have anywhere near the funds necessary to make it happen. Since we'd bought the house only two years ago, we'd been trying to put money away every month, but there were times when real life intervened. A new roof and hot water tank had helped derail the savings process for a few months. We remained hopeful that it would happen within the next couple of years.

Five weeks ago, my dream had been replaced by a nightmare. My new goal in life was to simply make it through a day without crying, and my restaurant ownership dreams had been put aside indefinitely.

After the accident, I'd asked my mother to call Sunnyside and tell them I wouldn't be returning. I'd only been there for a few months, and it wasn't fair to leave them hanging, although they'd been very supportive of my situation.

Even selling the house had crossed my mind a few times in the last couple of weeks. The first time the real estate agent showed us the light-blue Cape Cod, Dylan and I both instantly fell in love with its charm. Although only about fourteen hundred square feet, it was perfect for us, with its large bay window, hardwood floors, and steepled roof.

Now, however, it was difficult to stay here alone. There were memories of Dylan everywhere I looked, such as the empty window boxes built into the white shutters where we'd planted annuals together every spring. I missed so many things about him—his deep-throated chuckle, the way he held me in his strong arms on lazy Sunday mornings in bed, and the long walks we'd take, hand in hand, after dinner on picturesque autumn days, much like this one. Early November in Harvest Park, although chilly, was the perfect time of year to watch multicolored leaves fall from the trees.

The house was an ideal home for a young married couple and even had the classic white picket fence in the backyard. The only things missing were the standard two-point-five kids and dog, which I'd mistakenly thought we had plenty of time for.

ACKNOWLEDGMENTS

This book was written during the pandemic, a strange and scary time for many, including myself. I was grateful for the opportunity to escape into my own pretend world for a while and truly hope that readers enjoy the result.

Thank you to my publisher, Sourcebooks, for giving me the opportunity to tell my stories. A special thanks to my editor, Margaret Johnston, who is a joy to work with and always makes my writing better.

To my literary agent, Nikki Terpilowski, thank you for being in my corner. I appreciate everything you do for my career.

Profound thanks to retired police captain Terrance Buchanan for faithfully answering my questions and to firefighter Joseph Collins, whose help was instrumental in this book.

To my dear friends and beta readers Constance Atwater and Kathy Kennedy—thank you for your honesty and always coming through for me! Kim Davis, I so appreciate the delicious pizzelle recipe and all the other ones you've created for my books. Your talent never ceases to amaze me.

A special thank-you to my favorite bloggers: Dru Ann Love, Lisa Kelley, Missi Stockwell, and Kim Davis, for all that they do to support me and other cozy mystery authors. You ladies are the best!

Last but not least, thank you to my family for their unfailing support, especially my husband, Frank. After thirty-one years, you have never let me down. I love you.

ABOUT THE AUTHOR

USA Today bestselling author Catherine Bruns lives in Upstate New York with an all-male household that consists of her very patient husband, sons, and several spoiled pets. Catherine has a B.A. in both English and Performing Arts and is a former newspaper reporter and press release writer. In her spare time, she loves to bake, read, and attend live theater performances. Her book *For Sale by Killer* was the 2019 recipient of the Daphne du Maurier Award for Mainstream Mystery/Suspense. Readers are invited to visit her website at catherinebruns.net.